WYOMING SHOWDOWN

WYOMING SHOWDOWN

RUSTY DAVIS

FIVE STAR
A part of Gale, Cengage Learning

GALE
CENGAGE Learning·

Farmington Hills, Mich • San Francisco • New York • Waterville, Maine
Meriden, Conn • Mason, Ohio • Chicago

GALE
CENGAGE Learning·

LIBRARY OF CONGRESS CATALOGING-IN-PUBLICATION DATA

Davis, Rusty.
    Wyoming showdown / by Rusty Davis. — First edition.
        pages cm
        ISBN 978-1-4328-3066-3 (hardcover) — ISBN 1-4328-3066-X (hardcover) — ISBN 978-1-4328-3064-9 (ebook) — ISBN 1-4328-3064-3 (ebook)
        1. Wyoming—Fiction. 2. Western stories. I. Title.
    PS3604.A9755W96 2015
    813'.6—dc23   2015008988

First Edition. First Printing: September 2015
Find us on Facebook– https://www.facebook.com/FiveStarCengage
Visit our website– http://www.gale.cengage.com/fivestar/
Contact Five Star™ Publishing at FiveStar@cengage.com

Printed in the United States of America
1 2 3 4 5 6 7 19 18 17 16 15

WYOMING SHOWDOWN

CHAPTER ONE

Wispy dust blew across the hard-baked packed dirt of Broken Corners' one and only street. It left a gritty coat of white on horses and men who had long since inured themselves to the omnipresent irritant. Along both sides of the short space of buildings that marked the town, cracked, sunbaked, weather-beaten boards gleamed through the flecked paint of the false-fronted buildings. Deep gray clouds far off to the west spoke of looming rain, rain that would slake the thirst of wilting corn while turning the town's pitted street into an impassable trough of Wyoming mud. That would be another day—a day when life was lived according to its usual routine and the street would be all but empty because everyone had work to do on the ranches and farms that spread around the small settlement.

Today, Broken Corners' one street was filled to overflowing. Knots of men and boys gathered along the hitching rails by the hotel and the store. Voices rose and faded like the rolls and swells of the sea as their tension of anticipation grew. The pounding of the boys as they ran along the duckboards added drumbeat-like spikes of tension as men waited. Women remained inside, where they pushed aside curtains as they pretended to dust furniture or straighten displays in the stores. More than one woman wished men would simply kill each other far from town so that these gory spectacles could be avoided. Many also feared that—like the town over the hill—men who had wagers on one man or the other might turn the gunfight into an occasion for a violent brawl. The women knew full well who would have to sew up the wounded.

However, even the women who disapproved knew that the fuss was to be expected. In this late summer of 1868, little varied the workaday life in a hard-bitten Wyoming frontier town as much as the exhilarating spectacle of two armed men walking out into the street with each planning to kill the other in a gunfight. Unlike the times when drunken cowboys staggered out of the saloon and fired at each other, being as likely to hit the sky as the man they were angry with, this showdown was for real. The deadliest bounty hunter in all of Wyoming had challenged one of the most famous outlaws of the territory, a man with a string of killings who always came back to Broken Corners.

The time for the showdown had been set in a note delivered to the outlaw that morning. Advance notice gave the crowd time to grow. There was more attendance than for the traveling preacher. Men argued over whose watch was right, as if any of them were. One thing they knew as the sun passed its peak: It was almost time.

From the direction of the hills that shimmered distantly through the heat, a lone rider slowly neared the scraggly collection of buildings. The man had been resting in the shade of the trees by the craggy brook a mile to the west. One of the men coming into town to see the gunfight insisted that had Red Jim gone out to shoot down his adversary, it would have been easy because the gunfighter was sleeping. The truth was not quite that simple, but the bounty hunter knew that when there was nothing to do but wait, he might as well be comfortable. He had done this often enough, after all. All he had wanted while he waited was a place to be alone.

Now, he seemed indifferent as the horse walked down the street. He dismounted and hitched his mount to a rail, talking quietly to the horse for a moment. He smiled at the animal as if this was another day, another town. The horse was a giant black stallion with a white mark on his forehead. To a man, the townspeople and ranchers admired the animal, which combined beauty, strength, and speed. Plans were already being made to sell him or steal him when the stranger would need him no more, so confident that today's drama would end in the way all others before had finished—Red Jim standing tall with a smoking weapon in his hand and the lifeless body of a challenger who was not quite fast enough being dragged away to be buried at the edge of town in what was the beginning of a gunfighters' cemetery.

The man who walked away from the horse did not impress the onlookers. He was medium-sized, carelessly dressed, and thin in the face. His boots looked old. His clothes were worn and covered with trail dust. Saloon bums often dressed better. The flat-crowned black hat was nondescript. Beneath it, his face was shadowed by the hat, hidden by a beard and muted beneath the layers of dirt. The eyes that burned holes from beneath the brim radiated intensity that was in contrast with the rest of his actions, but not many townsfolk had ventured close enough to look. They did notice the pistol strapped to his right leg below the hip in a gun belt that seemed to be as much a part of the man as his arms and legs. They knew his name was Rourke. What he was trying to do this day he had done before. Some said he had killed fifty men; others put the number lower. Despite the lack of information, all were convinced he was deadlier than almost anyone else—except for Red Jim. On that one, they were not yet convinced. They knew what Red Jim could do. There were graves on the edge of town to prove it. They had told this to the man when he issued his challenge to Red Jim. The man accepted the information without comment. If he cared, it didn't show.

As the man walked nonchalantly toward the saloon, one boy detached himself from the crowd, losing his hat along the way but not bothering to fetch it.

"Toby," the man drawled as he nodded at the youth, who was barefoot in the dirt. The boy had been his source of information for finding Red Jim when he rode through the town a day back. So far, the showdown had earned the lad a quarter.

"Mr. Rourke," stammered the boy. "Care for your horse? The stable takes good care of animals. The rates are cheap. I promise to groom him myself." The last was said with pride.

The man smiled. The boy would be in the crowd with the rest, not in the stable. However, maybe the horse would get fed before they left. Then again, who knew? He reached into his pants and tossed the boy three silver dollars. "Make sure he eats when the doin's is done. The rest is to care for him and if he needs to be sold, make sure he goes to a good home, you understand?"

The boy gulped. He didn't think gunfighters thought about being killed. But three whole dollars was more money than he had ever seen in his life. He wondered if he should ask if he had to give the money back in case Rourke lived. It didn't seem the right thing to ask. Not sure whether to wish the man luck, he nodded, fingering the coins and hearing the musical jingle in his hands he knew he would never forget.

The man made a show of checking his pocket watch, which said it had reached three, the time he had said he would be coming for Red Jim. He put the watch away with a sigh that could have been sadness or boredom. "Can't keep a man waiting, can we?" he said softy, tousling the hatless Toby's unruly hair as he walked down the middle of the street toward the saloon and the rest of the town.

"Mr. Rourke?"

"Yes, Toby?"

"He's been drinkin' in there all day." Rourke nodded at the information. A man drank for courage or out of fear. Either way, it was good to know.

The man started to leave and then looked back. "Toby? Your money, live or die, so's you don't have to feel disappointed if I don't get dead." Toby said nothing, but he saw the man's eyes crinkle and a faint hint of a smile crease the tanned face and part the dust-covered beard.

Rourke ran his hand across his whiskers. The beard had grown out the way it did on the trail, and the grimy lines carved by wind and worry into his face spoke of hard nights and worse days. He took his hat off a moment. His hair whipped in the wind. No one could have guessed his age. Between thirty and death, give or take. He walked without the energy of the young or the pain of the old, but with a slowness and sureness born of experience in the work he was doing. He was not as tall as he seemed from a distance, thin but somehow substantial, as if there was strength underneath. He moved slowly but with an inexorable purpose.

He put his hat back on and adjusted it, pausing to drink in everything around him. He could see and hear and feel all of it, the way he could when it was time for a showdown. Why it was that a man came fully alive when death was close was a mystery to him, but it was as true now as it had been at Shiloh and Vicksburg. From the street, fragments of conversation flew by: who would win; who was faster; he had a chance; he didn't have a chance. Nothing changes, he thought, except what goes on inside. Everything was sharper and more intense. It was another walk, another town, another round. Win or lose wasn't in the cards. It was a chore to finish and ride out. The hills were calling with their promise of silence and solitude.

As always when he stood in the street facing a man, he thought of her briefly. Hair wild in the wind the way it was back when she fled Nashville. That white blouse she loved when she put her long red hair in that big pile on her head to go see the play actor in Richmond. Winter of '63. Long time ago now. He drifted more and more these days. Someday he'd pay the price. The High Plains were safer, better. Alone was better now. But he wasn't a farmer or a rancher or a guide for the miserable Army. He was what he was and it was time to go to work.

Rourke looked toward the men gathered by the saloon. "Tell Red Jim I'm here to take him prisoner or kill him—whichever he wants," the man said, adding sarcastically, "Hate to keep the whole town waitin'."

One of the men separated himself from the crowd and entered the saloon. The noise was building inside. Boys who had been wide-eyed at seeing a for-real famous gunfighter drink and smoke and swear scampered out first. Rourke's mouth twitched in a grimace or smile. Was a time he would have been there. Big thrill to see a man die. Like everything else, when you live on the edge of civilization and face raw nature every day, death becomes part of life.

More men spilled out. Some were still eating. A few held glasses of liquid. Well, Rourke thought, this was good for somebody's business. There were men in riding clothes; a couple in suits. Maybe the mayor, if there was one, would want to make a speech. Then he and Red Jim could both shoot him. That would be different. The smile came unbidden at the thought but faded fast.

He could hear yelling inside the saloon and saw men jostle at the hitching-post rails. The batwings of the saloon were flung open. Red Jim stood there a minute and looked at his prey. Red Jim lived a step over the line, but the line was drawn differently now that Wyoming was a for-real Territory and plans were being made to become a state. Killers couldn't be allowed to kill because it didn't look civilized. The Territory put up the reward after Red Jim's last spree.

Red Jim was a big, handsome man, clean-shaven with his hair trimmed and neat under the broad brim of the light-colored hat that perched on the back of his head. Although Red Jim came out of the saloon laughing with the cloud of sycophants that followed frontier killers whose fame exceeded their worth, Rourke wondered what was going on inside. Usually, all liquor did was fill in the holes nerves had bored into a man's fears beneath the layers of self-confidence. Rourke's gut instinct told him that Red Jim knew something hollow about himself no one else knew. Now Rourke knew, too.

Red Jim moved away from them and stood alone. Rourke waited. Red Jim's whiskey nerves were going to twang faster and higher, the longer it took. Red Jim looked for a place to stand that would give him an edge, because any edge, no matter how small, beat none at all. He chose a place in the deepening shadows. Rourke would have to aim from the sun into the gloom. Red Jim glared defiantly at Rourke. "Want me, bounty hunter, come and get me."

"Now that you're done dancin', Jim, guess we can get this over with," drawled Rourke softly. "I got to tell you that the Territory of Wyoming wants you to stop killin' folks. I'm here to take you in. You can surrender and take your chances at the trial. Only way you come out of this alive."

"I don't give up my gun to nobody, and if the old women what run the Territory are so sudden-like squeamish over what I done, let them come get me, Rourke. Walk away while you can."

The conversation over in the expected way, Rourke shrugged. Talking was a waste of time, but the folks who ran the Territory wanted it to appear legal. When you take a man's money, Rourke thought, you got to bend to his ways, even when it's plain stupid.

Taking in one long deep breath and letting it out gradually, Rourke walked toward Red Jim, closing the 100-foot gap between them a foot at a time. Slowly. Very slowly. The living fear death; the dead inside fear living. Let the one with the greater fear feel the pressure and the tension and the sweat in the small of the back and feel guts turning to water and the iron in the soul to rust.

Rourke could hear his boots crunching in the stones and gravel of the street. At least it wasn't mud. He'd been watching those clouds earlier and wondering if the rain would hold off. Man would sound ridiculous walking through mud; look pretty silly, too. The image of two muddy men trying to be dignified in a showdown made his lips twitch in another pale smile—an action that caused a ripple through the watchers who were ready for fear and bluster and death, not an empty face of unconcern that greeted a showdown with a flickering smile.

Red Jim wiped his nerve-slick hands down his shirtfront, and lowered his right toward the handle of his gun, slung below his right hip. Looking like a snake poised to strike, his eyes were all that moved as he watched Rourke. The dark-garbed figure moved closer, slowly.

Rourke could feel the sun on his shoulders, the wind catching once again the long hair hanging down by his shirt collar. A distant crow was complaining. Somebody's loose dog was barking. A woman not too far off was baking bread. At moments like this, he was one with everything. Time stood still.

Not for Red Jim. The outlaw's hand went to his gun in a frenzied draw while Rourke was still more than 30 feet away. The Colt revolver boomed across the town, echoing off the high false fronts of the stores and saloon. The watchers strained to see which man would fall. Both still stood. Red Jim's gun trailed a wispy film of smoke. Rourke had not yet cleared leather. He was walking, slowly, deliberately. Red Jim cursed. He'd never seen a man shrug off death and look at him now, only 20 feet away, with more curiosity than fear. He thumbed back the hammer of the gun and took careful aim. The gun fired but the sound was lost in two deeper explosions that filled the street. The crowd gasped. The outlaw hurled into the air like the bucking of a powerful mustang. He landed in the dirt and kicked up a puff of dust.

Red Jim could taste the dust, mixed with something foul in his mouth. The sun was in his eyes, blinding him. There was pain in his chest. He touched it. Wet hands. Red? Something dark, but he couldn't see colors very well. There was darkness; the man standing over him blotted out the sun. It was cold in the shadows. He wanted to speak.

Rourke looked down on the dying man. Red Jim's eyes were desperate with effort. Rourke bent down. The outlaw tried to lift up his head.

"They . . . terr . . . turn . . . you, too," the outlaw whispered amid blood and foam bubbling from his mouth and distorting the words.

Rourke's lips were saying something Red Jim could not hear over the roaring that was filling his ears. Rourke turned away and was replaced in Red Jim's fuzzy-edged vision by the gloating, grinning face of a man who fifteen minutes ago drank with him in the bar. He tried to spit blood in the turncoat's face, but only left a red trail oozing down his face into the dust. Then all the roaring turned to a deep quiet. Then darker than black.

Red Jim died in the dust, two .45 slugs in his chest. As he walked away, Rourke thought about the swift end of the man who had killed and raped and burned and died. He thought of the Old Judge, dying slowly with the blood in his lungs after spending a lifetime trying to make things right. Justice? Not in this life, partner. He wondered for a moment what the man's dying words meant. Probably nothing.

He called to Toby to feed and saddle Red Jim's horse. Next, he needed provisions. Whatever he could take that was edible he'd take. It would be better than taking time to cook his own. He was facing a three-day ride with a dead man strapped to a horse, and he didn't want to travel any slower than he had to. The dead were quiet and mostly good company, but after a while they stank.

The town photographer took a picture of the dead outlaw. He wanted one of Rourke with Red Jim's corpse. Rourke said he'd do it if he could shoot at the camera while he did so. The man left him alone after that.

In an hour, he was ready. He flung Red Jim on the outlaw's horse and tied his hands and feet to hold him there. He couldn't lose the man until the Territory had its proof and he wanted his bounty. At his request, the hostler threw in a bag of grain for each of the horses. Rourke guessed the boy would sell Red Jim's old saddle, which seemed to have disappeared. Next time through, that boy will own the town, he thought. A ghost of a smile caught his mouth at the thought of the young man using the outlaw's death as a step up toward prosperity. He cantered out of Broken Corners, taking a quick look around. The place was like so many others—buildings where the trails crossed. The coal mines were to the south along with the railroad. Maybe it would grow. Maybe it would wither and die. Then who would remember Red Jim?

Those who saw the man calmly gun down a man they all had feared to cross could not tell whether they were more chilled by his indifference to death or the chilling smile painted on his face as he left the town. Red Jim had been a violent man, they all would later agree. This Rourke, however, was a killer without emotions, without a soul. In the wake of the gunfight that killed the town's legendary bad man, few were truly glad he had come. All were glad he was leaving.

CHAPTER TWO

Rawhide, Wyoming, was always noisy. The place barely had 1,000 people, but there were fully 20 saloons. Rourke hated the town, which seemed to want to grow into the territorial capital as if getting bigger and dirtier would make it all better. There were too many people. Comings and goings from the nearby Overland Trail. Drunks underfoot everywhere. Fort Laramie was a long day's ride away to the northeast, but for some reason the town's saloons seemed to be on the way of cavalry troopers returning from the fort's far-flung scouting missions to keep one eye on the Indians and the other on the flood of settlers along the Oregon Trail to the north. Nobody had been scalped in a saloon, Rourke mused. Maybe they could say their visits were working.

He had hitched Star to the rail away from most of the horses on account of Red Jim stinking so badly. He walked past the open saloon doors of the Last Chance Saloon, the biggest of the bunch and the one designed to be the most raucous possible temptation for passing cowboys desperate to be parted from their wages. Loud, bad music and louder voices surged into his path like a physical presence, surrounded him, and then faded away as he moved along. Rourke grimaced and kept moving down the duckboards until he was outside the office of the territorial administration, which, as Rourke reckoned time, was all of about two months old. He peered through the glass door. Government didn't look any better in Wyoming than it did anywhere else—fellas in funny clothes who shuffled papers a lot and pretended they were more important than they were.

Rourke grimaced and put his hand on the knob to open the door. No matter how much he hated it, the territorial administration was here. It had to be convinced the man they wanted was dead or no one would pay him the money he needed to buy provisions. A man did what he had to do, even if it meant dragging a dead, stinking corpse around the High Plains for three days. Star didn't like it; he liked being alone about as much as Rourke did. Smarter horse than most people. Didn't like other horses much, either. He wondered if Star objected to the dead man in principle or just the smell. "Wonder what we smell like to a horse," he mused.

"How should I know?" responded the smartly dressed young man wearing an Eastern-styled suit who had come up behind him and was now standing next to him. "You have been out there too long when you wonder what your horse thinks of the way you smell."

"Probably true," said Rourke, laughing to cover his embarrassment.

He looked at his friend. Steve Owens worked for Territorial Assistant Administrator Andrew Dickinson. Steve was a genial young man, with softer and whiter skin than the men who rode the range. Blue eyes beamed contentedly from his full, round face. The blond hair beneath his derby hat was, as always, perfectly trimmed. He'd been to college in the East for a while before coming back when his father's health started to fail. He was old Judge Owens' son, which made him Rourke's friend. Rourke became one of the few men the judge liked and respected when Rourke had stopped a mob of vigilantes from hanging a man before the judge got the man into his court. The judge had no tolerance for vigilantes. "Hang 'em legal," he'd say. Steve was good to talk to, good to laugh with, but good to get away from. Young Steve often nagged Rourke to ape the fashions of the East. The man had the odd idea that the West would somehow be a better place if it were more like the East. Funny notions a man gets, Rourke mused. Owens dug right in.

"Look at you. Grown man talking to yourself. You ought to be married, raising a family, settling down like I'm going to do once I get the money. You should be wearing respectable clothes." Owens gestured to his fancy vest and suit that Rourke thought looked ridiculous.

"Rather do what I'm doin'."

"And what is that?"

A splash of conversation ended Rourke's rising irritation and announced the arrival of Territorial Assistant Administrator Andrew Dickinson, who could no more be silent making his way through a crowd than Rourke could speak to a soul in one. He was a tall, rail-thin man with dark eyes. A black mustache luxuriated beneath a hawkish nose. A mouth that was quick to smile when others were around.

He shook Rourke's trail-stained hand warmly and smiled. In Wyoming Territory, a man didn't worry about the state of cleanliness when he greeted a man; only what there was inside counted. Dickinson had been a Yankee cavalry in the war; Rourke a Texas scout. In the way of most real men, the bond of fighting and suffering was stronger than any cause that started the war. They had been unlikely friends since they met in '66. Dickinson came west to make a name for himself. Rourke drifted along with others heading westward because there were too many loaded memories everywhere else.

The men walked down the crowded duckboards to the hitching rail where Star stood patiently next to Red Jim's horse and its untidy burden.

"Well, that's him," remarked Dickinson, looking at the dead outlaw's face.

"Didn't know you knew him," Rourke remarked.

Dickinson looked flustered. Rourke guessed no one wanted to admit knowing a man who had been declared a dangerous outlaw. "I, um, saw him once before we were a Territory," Dickinson said lamely. "That was back a year or two ago. I can't rightly remember. It doesn't matter." Dickinson resumed his usual brisk tone. "Let's get the formalities over. With you as the Territory's witness, Mr. Owens, are we agreed that this is the body of the man known as Red Jim and the man we have a $100 reward on?"

"Nope."

Dickinson's head swiveled to Rourke.

"Two hundred dollars, as you know right well, Andy."

Dickinson looked back at Owens, who nodded. Dickinson shrugged. Rourke noted the man didn't blush. He figured his old friend was getting used to throwing Territory money around.

"Well, then, it's only money." He stared at the dead outlaw, who'd made the territorial wanted list—one of its very first acts as a government—after killing a rancher and his family. "He stinks. Owens, find somebody to bury him decently and cheaply and if not, cheaply will do fine. Then see if this poor territorial government can find enough money to meet the needs of our greedy bounty hunter friend, who will be waiting with me."

"Me 'n' Star are going out to the hills up northwest toward Indian Country in the morning, Andy, so don't be setting plans for me. This ought to buy me enough flour to get through the winter and a good long rifle and some stuff to trade with my friends the Sioux and maybe we can talk in the spring. Prob'ly be something I want to do then, but I can't think of what it might be right now. Workin' all year ain't good for a man."

"Listen to some advice, my good friend," said Dickinson as he threw an arm around Rourke's slight shoulders. Rourke smelled something that stunk all sweet like the stuff ladies wore.

He crinkled his nose. "Cooped up in some hideous mountain cabin of your own construction you would go positively insane for the lack of anything to do. I know you and those heathens get along because none of you actually like to talk, but you cannot escape civilization so easily. I speak as your friend and one concerned for your welfare. There is much to do before winter."

"Yup. Build a cabin."

"I had some other thoughts on that subject, and let me share them with you later over dinner. I am sure you need to eat something other than whatever disgusting mess you have cooked for yourself these past days."

Owens was grinning as he hooked his thumbs into the pockets of his vest and self-assuredly posed for all to see—the picture of what Wyoming could become. The administrator was a top-notch persuader when he had a mind to be, and whatever he wanted, Owens would bet that Rourke would end up doing it.

Rourke thought it over. Somebody else's cooking would be good, and if Andy wanted to fill him up he could afford to listen to and then ignore whatever was being said. "Deal, but money first."

The words were barely out of his mouth when Owens reached into his jacket, pulled out a slip of paper and a pencil, wrote briefly on it, and smartly handed it to Dickinson. Dickinson passed it to Rourke. "Take that to the bank," Dickinson said. "I do not keep the vast sums needed to appease greedy bounty hunters in my pockets, you know."

Rourke took the paper, looked at it. Checks they called them, for some reason. Rourke had become suspicious of paper money in the war, when it became all but worthless. Paper would never replace the feel of a gold coin in his pocket. But he nodded and went along down the street toward the bank. He did not see Owens and Dickinson talking behind his back in what looked like an argument.

Rourke looked along the main street of Rawhide a minute, sizing up the place. It had grown since spring. He wanted none of it. He regretted accepting the dinner invitation. Then again, it was a day when the arm was hurting again. Still. Shiloh would be with him until the day he died. Even if it left his mind, there was a piece of Yankee lead that was never going to leave his body.

Rourke's boots made a lot of noise on the boards as he clomped through the noisy crowd of people going someplace. He wasn't one of the cowboys who wore silver jangling spurs. He had never had any. Star wasn't some animal to be hurt. The horse was intelligent enough to know when they needed to get out of someplace in a hurry. Spurs in a town were to impress somebody. Rourke didn't care who thought what, as long as they kept their fool mouths shut around him. The boots were pretty old and smelled, and the nail where he put the right heel back on in the spring was coming loose. However, he'd worn these boots when he rode away from Johnston's army in '65. Getting rid of them was like losin' an old friend. Well, he'd cash that check first and then see what money bought these days.

The bank looked like little town banks everywhere—a short row of tellers, a pompous-looking guy in a gray Eastern suit at a wooden roll-top desk, and a couple of professionally smiley women behind the teller windows. One of the few places a woman actually worked. Everybody overdressed but not too fancy. An old man looked at him as he walked in. The line for the two tellers was short.

The young woman teller who took the check looked puzzled.

"This is a lot of money. The administrator should have come with you," she scolded Rourke. "We have to verify this is genuine. Please see Mr. Stafford at the desk. He knows Mr. Dickinson's signature."

Rourke went to wait some more. He looked around. Working

indoors. Talking. Must be nice for the folks that do it, he thought. The rancher ahead of him was gabbing with the banker fella. The banker was gabbing back with the extra chin he was growing flapping the same way his arms did—animated and smiley.

A gunshot ended his thoughts. Another pistol shot followed. Screams flew about the bank like the scattering of pigeons. Customers darted instinctively away. The banker had already ducked behind his desk.

"Everybody freeze!" Two bandana-masked cowboys stood there with weapons—one a shotgun, one some kind of long-barreled revolver. The revolver fired into the ceiling. Dust flew.

Three shots wasted, thought Rourke.

"Down, all of you. Down!"

The blur at the edge of his vision turned into a screaming old man as the speaker fired one bullet into the old man guard, who fell, making pitiful noises. The tiny pistol he had been pointing at the robber skittered across the floor to rest by the windows.

"I said to get down!"

Eyes above a bandana that was pulled up as a mask were looking right at Rourke. He shook his head as if not comprehending and put his arms out in a universal gesture of helplessness and confusion.

The man with the gun gestured with it. "Get down on the floor, range bum, or I'll kill you."

It was not the place for a discussion about his appearance. Rourke slowly got down, face down as he was told, making pitiful meek noises. The robber waited until he was down, then turned away. Rourke rolled fast.

Twin explosions shattered the remaining nerves of the bank's customers. New screams rocked the bank. The long-barreled revolver fired its last bullet into the polished wood as the robber crumpled to the floor clutching his right thigh.

With smoke curling from the end of the old .45 Remington revolver, Rourke moved fast. He stepped on the wrist of the shooter. Hard. The gun was free. He kicked it to the far end of the bank, and looked up to see the shotgun pointed at his guts.

"Drop it," said the man in the mask, holding the shotgun with his right hand and clutching a woman with his left. Somebody's wife on an errand.

"Don't worry none, ma'am," said Rourke. "Might get a bit loud but you ain't gonna get hurt."

"Drop the gun or I kill her," said the robber.

"Nope," replied Rourke. "It's over, podna. You got the choice of giving it up or gettin' shot. You ain't gonna get no money, you ain't gonna get outta here. Put the big popgun down or get hurt."

"I'll kill her," repeated the robber, moving toward the door.

"Don't work that way, son," said Rourke, shaking his head in what could have been sympathy for the man or an assessment of the robber's stupidity. "Use your head for somethin' other than a place to put that hat. When you get to the door, you got to either use your gun hand for the door and I kill you or you let go of her and I kill you. If she opens the door, and I don't know as how she can shaking the way the poor woman is, she's far enough away that I have enough space to kill you. And if you fire one-handed the way it is now, you're as like to ventilate the ceiling as get me, because you ain't never done this before and your body's jangling with the shakes. Now put the thing down; let me get help for the old fella you boys shot cuz if he dies you are in a whole different world of trouble, and maybe even we get some help for your partner so he don't die, too."

Silence built. Rourke knew he had wasted his time. He was glad none of the customers were behind him. They had had the good sense to crawl away when it became clear a showdown

24

was building.

The eyes above the bandana stared back impassively. The arm holding the shotgun began to twitch as muscles got the word from the brain to fire.

Rourke fired from the hip, bullet sending bones, muscle, and blood from the man's right arm all over the female hostage, whom Rourke tossed aside after clearing the space between them in three huge leaps. She landed with a sound of pain. Distracted, he looked, almost not seeing the masked outlaw reach toward his hip with his left arm.

The next boom of the gun ended it. The impact of the bullet slammed the would-be robber against a wall, where he lay in a crumpled ball. Blood spurted briefly but was already starting to slow as Rourke put his gun away.

"Fool, boy! For nuthin'!" Rourke exclaimed. He took three steps over to where the dead man lay, his boots the only noise in the bank. No pulse. One in the heart doesn't usually give a man much time to make his peace before dyin'. The other one was alive, and probably not bleeding out.

The guard was half-conscious. Rourke guessed he'd live. Not much blood, which was good.

"Hang in there, podna. We got 'em. You made it happen, you're gonna be a hero, so don't you go and die now and spoil all of that."

The man's lips moved. He tried to smile. Rourke felt better. He knew from the war that if the wounded could smile, they would usually live.

"Anybody a nurse or some such can help this fella?" he called out, knowing his record for playing doctor was almost on par with his cooking. "Maybe one of you can fetch a doctor or whatever you all have here?"

Nobody moved.

"Hang it all, people, this fella tried to save you. Now, can somebody help him here?"

An older woman stepped forward. "My men are always getting hurt," she said. "I can help him until Doc comes."

"He needs bandaging and to have someone with him, ma'am, when he starts to go into shock. Grab anybody you can to give you a hand." Satisfied that the guard would be about as cared for as he could be until whatever Rawhide had for a doctor arrived, Rourke walked away to wait outside. Whatever passed for law might shoot first and ask questions later.

A middle-aged man with a badge and a belly was huffing down the walk. There was a star pinned to the brown leather vest he wore over the white-and-blue striped shirt underneath. He moved fast past Rourke, bellowing questions and orders. In a minute or two, he was back outside, staring at Rourke.

"You done this?"

"Yup." Rourke stared back, waiting to see what followed. Put a star on a man and it changed him.

"Obliged." The man stuck out a hand. "Dan Wheeler. Sheriff. Sort of. They want the drunken cowboys thrown out of town but not too hard or they don't make money. Never had bank robbers before."

"Progress, podna."

"Tell the Territory that, sonny. Since the war ended, been nothin' but changes and troubles. Both of those boys in there had their day ridin'. Jim Lynch, the dead one, had a small spread not far from the North Platte. Last year the drought got him. He tried this and that but nothin' came out right. Fella you shot in the leg, Mel Calhoun, was breakin' horses at the Lazy S but they let the man go because the Army started buyin' from other ranchers. Mel said they was lookin' to get a stake and pull out to California. Leastways they don't have kin to tell. Lynch's woman left for Denver when he started drinking in the summer. Mel never got married yet. Maybe in the East they say this all comes down to progress for the better, but, friend, out here it looks like a lot of lives thrown on the pile." The sheriff's massive gray mustache hung down over both lips, giving his face the look of a sad walrus, Rourke thought. "Well, I guess you are passin' through and this is all the same to you, but it bothers an old man. Just glad I don't live down where the railroad is being built. Ranchers talk about the railroad like the Second Coming, but all I see are drunks and shootings."

"Maybe that's progress, Sheriff."

The lawman spat in the dirt. He glared at Rourke. "What I want, son, is for the Territory in its almighty wisdom to find a way to pay for somebody to control this progress they want. But the Territory don't know which end . . . well, speaking of progress, here they come now."

Owens and Dickinson were walking swiftly, looking agitated. They stopped when they saw Rourke talking with the sheriff. For a minute, Rourke saw something like alarm pass across their faces. He waved. They waved back. The sheriff watched him with shrewd, narrow eyes that read faces by the score every day, a light going on behind them.

"You that Texas bounty hunter who brought in Red Jim?"

"Rourke's the name, Sheriff."

Wheeler grimaced. "Well, son, Jim was too wild and too crazy to understand that the law wasn't gonna let him kill just anyone just any time, but you ought to know that in his day, there were folks in Nebraska Territory, who are now the almighty of Wyoming Territory, who thought of him as the man with the gun who could handle folks they didn't like. Sound like anyone you know?"

Rourke knew only that Red Jim killed because the man liked killing. If there had been a pattern, he hadn't noticed it. Then again, he was never around in one place long enough to pay attention. Wheeler's words reminded him of Red Jim's final utterings, but in a country where facts were as rare as water, gossip was always there to be had instead. "Interesting, Sheriff. Thanks for the news."

Wheeler gave Rourke a long look to see if he was being mocked. Rourke returned the gaze levelly. "All right, son, we understand each other. Now, let me tell the high and mighty of the Territory what happened in my own way. They your friends?"

"We go back."

"Lots of folks go back; not so many go forward," Wheeler said. "And don't say I didn't warn you. Now, don't say nothin' about this. Not one word. Mel Calhoun was a fool on a fool's errand and he's guilty of being stupid. I'm not sendin' him to hang or prison if I can get him out of it. We got a problem with that, son?"

"Your town, your people, your law," replied Rourke. "You convince your people that fella was shot by accident, it's no skin off my nose. Never liked watchin' a hangin' myself. Figgered the need of folks to hang a man was like one of them contagious diseases that's likely to spread."

Wheeler grunted. "Half the folks here been caught actin' stupid at least once, Rourke. They know the way it works. I'll get Mel out of town quick and he can take his chances some other place."

Rourke shrugged.

The conversation was short. Dickinson and Owens made appropriate noises about the need for more lawmen now that the Territory was growing. The sheriff went to arrange for the dead man to be taken away and for someone to care for the wounded guard and wounded "bystander."

"Come on, Rourke," said Dickinson. "The bank will be too crowded for a while. We can go to my office and have a drink. Better than what you can get at the saloon. Give me the check and I will have the money delivered."

Shrugging, not caring for a drink he wouldn't drink, Rourke handed the check to Dickinson, who gave it to Owens. The young man walked into the bank while Rourke walked along with Dickinson. Truth was, he'd had about all of the people he could stand for a while and he wanted to go someplace where the nearest person was an Indian a mile away wondering if he had anything worth killing for. The Indians he'd met last winter didn't seem to mind one white man putting up a cabin, once they realized he was all alone and not planning to stay. They'd had their scraps, settled things out in the open, and agreed that too much of that kind of thing was not good for anybody. Not like this talk to cover up facts. It was pretty plain Sheriff Dan Wheeler had a grudge against Andy and Steve, and they had hard feelings right back. That's what happened when people lived too close to each other and saw each other too often, Rourke told himself.

He was thinking about the feeling of last winter when there was nothing outside that cabin door but white for miles around for weeks on end, when he heard the woman scream.

Across the muddy, rut-filled street, a massive man had grabbed the arm of a young woman dressed in Eastern clothes and was half-dragging her across the duckboards. Her hat had tumbled off of her head and was ground up as passersby and wagons trampled it. Rourke and Dickinson jumped out into the street, narrowly missing being run over by a wagon of barrels, and ran through the mud and dirt to where the man—a full head taller than Rourke—was talking to the woman incoherently. She was telling him something in a tone that reminded Rourke of the camp followers around Richmond, but he didn't stop to take in the words.

"Let her go!" Rourke bellowed. Four years of soldiering had taught him to make his voice carry to get men's attention. It worked again.

The man stopped. Squinting out from a fog of cheap liquor, he looked at Rourke. "Do I know you?"

"My sister," replied Dickinson smoothly, taking the woman's arm and smiling at the giant miner. "I think you might need another drink there, my good friend. Tell them it's on the Territory." Dickinson pushed the giant of a miner down the duckboards, where he lurched and staggered before veering into one of the saloons. Dickinson's eyes met Rourke's and he chuckled.

"Miss Harwood, my apologies," Dickinson said. "They are usually only dangerous to themselves, but sometimes the mining men have a bit too much to drink."

"You never said . . ." she raved. Rourke wasn't sure if Dickinson squeezed her arm or she was rambling. "What kind of drunken . . ."

"Miss Harwood, this is the West and these things happen, but you are safe, now." Dickinson seemed to be smiling through clenched teeth.

"Show's over, folks," Dickinson yelled. "Move along."

"Drunks out here are like twisters, miss," said Rourke. "You got to learn to get out of the way and they don't cause you no hurt."

The woman glared at him for a second. Rourke watched the Eastern woman. She turned, looking into the crowd. She didn't look as scared now as much as she did concerned—as though something was wrong. Not much relief at being rescued. She didn't seem to have heard him. Must have come to town with family or something, Rourke thought. Maybe a husband? Woman that pretty wouldn't remain unmarried very long in a place like this. Clothes looked Eastern. He remembered how women dressed back East. "How do I ever move in this ridiculous outfit?" Lorraine had told him once when they went to a fancy fine dinner at a Richmond social event. He shook his head. What's gone is gone. The woman was pretty, though. Her husband should have kept a better eye on her. Maybe they came from the East. He wanted to get her away from the saloon the miner had entered. She was compliant as he helped guide her along the duckboards, but she was clearly not very happy about being touched by hands that were roughened by a thousand chores without gloves and, despite an effort to wipe them in the dirt, still stained with blood from the shootout at the bank. She kept scanning the crowd.

An Eastern-dressed, gray-haired man pushed people out of the way as though used to being obeyed. He started to shoulder Rourke aside until Rourke grabbed him by the shoulders of his suit and put him against the wall of the saloon. "Easy, podna," he growled. "Had about enough of them Rawhide manners to last the day. Now give the girl room."

The man disengaged himself from Rourke's grip. Dickinson materialized at his shoulder with a horrified look on his face.

"Bill Harwood," said the man, nodding at the girl, "My daughter." He was about Rourke's height, bigger built and ruddy-faced. Although dressed in an Eastern suit, he had the look of a man who knew his way around the saddle. He had a bluff, open, honest face. His hair was going to gray, but he looked like a powerful and dominating man in charge rather than a man getting old. "I know that they told me this was a town where miners went wild but I never saw anything like that in my life. I will speak to the territorial governor about this."

A woman standing behind him, clearly the girl's mother from the similarity of their appearance, added emphatically her opinion of Rawhide, Wyoming, and everyone in it. The girl dimly radiated her distaste for everyone and everything within sight, including the rescuer who looked little different from the drunk who had accosted her. Everybody stared at Dickinson as if they expected him to do something. Rourke felt a smile coming on. No good deed goes unpunished, he told himself. He was about

31

ready to tell them to find themselves another rescuer when Dickinson came forward to interject himself.

"Territorial Assistant Administrator Andrew Dickinson, sir," he said addressing Harwood. "I don't know if you remember me but we met yesterday. No one regrets this terrible incident more than I do. Please, come and take a minute, if your time permits, and we can discuss this sad state of affairs. May I escort you and your wife and daughter to the hotel?" For a second, there was some expression on Dickinson's face Rourke could not place. Fear? Something odd, like Dickinson was saying one thing with his eyes and another with his mouth.

Harwood laughed loudly, and commented that he liked to see a territorial administrator in shirtsleeves. "I know this is the West, and the ruffians here are a legend, but I hope you will make an effort to control the town here, sir," he said to Andy in the pompous, formal style of Easterners. He told Dickinson that as soon as he saw his wife and daughter to their hotel he'd find the territorial offices.

There was a brief test of wills between the man and wife. She insisted with some asperity that she could walk through the chaos of the town as well without him as with him for all the good that he did in protecting her and that her tiny pistol would make the next man who said a cross word sorry. In the end a compromise was arranged: Bill Harwood would accompany Dickinson to the territory offices for some reason Rourke could not fathom, while Rourke and Owens would walk the women to the hotel. Dickinson said Harwood would join them for dinner later.

Rourke balked at escorting the women. "If you wasn't married to Caroline you'd be walking them two silly women and I could go on my way. They don't need only Owens to escort them. You been changing and it ain't good for you."

"Being married to Caroline is very good for me," Dickinson

chortled, "and it's about time you took some interest in women." He read Rourke's face. The lack of expression registered. "I'm so sorry, Rourke. I forgot about Lorraine."

"S'alright, Andy. She's been gone three years now, about. Funny that she's been gone longer than the little time we had together. Sometimes I look back and I wonder if it was my life or somebody else's, it's so far long behind. World goes on. So they say." There was a wistful sadness in his face.

Dickinson retreated with Harwood. Rourke saw them talking in low tones and wondered that they could be good friends on such a short acquaintance. He guessed Dickinson would run for President someday, or something. The man was on his way up to someplace beyond Rawhide, Wyoming. Well, ambition had never bitten Rourke and he doubted it would. He supposed he could overlook it in other people if he tried real hard. The problem was that when ambition was done with folks, there were often no traces left of the people they used to be.

The women had waited at a discreet distance. Rourke thought they looked less like a mother and daughter than sisters, although the difference in ages was clearer when you looked closely. There was something harder about them than he expected, as though they had seen all this before and the fussing about the ham-handed drunk was for show. They seemed happy to ignore Rourke, but he tried to remember his manners for Andy's sake.

"You folks travelin' through? Goin' far?" he asked the girl.

She looked at him with barely concealed contempt. "Don't you know anything? My father owns half of this territory. We have a large house waiting for us not far from here at a place called Green Hills. The purchase has taken months and we are finally here to move in, that is if we can reach our new home without further assaults from your Western ruffians."

Well, no matter how much the girl looked like a pretty lady

that would sip tea, blush at swear words, and sew silly things they stuck on walls, she seemed to have recovered her health pretty quickly and was acting about as cozy and needy as a rattler so there was no sense worrying about her. Maybe the miner got the better end of the deal. He frowned. He knew the ranches in the area. Green Hills was a big piece of land, but it had been abandoned for years, as he recalled. Didn't matter. These folks looked like they could buy about anything. The hotel was there and they could go be snobbish to somebody else.

"Yes, ma'am, Miss. Enjoy the rest of your trip. Gets real dusty on them back roads, so bring water."

"I am sure that will be attended to," she replied distantly. "But thank you for your concern."

He was dismissed. He'd heard the tone from them Richmond ladies during the war. It was like they all were in the same play reading the same lines. Lorraine would mock them, before the sickness. Memories didn't stay buried like dead people. All he wanted was to get out of there, so that's what he did. He tipped his hat as she walked off with the older woman into the dimness of the hotel, not looking back. Owens said he would stay at the hotel for some unknown reason. Rourke didn't much care. He wanted to get away.

He retraced his steps to Star and then found the only decent place he knew in the town. He never trusted anyone to care for Star, so he slept in the stall on a blanket. They slept like that on the prairie. The horse kept away nightmares, mostly. If the horse objected to Rourke's presence, he'd never kicked Rourke upside the head to indicate his displeasure.

Bear Wallace, the giant of a man who kept the stable, was glad to see Rourke. He even smiled a rare grin, parting the huge bush of black beard that gave him his name. Rourke always paid extra, and paid up front. The horse was more like a pet than a work animal, but from the dust covering them both, they looked like they'd been riding awhile. Wallace knew that he could spend the night elsewhere whenever Rourke stayed, because Rourke would stay with his horse and he slept lightly. Rourke was odd. He talked to himself, and to the horse more, but he was deadly with a gun. Wallace had seen the results himself. Rourke would inevitably check on all the animals, for whom Wallace often felt a greater affection than most of their riders. He recalled once catching Rourke feeding cream to the barn cats.

The shadows were filling Rawhide's main street as Rourke emerged from the stable, feeling slightly refreshed by some time with critters he understood. Owens was still where Rourke had left him near the door to the hotel, enjoying his fill of looking at whatever young fellas liked to look at—mostly women, Rourke guessed, from the way Owens was staring at someone. Owens had talked about having a woman of his own, but the man didn't act as if he did. Maybe that was what being young was about. Rourke yelled his name in the young man's ear before he heard. Owens greeted Rourke with a shame-faced grin.

"Rourke, tonight you get a taste of the good life," Owens exclaimed. "We will be eating at Mr. Dickinson's house. Mr. Harwood and some other important people will be there. They should be arriving any minute, so let's go."

Rourke didn't like the way Owens stressed the word "important." Back in the Army, even in the Confederacy, it meant pompous blowhards. "My money coming any minute, Steve?"

The young man blushed. "Forgot, Rourke. Plumb forgot." He handed Rourke an envelope heavy with coins. "All $200 is there. Knowing how you feel about paper money, we didn't give you any."

"Paper's no good out there," replied Rourke, motioning toward the hills. "Man wants money, he wants real money, not phony paper." He walked with Owens away from the main street of Rawhide to where a few houses had been built, set back from what was as close to a street as there was likely to be. Rourke grimaced. "You know what Andy wants? Can't he come tell me man to man without all this?"

"That's for him to tell you," Owens replied. "Now that we're a Territory, we have to make changes for the better. You know you're going to end up doing what the administrator wants done, though."

"Nope," replied Rourke. "Got my fill of people. Time to get away. Reckon you and Andy can keep the Territory from going to pieces without me." He was uneasy around people. When they were out on the Plains in ones and twos they weren't usually too bad, but coop 'em up in a town and they took the strangest notions about life.

Now that he had his money, all he needed was a good rest with Star. Maybe they could head out the next day or the day after. Bad things happened to a riding man when he stayed put. There was a place by a stream about fifty miles north he knew would be good for the winter. Indian land, but he'd get extra stuff to trade or that they could steal, whichever they seemed to like more. When it was warrior-to-warrior, it was simple, even if nobody could talk anybody else's language. He was thinking about the winter and not paying attention to the present.

He was so lost in thought, he barely noticed when they arrived at the door to Dickinson's house to be greeted by a woman about his own age in a pink, frilly dress whose smile seemed a little plastered on her face to Rourke's frame of mind. Then again, she had been smiling the whole time while he was thinking about being 50 miles from anywhere and anybody's smile had a right to be tired after a while.

"Hello, Caroline," he said, having met Dickinson's wife once before. "Um, you want me to wipe my boots?"

"You would be the only one today who has, Rourke," she

replied with a small laugh. "Come on in. The men are gathered in the dining room. I will tell the cook you are here. As I recall you much prefer eating to talking."

"Got that right, ma'am."

"Steven, take Rourke to the parlor," Caroline said, turning away with her formal smile still firmly in place. "Fix him what he wants to drink."

All Rourke knew about Caroline Dickinson was that Andy Dickinson had met her in Illinois or someplace like that. She seemed to sort people into two piles—the ones that were of use to her husband and those who were not. Rourke was in the first group, since he helped Andy look good by chasing bad guys. But Caroline, who was almost as tall as Andy and smiled a lot less often except for company, always seemed to be assessing him. She was thin, very thin to Rourke's way of thinking, with angular features and dark eyes that were always serious. She had her hair in some fashion Rourke figured was what women in the East wore, piled up with pieces hanging down on the side. Lorraine had done that once, he recalled, and they both had had a chuckle over it.

Dickinson met him at the doorway to a room that seemed far too small for the amount of furniture in it. Rourke recalled rooms like that in Richmond. Sometimes the padded things were comfortable and sometimes they were like a saddle. There was a rug on the floor, paintings on the walls, and three men eying him expectantly. He swallowed at what was to come and allowed Andy to lead him into the room.

"You have met Bill Harwood briefly," Dickinson said, nodding at the distinguished-looking man. Harwood gripped Rourke's hand tightly and smiled as they shook hands. "His daughter, Elizabeth, and his wife, Mary, you have also met. This is Gilbert Harrison, a rancher up north a ways, and this is Pete Treadwell, another rancher whose land is off south of Green

Hills. Gilbert and Pete wanted to talk with me, and since Bill is getting settled, I thought he ought to join us to see the lay of the land out here. Let's have dinner first and then we'll talk business."

Harrison was a tall, lean middle-aged man who had clearly grown old in the saddle. He surveyed Rourke at a glance as though he had inspected stray riders his whole life. Treadwell was a short, stocky man not much older than Rourke. He pumped Rourke's hand vigorously and looked at Rourke with pugnacious determination as though there was something more than dinner on his mind. Neither spoke beyond a muttered greeting.

The women had nodded politely. Mary Harwood looked as though she had missed a few meals along the way and was never going to miss one again. There was a determination in her jaw and a look about the eyes that told Rourke a story he had seen a thousand times before. Being from the East didn't mean always being rich. He knew that. She was wearing some dark dress with a little bit of white lace ringing the throat. Her light brown hair was swept back in a bun that accentuated the severity of her face.

Her daughter, Elizabeth, had jet black curls flowing down around a heart-shaped face. Her large brown eyes and small nose gave her face the look of youthful innocence. She had nodded politely to Rourke when he entered, and given him a slight, shy smile, but otherwise kept her eyes averted. She was tiny, with very small, white hands below the lacy cuffs of something frilly and white that was mostly covered by a jacket of some kind of velvet. Rourke was wondering why she was not snappish the way she had been on the street earlier. Probably she had been called to task for her behavior by her mother, Rourke thought, wishing he had never agreed to this foolishness.

Dickinson was carrying on a conversation with the room at

large, since the women didn't say much and the ranchers not much more. Caroline swept in to announce dinner. She and Dickinson exchanged smiles, but Rourke caught a side glance and heard something muttered that was clearly not pleasant and also not meant for the guests to hear.

Rourke put aside worries as the cook and a maid brought in plates with large, juicy steaks that looked a lot more edible than anything Rourke ever cooked. Afterward there was pie. Throughout there was coffee that tasted the way Rourke remembered real coffee tasting.

Much of the conversation was about the railroad. The Union Pacific was laying track through the southern end of the Territory. There was talk of a line coming up to Rawhide from there, once the transcontinental railroad became a reality. They saw the railroad in a very different light from the way Rourke saw it. It was the gateway to progress. It would connect Wyoming with the East. The railroad would create new needs with the coal that would be mined in southern Wyoming.

There was worry about the Indians, but Red Cloud had the Sioux under control, and the Army had learned from the Fetterman massacre and its 80-some dead cavalry troopers that leaving Indian land alone made a lot of good sense. The immigrants coming overland didn't want to hear that, though. The Oregon Trail was about a day north of Rawhide, and this had been a busy year. Travelers wanted supplies, and many times they ran out of energy by the time they reached Wyoming. They all agreed that U.S. Grant was a better general than he was likely to be a president but that Andy Johnson had been plumb useless. Even the Territory men agreed that this far West, it wouldn't matter much because Washington couldn't do anything right if it tried.

The ladies said very few words. When the meal was over, they excused themselves to chat in the parlor.

"Now you can talk your business," Caroline admonished Dickinson. Elizabeth Harwood, who had looked at Rourke from under her eyelashes off and on throughout the meal, gave him a small smile as they left. Owens, sitting across the table from Rourke, gave the young woman a quick glance and then looked down at the table. Rourke assumed the girl was simply fascinated with seeing a real cowboy. She was more or less pretty, though, in a different kind of way. Something to look at, but not like a real person.

Caroline Dickinson sighed as the two Harwood women prattled on and on. The longer they talked, the more she wished Andrew and the men would finish their conversation so she could be rid of them. She knew little about the Harwoods, only that Andrew was certain they would be suitable. She hoped so. Andrew's judgments were often at variance with hers. She knew they only had to worry about the men, but women of any intelligence, with the least bit of a discerning eye, would immediately know the truth. Fortunately, in this case, few in Wyoming Territory aside from her had such discernment and refinement.

Rourke was a good example. Andrew had the highest confidence that he was exactly what they needed. She was less convinced. Although the man was, unlike a certain past associate she now knew she never needed to worry about again, someone she would allow in her house, he was far too reserved and far too remote for her taste. She liked things simple. People who had a role in her plans should fill that role and nothing more. Rourke's predecessor was crude and foul, but could be easily controlled with women, drink, and money. Despite Andrew's confidence that Rourke could be controlled by the power of their friendship, she was not certain that anyone could control the man. She did not think he could be bent to Andrew's will, but as a woman, there were very clear lines on how far she could offer advice to her husband. She had thought this meeting was a risk, but with those two ranchers howling about rustling, she supposed that Andrew was right. The Territory had to do something, or at least look like it was doing something. She saw Rourke noticing Elizabeth Harwood's well-coached efforts to attract his attention, but he seemed far less interested than that simple Steve Owens did in the girl. Dragging the women into this only complicated things, she had told Andrew. Of course, being a man, he did not listen!

The rest of them were nothing. Gil Harrison had raised horses all his life, never married, and would one day die on that two-bit ranch of his that took up far too much land for what he got out of it. He lived lightly on his land, and when he was gone, it would be as though he had never been.

Pete Treadwell was very different. She recognized him as an aggressive rival who wanted more and more land for his miserable wife and their brats. He was not raising horses; he was sinking deep roots. She recalled the visit to the Treadwell farm where the woman had the temerity to ask Caroline to help milk the family's cow!

As for young Steve Owens, he was useless. Andrew said the young man was good to have around because people liked him, and he wasn't bright enough to do anything other than what he was told. She thought he would be a liability. Even though he told everyone he had a woman and was planning to settle down, Caroline knew the truth was very, very different. Men!

The Harwoods, of course, were quite suitable in many ways. She could see why Andrew chose them on his trip back East. She hoped they would not prove difficult. She looked around the cramped room as the Harwood women talked—now about bonnets. Caroline had the clear insight that if she suddenly talked about far less proper subjects, the women would lose their affectations, but she did not actually want to know them.

They had a purpose, and that was all that mattered. What she
didn't know she could never betray in a word or a glance. As
she inventoried her possessions, she was thinking of what she
would need in a few months, when a new and larger house
would be hers, at least until such time as Andrew would be
governor or a senator. Until that time, she would make sacrifices
for their future. And so she smiled back at Mary Harwood and
inquired about the fashions in New York City as if it really
mattered.

Dickinson was handing out cigars, not offering one to Rourke,
who couldn't stand the things, when Harrison spoke up. "Well,
this was a good meal, Andy, and I hate to put a sour taste in
anyone's mouth but me and Pete want this rustling under
control, or we're going to have to go to the Army about it or
someone about it. Not personal, you understand. I can't bleed
stock. Even if it is a horse or two at a time, it adds up in a year.
I'm so small I can't take those losses. And let me tell you that,
by God, I shouldn't have to stand for it!"

Treadwell nodded. "We need a posse to catch the rustlers.
Territory ought to do the job. Round 'em up. String 'em up."

"Pete, maybe if I knew where to send that posse, I could
round one up, but the Territory can't deputize a bunch of men
to ride around and look."

"There may be another way," said Harwood thoughtfully.
Dickinson stopped and waited for the new rancher to continue.
His eyes, however, glanced at Rourke. Rourke saw the glance,
and wondered if his old friend and the rancher had scripted
what was coming next.

"Now, I know I'm new to this range and since I have no clear
idea what was left to me on Green Hills when the old owner
died in the spring and I took over, I accept that as a loss," Harwood said. "For all I know, my stock drifted onto your ranges.

But I did not become a success in New York City by letting anyone take anything from me at any time. I think we need to take an active approach to finding the rustlers."

Treadwell cut in. "You sayin' I took your horses?" The tone made the challenge clear.

"I'm saying that when no one minds the ranch, horses run free," Harwood said, palms upturned. "I investigated this business before I came out here. I know a free horse without a brand is fair game. If you've found a few this summer to make up your losses, fine with me. What I'm trying to say—"

"—is that I'm a horse thief," Treadwell said, starting to stand.

Dickinson waved his hands at both men. "I think Mr. Harwood is saying that finding strays and taking branded stock are different things, Pete." He turned to Harwood, looking more exasperated than Rourke thought he would, given the fact that all Easterners thought about rustling as though it was nothing. "Rustling is not about money out here, Bill. It's about a man's honor."

"Well, I offer an apology for an offense," Harwood said. "What I am trying to say is that we need to be out there looking for the rustlers all the time, not when we are missing horses, and that we need to look for large numbers, not just strays."

Harrison snorted. "Green Hills has a lot of land, suppose you got a crew to match," he said. "Me and Pete, we're shirttail outfits. Couple riders, some extras now and then. We don't have anyone to ride around and look for trouble."

Harwood turned to Rourke. "Andy Dickinson says you are good at finding people," he said smoothly.

"I hunt folks with bounties on their heads, if that's what you mean," Rourke said, having a very bad feeling about where the discussion was going to go.

"Well, in this case, we don't know who to find because we don't know who it is, but we all believe that someone is rustling horses." Harwood looked at Harrison and Treadwell. They nodded.

"Lost five head in 10 years and I lost eight head this summer," said Harrison. Treadwell muttered something and started getting red in the face again.

"My new stock is on its way to Green Hills," said Harwood, "so I haven't been hit yet. I want it stopped now. These men and I may compete when it comes to other matters, but that's business. I think we should hire you to stop the rustling. Andy says you're the man. Here's my offer: I have a lot of young fellows who can ride all day and ride all night, but I don't know that some of them have a lick of sense in them. I can tell from the way you handle yourself and the way Dickinson talked about you that you have a reputation as a man who gets things done. I'm going to need men like that to get things done at Green Hills. Between you and me, the Army is going to build more forts out here, and will need more horses. With even more settlers on the way and more of your Texans driving cattle up here every year, there is going to be a market for horses far beyond the Army.

"I built gun factories back East, but I got tired of the life back there. It was stifling and it was snobbish. I finally decided that I wanted to throw it all over and make my mark in something new. Now, you might be saying that a man my age is a fool for leaving all that behind—Lord knows I think my wife says that when I was not around—but you know, there's no sense in a man having dreams if he lets them wither on the vine. So, I'm here, and I'm investing and building for the long haul. I know I've got some lean times and lean seasons, but I've studied the way things work and I know I can succeed." He pounded the table. "But I'm not going to have thieves around. I want to help these men and track down the rustlers. I'll put you on the Green Hills payroll and you work for all of us until this rustling is over. Then, once you see what kind of outfit I run, I think you will want to stay on. What do you say?"

Rourke looked at Harrison, who seemed to be studying Harwood more than anything else. "You been here the longest. You got a thought? Stealin' horses usually means you got to know the country because you got to have a place to keep 'em. Somebody who got fired or got mad or never found a rule they couldn't break you can think of as the likely thief?"

There was a fleeting glance between Harrison and Treadwell. Something unsaid. Harrison shrugged. "Lot of wild boys come out here since the war ended," he told Rourke. "Now the railroad down south brings folks from all over creation to Wyoming. Those camps are wild, Rourke. My guess is that someone thinks he found an easier way to get rich without workin'. Few head here, few head there—eventually a man could make himself a living. Army never asks questions. Me and Pete can't say anything certain, but we think the Army has to know some of what they get is stolen. That's why we got to go there next if the Territory won't do anything for us."

Treadwell finally exploded. "My ranch is going to go under if we don't stop this! Now, I'm not an old-timer here, I came here after the war. I raised horses in Nebraska and I can do it here. I want this stopped before the spring. If we lose next year the way we did this year, Bill won't be the biggest rancher here, he'll be the only rancher here!"

Dickinson laid his hand on Rourke's arm and looked his old friend in the face. He spoke lowly and urgently. "Rourke, Wyoming is the youngest Territory in the country. We can be the next state if we move fast. Think what that means. Law. Order. Peace. Prosperity for all the people who want to live in peace. If the politicians in Washington think that we are a lawless hole of rustlers, that will work against us. I know you've been drifting since the war, but you know what it was like to have dreams of settling down. Wyoming can be a place for people who have those dreams, Rourke. I want to make the Territory a safe place for families. I'm your friend, Rourke. There are other men we can hire, but you need this job. In a few years, if you keep going the way you are from bounty to bounty, you will see the ranches and the farms and wish you had not let all of it pass you by. We're asking you to help us take a stand and also put down some roots."

It was as good a speech as any Rourke had ever heard. It reminded him of the way his back ached after days of tracking Red Jim, and the way the grit got into every pore of his skin when he was out in the wind riding for days to pick up an outlaw's trail.

"I'm not a gunman," said Treadwell. "You are. You can stand up to them."

"Rustlers only stop when you kill them," said Harrison. "Not my kind of work. We need you."

Rourke wished they would all stop talking. He wished he was far off alone. He knew that if Lorraine had not died, he'd have been one of the men trying to start a new life. He could feel an obligation to do something that was probably right, but he didn't want to be around people. He also had the feeling that something in all this wasn't right, but how anything could be wrong in a bunch of ranchers trying to stop rustling was beyond him. He rubbed the scar by his left eye where a Yankee bayonet almost blinded him at Shiloh. It always throbbed when he was feeling penned in without a road out.

"Think about it, Rourke," said Harwood, who was keenly watching the emotions that were plain on Rourke's face. "Why don't you do this? Take a day or so and come visit our ranches. See what we are building. I think you'll want to be part of it, Rourke, but I don't ever want to push a man into making up his mind."

"Well, it's still early," Rourke said, not wanting to either say yes or no. "Don't have to go north right yet. Guess I could look around a little, ride out and see the lay of the land. I don't know about that job you want me to do. That sounds like the law and I'm not the law." He paused. "I'll think on it."

"That's all we could ask of you, Rourke," said Dickinson. "You've just ridden in and we know you need a little time. Gilbert and Pete are riding back out to their ranches in the morning, and Bill will be heading to Green Hills in a few days. We wanted to speak to you tonight because we were all here and, well, you showed up like the answer to a prayer. Think on it, cowboy, and make sure you come see me about it before you leave." He finished with the tight, small smile of a salesman who knows his words have been effective.

Treadwell scraped back his chair from the table. "If we're done with business, I have to see a man about a card game. Tomorrow it's back to the kids, but tonight I want to see if I still know how to play poker. That is, 'slong as I don't lose any money, or Abby will never let me out again!" He nodded to Rourke and strode aggressively out of the house.

"Anything you can do will help," said Harrison. "There were some ranchers I knew on the North Platte who were hit by a gang this summer. Just about cleaned out. I know they went to the Army; can't believe sodbusters on the way to Oregon bought 'em all. No proof. Even if we had proof, we can't just take a few days away to bring our case to the Army. Ranches like ours are always short-handed. Now I'm going to have a drink with my boys before we ride back in the morning." He shook hands with Rourke and moved away.

Rourke excused himself then and followed the ranchers out into the night. Harwood and Dickinson walked Rourke to the doorway, where they watched him look up and down the street, loosen the gun in its holster, and then shut the door softly behind him with the wariness of a man ready for anything. Long after Rourke was gone, they sat and talked in low tones.

CHAPTER THREE

"Hands up or die!" growled the voice behind him as a gun barrel was shoved into the muscles of Rourke's back.

Talking about the future had unsettled Rourke. From the closing chaotic violence of the Civil War's conclusion to the ever-vigilant life on the Plains, he lived to survive day to day. Tomorrow only mattered when he had survived today. He had paced the stable awhile until the horses started looking at him. Then he walked from the back of the stable out past the corral to the edge of the foothills and walked some more until he returned no less pleased with himself than he was when he left. Finally, as the promise of dawn was filtering across the sky, he had slept. When he woke, he was wooly-headed. Too much food, he told himself. Too much talk. But he could not get the ideas of roots and settling down out of his head, even though he knew they were things for other men, not him.

He had gone to grab a pitchfork to clean out Star's stall, his mind far from his surroundings. For a moment, he froze. The gun pushed harder. Then Rourke broke into an unlikely grin when the reflexes of surprise and compliance had finished and he recognized the voice.

"Cal, you are in a heap of trouble for that one," Rourke drawled, with his Texas roots showing. He put his arms down and turned to face the figure who had stepped from the shadows.

"You're mad because I got you good this time," replied the smirking young woman, dressed in a man's checked shirt and jeans. A battered once-tan cowboy hat covered light-colored hair that spilled down her back in a long single braid that blended browns, reds, and yellows—reflecting endless exposure to the weather. The greasy, trail-stained jacket she wore was short enough in the arms that an expanse of tanned, sturdy forearm was visible. She put the massive gun back into the holster that dragged below her hip with a smirk firmly planted on her face to celebrate having achieved total and complete surprise. She let him drink in the sight of her, celebrating her triumph over the most watchful man she ever knew before she continued.

"You know we spend this time around Rawhide, assuming you even know what month it is. I heard you rode in. Were you planning to look for us or not? Or, now that you caught some famous outlaw and have all this reward money to spend, are you too good for your old friends?" she asked archly.

Caledonia MacReynolds was the only living person who could make Rourke smile simply by walking into his line of sight. She was as wild and untamed as the wind and had long since developed a fierce loyalty to the man who had saved her father, a traveling smith, from being killed a couple of years back. She was without tact or guile or deception. The gray-edged blue eyes he saw shining out from her fine-boned face always reminded him of the January sky when it cleared after snow. She was his height, which made her tall for a woman, with strong hands from helping her father and working with horses, her special love. There was no horse she could not ride, as there was no person on the face of the earth who could make her do anything she chose not to do. Her face was red and ruddy from the wind and weather.

The smile she wore was not put on to be polite, but an extension of what she felt when this very strange man, who was unlike anyone she ever knew, rode into her life. Star, who disliked almost everyone, adored her. The stallion would let Cal kiss him on the nose, something not even Rourke would dare to try. And now the girl had become a woman, somehow in some way that had changed since the spring when he saw her last, Rourke realized. She caught him staring and laughed out loud at him.

"I'm called a woman, Rourke. You know? People? Humans? Two-legged critters? Maybe you could say hello to me, or do you only talk to Star these days?" she teased. "Or have you forgotten what people look like spending all your time out riding around doing who knows what and only meeting friends like Red Jim? Did I ever tell you Star tells me everything you say to him? I know exactly what you said coming over the ridge. You told him that you were looking forward to seeing your old friends, right, Rourke? Well, cowboy?" The bantering tone sounded a lot like what girls did when they flirted with younger men. He shrugged to buy a minute. Feelings for women had died with Lorraine. He figured they were going to stay dead. As he looked at Cal looking back at him as though he really mattered to her, he realized that maybe those emotions had received a premature obituary.

"As I recall, I told Star all that quiet we had out on the Plains was like to be ruined as soon as I saw you," he said, falling into his more familiar teasing with her as if it was the day after the last time he saw her months back. "Got somethin' to say for once instead of runnin' on about the weather the way you do as if you could really predict it?"

"I can predict weather better'n anyone else you know. You would have been on the other side of that river back in Dakota when it flooded if you hadn't listened to me for once in your life and I know that and you know that so don't get all high and mighty on me there, mister!" She pointed a finger in his face as she gloated at the memory she invoked. He couldn't help but smile back. She had that effect on him. "Well, lazybones, go on with your stable work! You are going to have a job to do for me here and don't try to get out of it! You can either say yes now and save time or you can say yes later! Dad and I are camped down at Ellsworth Creek. I will come by to collect you at dinner time, unless you plan to eat with your horse as well as sleep with him." With that, she flounced away, something that definitely caught a man's attention when done in pants, he reflected. He watched her until she was gone from view, wondering at how this little girl had changed into a woman and also realizing he was not quite as sure about the nature of his feelings for her as he used to be. He was unaware that he was grinning like a boy; it was a look only Cal could summon.

Cal was whistling as she walked down the street to the rail where she had hitched her horse. Rourke had been glad to see her, no doubt of that! She was surprised how glad she had been to see him, since they bumped into each other here and there every few months and that was the way things were. Maybe things were changing, like everything else lately. At least Rourke was predictable. She did not want to have to comb the streets of Rawhide looking for him. There were places cowboys went she wasn't going to go.

There was a well-dressed young man in an Eastern suit watching her walk to her horse. She did not like the look in his eyes. She hefted the heavy Colt Pa had given her, just to be sure she hadn't forgotten it. It dragged on her hip and the belt chafed her waist, but she never went into a town without it. A girl in the West knew that men were men, and that when they were drunk or in the mood, a gun was the only way to make them listen to reason.

The man was still standing in the doorway of the fancy hotel building. Another man in fancy clothes walked by—an older man. They both looked around furtively as they hurried down the alley that ran between buildings.

Men up to no good. She boosted herself into the saddle and turned her horse down the street. A woman in a pale blue dress and a silly Eastern hat gave her a long look, as though Cal was doing something wrong. Cal wasn't sure, because the woman had some funny wide-brimmed hat with ribbons and gee-gaws on it, but it looked like the woman was crinkling her nose at Cal. For a second, she thought about what Rourke would tell her to do—put a bullet right through the lady's hat! That made her laugh. She laughed even harder when she realized she had been observed by Dan Wheeler, the town's sheriff and about the only person in Rawhide she liked.

He was grinning. She realized he probably had the same thought about what a proper use that hat would be as target practice. She grinned wider. She rose in her stirrups and took her hat off to the sheriff like a fancy riding cowboy. Wheeler did the same as she rode past, a broad grin splitting the weathered face. She touched her heels to her horse and they rode out of town, away from the scar of civilization and back to where they both belonged. Neither she nor Wheeler were aware of the hostile eyes of Caroline Dickinson as she felt once again the mockery of the frontier yokels—all of whom one day would be dust under her feet. Of that, regardless of how much it took to keep Andrew focused on what was important, she was very sure.

Rourke's grin faded quickly as Cal left. He started the chores he had set out to do. Long inured to doing work with his body while his mind was elsewhere, Rourke wondered how the girl had found him and what she wanted. Whatever Cal wanted he'd end up doing. He'd never said no to the girl in all the time he had known her.

Rourke felt the unaccustomed weight of the money in his

pocket as he worked. He was about as rich as he could recall being in the last three years. Even a winter of supplies wouldn't eat up all the money. Well, there would be something. There always was. In fact, now that he thought of his meeting with Cal, he could think of something right off.

He supposed he ought to clean up and get new clothes, but that could come later. Cal had seen him looking a lot worse, that was for sure. He wondered what was up. Her Old Man was always at the edge of trouble, always in some scheme, and always somehow or other one step ahead of getting caught. Even when the evidence was pretty plain, like when those fellas about had him ready for a necktie party the first time he'd met Ezekiel, Zeke could no more tell the truth for a whole day than Cal could lie.

Different as night and day, they were an inseparable pair. Cal's mom was long since dead. Like a lot of the men who raised girls alone out on the Plains, Zeke had brought up the girl with an odd mix of wildness and civilization. Rourke had never seen her in a dress, and such sewing as she did usually was either sewing her pa together or fixing rips in clothing that could not be replaced because there was no money for such things.

The girl could read, though—probably better than most of the cowboys. She knew her Bible. Zeke worshipped her now that she was, so he had told Rourke back in the spring, growing into the spitting image of her mother. Cal was unlike anyone he ever knew—and she was the one person Rourke felt was his to protect when he was around. For people who saw each other maybe three or four times a year, it didn't make sense, but not much in life ever did. He would think of her spirit in the wings of an eagle, feel her laugh on the gust of a west wind, and know her soul in the golden pure sunset of the sky without a sound to interrupt the spectacle. Yup, Cal was different from the rest.

Star was waiting. The horse knew his rider's moods; knew him better than anyone had ever known the man in Rourke's whole life. Animals knew more about people than people ever would. When a horse was alone with a man without the veneer of civilization, it was the horse that either paid the price for the man's bad temper or learned that his human was someone to trust, not fear. Rourke figured Star was his best friend and treated him that way. He didn't talk much, but when he did, he believed Star understood. More than once he wondered if God's eyes looked like the eyes of a horse, because those eyes seemed to know everything and somehow seemed sad about it all.

Rourke checked Star closely again for bruises, picked out some mud from a leg, sat down by his stuff, breathed in the smells of horses and hay, and before he knew it, was being rudely shaken awake by a smirking young woman who seemed to be frowning and laughing at the same time.

"Does the little baby need a nap?" Cal cooed as she stood over him with her arms folded. "I would have come by to tuck you in, but I have work to do!"

Since he'd spent most of the last two days without sleep, he knew there was a reason; she probably did, too, but there was no sense explaining. She had caught him again—her favorite activity. Trying to get out of it would make the tale worse. He grumbled something, managing not to curse because, even though Star wasn't really concerned about his talk, Cal had a very well-defined sense of which words she cared to hear and which she did not. Rourke had learned a couple of years ago that there was a huge difference between talking to soldiers and talking to Cal.

"Drivin' a man hard, Cal," he replied. "Gettin' to be a growed woman. Pore Zeke must be gettin' worn to ragged. 'Zat what this is about? He needs you to boss somebody else so's he can feel free enough to find trouble again?"

"Well, someone needs to look out for you or you would have missed dinner. Pa's waitin'. It's down the gully about a mile. And don't you dare talk about the things Pa does because he's my Pa and I might have to shoot you before dinner and you'll never get pie. I had to come and find you because we waited and waited. I'm hungry and it's not polite to eat without everyone present, or have you forgotten there is such a thing as manners?"

Star had been patient long enough. The horse wanted Cal's attention. Now was no different. He pushed Cal from behind, earning soft words for his trouble. Cal was amazed at the contrast between horse and rider. Star was always brushed and combed and cared for. Rourke was another story. He usually was more or less clean, not like some of the cowboys who smelled so bad that she was sure they never touched water the entire time they were on the trail. His clothes, however, were usually a mess, even by range standards. She noticed he had not spent any of his reward money on anything new. Men! Rourke used a pump to clean off his hands and face while Cal petted Star and gave him an apple she had brought.

"Done primping for the ball, cowboy?" she called. "I was hoping to eat some time tonight."

She smiled at the grumbling that answered her. Rourke kept most people at a distance. She knew very few people who could tease him the way she did. It struck her as odd. They would be apart months at a time, then when they saw each other it was as though all that time was only a long day apart.

"Been waitin' on you, Cal," he said as she pondered. "Or you gonna daydream all day 'sted of feeding me?"

"Pa's the one thinks you need to eat, Rourke. I wanted to see you actually eat your own cooking! Is it true you had to throw out all your cooking utensils because you used them and the stew got like a rock? That's what Pa says and we know he never lies!"

Her laugh in response to his glare was like water rippling out of the mountains over stones. "The rest of the world thinks you are some bounty hunter–gunfighter, Rourke, but I know you are another man who would die if no one cooks for you. How do you manage on the range? Does Star cook?"

He let her chatter. Just the laughter in her voice was worth hearing.

The barn was dark, but as they walked outside where she had left her horse, there were still traces of the sunset. The bantering stopped. A streak of gold filtered across the sky, and they watched it narrow to the width of a ribbon and finally turn to nothing as the band of black shading along the horizon announced the end of day.

Cal was watching Rourke. The man was almost as wild as the wolves he liked to play with when he camped with them. She knew he had been in the war and been married to a woman who died from disease, but the rest was closed. He would vanish, then reappear like her best friend, and one of the few men her pa liked and trusted. She knew he hunted men for money, but she figured it would turn to ranching eventually. But he seemed to be growing wilder, not tamer, in the seasons she had known him. He never spared a glance for much in the towns. She knew he avoided the dance halls and saloons. Her father had told her that once when they were looking for him in Leadville back in Colorado. And there was something about him that was touched by sunsets.

He held out a hand to touch her arm for a minute as they watched the sunset, as transfixed as she was with the delights that so many around them ignored in the rush to do something not near as important. They ended up watching the sun set with her hand on his arm. When it was done, they mounted and rode in contented companionable silence to where Cal and her father were camped.

The camp was not far from the creek, which after another dry summer, was barely a dark line against the dirt. The fire was blazing brightly, illuminating a large ungainly canvas-topped wagon. Two horses were tied loosely to trees at the edge of the clearing. Sitting on a downed log by the fire was Cal's father. Ezekiel MacReynolds had been many things in his life, many of which were best forgotten and few of which he would acknowledge around his daughter. His traveling blacksmith shop was known all through Nebraska, the Dakotas, Kansas, and Wyoming. He played the fiddle, told stories, brewed alcohol, and dispensed advice on healing, cattle, and flower gardens. The dispensing of the latter was occasionally done in the privacy of a lady's home until the usually long-absent or oft-away gentleman of the house became aware of the goings-on. Cal had grown up knowing that when men started chasing the wagon, it meant Pa had been up to something the adults would never explain.

Zeke had aged a lot since the spring. At a glance, Rourke could see that if death was not riding in the man's wagon, it was waiting not too far down the trail. Even if Cal could see Zeke's aging with her eyes, he knew her heart would never admit it. Ezekiel exchanged a few pleasantries about the weather, the Sioux, the Army, Cal's resemblance to the mother the girl never knew, and a few other topics. Zeke never moved, talked, or thought in straight lines. Tonight was no exception. Rourke waited. Life was like stud poker. Sooner or later, the hole card turned over. There was food aplenty, all cooked by Cal. In fact, the steak here under the stars, burned in places and raw in others, tasted better than the fancy one in the hotel. Cal kept looking at him in a funny way, as though trying to find out the answer without asking the question.

Finally, Ezekiel more or less blurted it out. "They's a rich family taking Green Hills, rich Eastern fools. Place up on that high table of land out there. Fella wants a blacksmith. There's an old shed that needs to fixin' up, but I been out there and everything I need is there. Me'n Cal are thinkin' of settlin' there 'stead of riding around in circles. Leastways give it a try. All this civilization cuttin' into my business so maybe I ought to try to join 'em if I can't whup 'em."

"Met the man," Rourke replied neutrally, catching Cal's poker face from the corner of his eye. "You've gotten the better of tougher men than him along the way, Ezekiel, if I remember correctly."

"I bet I have that, yes, sir," Ezekiel said with a smile. He liked being reminded of the days when his stubble was not white, his skin was not baked leather, and the women looked at him with more interest than pity. He had lived by his wits from the days before the Civil War, when it was hard to find a safe ground to stand on when Bleeding Kansas was erupting all around him. "Man's got money, man's got plans. Man was sayin' he needs some riders. Thought you ought to talk to him."

"Why?"

"Why? For John Brown's Body's sake you fool idiot, you need to do somethin' more than riding around the rest of your life. Fine when you're young. Ain't right for a man. Gets you crazy in the head to be riding forever. You spend your whole life moving and look back and there's nothin to show for it but the tracks the wind's blown over so nobody knows you ever passed by."

Rourke wondered which one of them Ezekiel was describing. Cal seemed to be very intent on this conversation. A flash of rare insight made him wonder whose words he was hearing, Ezekiel's or Cal's? "Don't like being crowded." He shrugged.

"Well, I got to get the shed fixed. It's only September. You got nowhere to go that fast. No posse after you. Even if you plan to winter with your friends the Sioux again, you show up now they'll hunt you for food. Was figgerin' maybe you could stay and help me on this one? You used to do carpenter stuff, so's you told me once awhile back. Winter won't be here for a while. Cal can cook better'n you. There'd be a place to stay. Mebbe you want to think about this ridin' thing. Mebbe not. Take a few days to think. Girl's a help but I need a man to get this built to rights. You happen to be here. Thought maybe it was something you'd want to do."

The casual tone belied the tension in the old man's body. Rourke gave the idea some thought. Depending on how rundown the shed was, rebuilding a place might take anywhere from a few days to a few weeks. He could still ride off to the north come October. Ezekiel was about what there was for friends west of the Mississippi and he guessed the old man didn't want his new employer to guess he could never do the work alone. Cal was great at a lot of things, but she hadn't been a carpenter before the war like he had. Bein' a man who was proud made it hard to ask, so it must have half-killed Zeke to speak up. Maybe that's why Cal was watching him the way a hawk tracks a mouse.

Then he looked directly at Cal. Her hands were folded as if she was a lady at some fancy place, but when he looked at her, the fingers were white from being pressed together so tight. Maybe she knew her daddy was sick. Maybe she was worried about the old man more than she let on. She was looking him back in the eye, deadly serious like he had never seen her before. There was no question what she wanted.

"This that job you were talkin' about?" he asked.

She nodded wordlessly, looking him in the eyes solemnly.

Rourke shrugged. He hadn't held much but a gun in his hands for a while. Maybe he could give something else a try.

Maybe all the nightmares would take some time off as well. Probably not, but it mattered to Cal, so there could only be one right answer. "Don't see why not. Couple weeks ain't gonna mean nothin'. Don't think I want to go be a rider punchin' livestock at my age, Zeke. Leave that for the young bucks that like to sit a saddle all day and call it fun. You promise me Cal's gonna cook?"

"She better," Ezekiel said. "Gonna starve or get poisoned if she don't, least the way I recall your cooking." He whooped at the joke. He stuck a wrinkled, calloused hand out. Rourke took it. He looked Cal in the eyes, and she was looking back with thanks as tension drained from her face. This mattered to her. It mattered a lot. The longer he looked, the bigger she smiled. If she'd smiled like that first off, he'd have said yes first off. Maybe not something she ought to know. Well, he'd find out why in time. If the old man needed help once the smith got going, he was sure they could find an assistant. He'd make sure of that before he left, and then he'd check on them after the winter.

"Guess the least you can do if you're gonna work me to death," Rourke told them, "is get me some of that pie that's hiding under that blanket."

The serious faces vanished, and the minutes flew as they told stories, exaggerated a few close calls that were nowhere near that much fun at the time, and enjoyed the rare feeling of wasting time without either watching their backs or feeling the pressure of undone work pushing them forward past the moment.

CHAPTER FOUR

Star's noises, the ones that said people were near, woke Rourke—never a good way to start any day. The stable was filled with sun. A man was standing outside Star's stall, calling his name far too loudly for Rourke to ignore. The judge's son. Rourke holstered the gun that had filled his hand by reflex.

"Can't a man sleep in peace around this town?" Rourke called, still lounging in the hay. Cal had told him there would be a surprise waiting around the middle of the day where she and her father were camping, so he had no reason to move much before then. He'd been up late thinking about Cal and Zeke and the idea of settling down. He still couldn't imagine it for him, there were too many restless ghosts gnawing at his spirit, but if Cal wanted to settle down he guessed she should find a man and get married. That notion didn't seem right, though, even though it should.

"You really do sleep with your horse?" Owens asked in astonishment as he peered in the stall. "I didn't believe it when I was told."

Rourke was irritated that habits that made proper sense to him should be laid out for anyone's disapproval. He was also annoyed that one of the few times he had ever wanted to sleep part of a morning away had been taken from him. He held his tongue, though, because Owens was the judge's son and young folks were known to be foolish. He also guessed this was more of that rustler business. The young man hadn't come by for the sole purpose of commenting on Rourke's sleeping habits. When Rourke didn't reply, the young man spoke up again.

"Mr. Dickinson wishes to see you."

"I'm busy."

"Sleeping with your horse?"

"Don't ask you none what you sleep with, so I don't see it's your business," Rourke grumbled as he rose, angry at being disturbed and stung by the sarcasm in Owens' voice. "Andy got a burr under his saddle?"

"He leaves on the stagecoach at noon today and he wanted to see you before he goes."

Rourke, blinking himself fully awake, watched Star watching him. He wished again the horse could tell him how absurd all this probably looked. "Tell Andy when I get Star fed and watered that I'll be by."

"Um. That could be difficult. It's already ten."

Rourke felt irritation swell within him. People and their watches! There was a whole day every day to live life. It was a waste of it to be constantly looking at a piece of metal to worry about why this or that wasn't happening.

"Andy wants something, he knows the way here," he told Owens obstinately. "Star needs food and I need to clean out the place. I got my plans already made, so he can come and talk but it ain't gonna change nothin'."

Rourke could not understand why anyone didn't like caring for horses. They made a lot less fuss than people. Maybe it smelled a bit to clean out stalls, but nobody was whining about whatever he missed. Familiar work and familiar smells were as good a way to start a day as any. Happiness was relative. He'd eaten about a week's worth of food the night before; he was going to help his friends. Nobody that he knew of was gunning for him. He had more money than he knew what to do with. Cal was around. Life didn't have much more than that to hold out as a promise.

Dickinson may have preferred to meet in his office but he knew his way around a stable, as he told Rourke when he came by later to see his friend. "Should I remind you that there are people begging for a chance to see me to air their grievances and complaints and beg for assistance from the territorial government. These many souls would not require that I walk into a filthy, stinking stable for the privilege of conversation," he told Rourke with a smile robbing his words of any possible sting.

"So see 'em," Rourke grunted, not slowing the pace of his work. Dickinson grinned broadly in response.

"When you are done shoveling and raking could you spare me a moment of your very valuable time?" Dickinson asked in a falsely arched tone.

"Only if I get that bread you brought as a bribe."

"I am amazed you can smell it."

"Gettin' to be a city boy, Andy. Not good for you. You was happier with nothin' to lose. Here, set."

Rourke pushed two barrels near each other. Dickinson hopped onto one, tossing the loaf of fresh bread to Rourke, who broke off a hunk and passed it back to Dickinson. They ate in silence a moment.

"I have a problem," Dickinson said.

"If I took your poker stake, it's not my fault. Just claiming what the reward poster offered."

"Not that." Dickinson waved his hand. "It's only money. I deeply care about what is best for the Territory, and any outbreak of vigilantes over rustling would be very damaging, which is what I think will happen if Treadwell is not appeased. Since you have apparently decided to go into the blacksmith business temporarily, and you prefer that to anything Bill Harwood or I could offer you in the way of employment, you should have some free time to ride Star around and maybe tell me some things I don't know about what's going on. This is my deal: You go when you go, but until you do, you look around on the Territory's behalf when Zeke and Cal are not turning you into a workhorse. Although the ranchers talk as though they were all on the same side, you and I know better. Everyone suspects the other fellow when these things happen. Treadwell is a hothead. Harwood wants to bully his way to the top. If I can keep them from killing each other before the snow flies, I figure time will heal all."

Rourke wondered a minute at how Andy could know what he was going to do when only he, Cal, and Zeke knew. Well, it wasn't a military secret, but it did set his mind to wondering for a minute if his friend, who was looking pretty smooth and sly and pretty much like one of the important people Andy and Rourke used to mock, was either up to something or in some kind of trouble. "For free?" he asked back.

"What do you want?" Dickinson replied, frowning at the unexpected reply.

"Zeke and Cal might have some needs after I leave. Zeke might be getting sick. You cover what they need. You keep an eye on Zeke, make sure Cal's not in trouble or needful or nothing, I do your work."

"Of course. Once you ride out, I will see that everything is taken care of." Dickinson plopped down from the barrel with his hand out. He thanked Rourke and turned away, then came back.

"Report only to me. Nothing in writing. Do not let the girl and her father know what I asked you. I don't want them involved. And watch what you say to Wheeler. He drinks too much and talks too much."

Rourke was not surprised Andy didn't like Wheeler. That had been plain earlier. But the secrecy around Cal and Zeke surprised him. "What's so secret, Andy?"

"Rourke, I can't tell you everything but you need to trust me that this is bigger than a couple of horses. When Zeke drinks, he talks, and I don't want everyone else hearing whatever you find out before I do!"

Rourke shrugged. It wasn't like Zeke or Cal were going to tell Andy what they were told he didn't want shared. When folks gave you stupid orders, the way they did in the war, you say you will obey and then do whatever gets the job done. "What about the judge's boy?" Rourke asked.

Dickinson had a bad news face on, the kind men wear when they want to be honest but fear the price. He looked very unhappy. "The boy's not as steady today as he was a few weeks ago, to tell you the honest truth. Thought he was settling down with that woman of his. Not really so sure anymore. I don't want things that I want secret shared in the saloon or along the bar at the hotel. Just report to me. I will decide what is safe to tell anyone."

Rourke looked like he had swallowed some traveling man's medicine. He'd looked out for the boy when the judge died, at least as much as he could when he wasn't someplace else, but a man was going to be what a man was going to be, and people were not like horses. Blood didn't always tell. Still, he knew many men out in the Territory had gone through more than a few rough days. Dickinson could be seeing ghosts. But since he was going to be staying nearby for a while, it wouldn't hurt to keep an eye out in case Owens had acquired some habits he didn't want to talk about.

"Understood, Andy. Whatever I do is for you and you alone."

With an expression of great relief, Dickinson nodded and made his way out of the stable and back into the world of people and politics that rarely looked around at the price of its progress.

Rourke chewed the rest of the bread and chewed a bit longer

on the conversation and the questions it raised in his mind. He talked it over with Star as he finished his chores. The sun wasn't quite at its peak. He went out to get himself looking a little more civilized. Cal and Zeke were moving out to Green Hills and he was supposed to be there as well in a day or two. There was no rush. It was always routine for him to get a bath and new clothes when he came to Rawhide. He let the beard stay, though, and didn't bother with his usual haircut. For some reason he couldn't place, he didn't want to look any more Eastern than he could. Well, if Cal had an objection, maybe he'd shave, but it was one less thing a man had to worry about.

There was a hint of self-mockery, though, as he went to the general store. He wondered if the unexpected care he took finding a shirt was because there was nothing but thin shirts at the store or he knew Cal fancied blues instead of the reds he usually wore. Well, it would be all over dirt in a day or two, he reasoned. If she liked it at the start, it wouldn't hurt. If she even noticed.

Rourke felt stiff in the new clothes he bought as he and Star rode out to the creek where Zeke and Cal were camped. Zeke liked having people as customers, but he wasn't much more interested in them as neighbors than Rourke. They had set up under some trees that were now starting to lose their leaves. A few yellows came down with the breeze. Rourke recalled Tennessee in the fall of '64. Franklin. His one and only glorious battle. A slaughter. It made scouting a much better alternative when he saw what fighting was like when the full armies met. He hadn't minded much at the time, but when it was over, that's when he realized how stupid it all was.

The voice he was realizing how much he liked hearing cut through his thoughts. "You gonna sit there all day and wait for a buzzard to peck you?"

"Cal, what if I was a customer wanting to get a shoe for my

horse? If that's how you greet the traveling public, I need to have a word with Ezekiel."

"Normal people don't sit on a horse and stare at a tree with their lips moving," she responded. "Since you're here, get down. There's coffee. And you will never guess who stopped by in case we had something to steal." She walked away, and then turned, a hint of a smile showing. " 'Spose they were all sold out of those red battle shirts you usually wear. Now you don't look like you got your flannels on, for once. And I like your beard because it will give me something to pull when I want to wake you up, so there!" And she turned back, not giving him a chance to reply and moving a little faster in case he didn't like the joke.

Rourke put Star in as much shade as there was and left him saddled. He wasn't staying long. Then he met one of the few links with the past that mattered—Thomas O'Toole. O'Toole was a tall man, well over six feet, with coal black hair and a thick black beard. He had a preference for loose-fitting clothes, which Rourke had said during the war was due to a need to find places to hide potatoes and chickens. Despite his preoccupation with whiskey and food, and his unofficial role as the chief forager of Rourke's scouting battalion, he was a thin man almost to the point of being bony. During the Famine, he had come from Ireland to New Orleans, and drifted down to Texas after a question regarding the killing of a gambler in a rigged card game. The question was only resolved when Rourke happened to show up in time to prevent O'Toole from being hung. As a result, throughout the war, O'Toole had been Rourke's shadow.

Peace had come as a shock to O'Toole, who had joined Rourke on the journey from the South to the West after the war ended. O'Toole had signed on with the U.S. Army as a scout, since he found staying in one place tiresome if not hazardous to his health. He felt most at home around soldiers. Rourke had last seen his old friend in the early part of the year, when he had made a trip to Fort Laramie. Now, the two men took inventory of each other as broad grins told the story of the depth of their friendship.

"Captain-General Your Worship, sir!"

"And is it on furlough you are, Sergeant?"

" 'Tis a scout, now, sir, and I appear to have misplaced meself and become lost. When I heard that Your Worship had met the good Red Jim I assumed you might be coming this way to collect a reward, so I have loitered and shirked my duty. While I was passing back and forth the horse threw a shoe. I happened to meet these good people, and this charming lass who loves to hear stories about the war."

Rourke grinned. O'Toole had been his right arm in the war. Some days, he missed it. Not the fighting. The men. The small unit had been winnowed by death to the point where everyone was closer than brothers. They shared the sense that they would survive, somehow, together. Then when the war ended, they scattered. O'Toole was the only one he had seen since 1865.

Rourke waited. O'Toole never got to the point quickly, especially when his Irish brogue was as strong and thick as it was today.

"It seems that your friend from the Territory who is the son of the judge you once knew stopped at the fort a few days ago while you were dancing the jig with your friend Red Jim, and suggested that there might be activities here needing a scout. Much of the conversation was behind closed doors with brandy, which is an affront to any man who drinks whiskey. For some reason known only to the spirits of chance, I happened to be the one selected, Your Lordship. What I was told was that there might be rustlers stealing horses. The Army needed to 'keep a keen eye on the situation to prevent undue action,' and all those lovely words the men with gold braid on their shoulders use when they have no idea what it is they mean but want someone else to do their dyin'."

Rourke was quiet. The Army always complicated anything, because no one ever knew whose side it was likely to be on. Rourke summarized the conversations with Dickinson and the ranchers. "They never mentioned the Army. Are you here to help me or watch me, Thomas?"

"There is that," said O'Toole, taking off his hat and wiping his brow. "I think, sir, that officers being officers, sir, they all want the best horses by any means possible. A trifling matter, sir. For certain it shall be cleared up in a trice."

Rourke wondered. The ranchers had a problem. Something had to be wrong. O'Toole had a nose for things that were wrong—especially for finding advantage in things that were wrong. Yet his oldest living friend was telling him it was a small matter. Thomas would know. Still, he was curious. "What did the judge's boy really want, Thomas?"

"There seemed to be concerns about a threat to the stability of justice and order, kind sir, but the way that young man talks he might have been expressing an opinion about pigs. Yon friend, so that you know, has a list of ambitions as long as Jeb Stuart's beard, sir, and there are officers at the fort who might be tempted to help make others wealthy if some of the glow of the gold reflects upon them, sir."

Rourke wondered. He knew that the judge's son and Dickinson were both ambitious, and had grown more so. Everyone knew that the goal of every territory was to attract settlers and become a state. Governor? A senator? Dickinson was young enough to be ambitious for it. The judge's son might have the same thoughts. Perhaps both wanted the credit for ending a ring of rustlers? Perhaps they were trying to fix a deal in Harwood's favor? If the Army was involved, Rourke would not be as free to settle things as he wished. But if the Army was there, it would also be hard for whoever was stealing—if anyone truly was and this was not a case of more anger than actual theft—to simply ride away unscathed. The Army was really what passed for law in Wyoming Territory as well as the prime customer for horses. But the fact that his good friend Andy would send the judge's son to the Army and not tell him was an itch that Rourke's mind kept trying to scratch. It was hard to imagine the judge's son taking that much initiative on his own. He had the funny feeling he had sometimes got in the war that something was going on that was below the surface, like when the generals were playing games that ended up costing men their lives. Friends change, he reminded himself.

Whatever the game, it was too deep for Rourke. "How did you end up here today? Are Cal and her pa suspected rustlers?" he asked O'Toole, who seemed to be studying Rourke intently.

"When I met these fine folks in Rawhide, your friends here suggested they would ply you with food and bend you to their will, and that they might avail upon you to ride with them for an adventure that sounds far too much like work. I decided to remain and pay my respects. From her reactions to the few scraps of truth I have fed her, the lass does not seem to know you at all," O'Toole added, with a gleam in his eye.

Rourke could not resist a smile in return. He knew that O'Toole did not need the facts to make the story a good one. He hoped Cal would understand that when she heard things that he had long ago decided were never to be discussed again. War was war. It was done. He and O'Toole and his battalion of scouts had left most of the rules and regulations behind while they scouted for Bragg and Johnston and finally Hood during the Civil War's fighting around Tennessee and Georgia. They lived on stolen food for months at a time, fired stolen guns, and rode stolen horses. But that was all in the past, and they were out in the Wyoming hills where the rules were what men made them, and the strongest one of all was to stand by your friends. O'Toole's instinct told him that something was amiss, and he was here to warn Rourke. That was friendship, not glib smiles and fine words. Rourke reminded himself he had become too quick to doubt and distrust everyone.

Cal watched the two men, staying out of earshot to give them a semblance of privacy. Rourke looked relaxed, so the man must be a good friend. Rourke never relaxed. Even last night around the fire, when some critter moved in the night, his hand had moved to his gun before any other part of him reacted. Rourke looked different now. The man was someone whom Rourke liked. There was amusement in their faces as they traded words. Well, whoever it was, he might be able to shed some light on the shadows of Rourke's past, and he also might be able to help keep them safe. Even though she was told a thousand times she did not have a head for these sorts of things, it did seem to her that Pa's plans usually ended up with them running fast away from people with guns. A different ending would be nice, if only for a change.

She thought she saw a little doe. She followed her trail. She had walked quite a ways from the wagon and had left it behind, along with her gun, when she caught the sense of unease that was in the woods. Then she realized how quiet it was, except for the birds up at the top of the towering pines. Usually the undergrowth would be crackling this time of year with deer and squirrels. She had gone on enough scouts to know the signs. It was almost impossible to move and not make noise. She stopped, debating whether it would be smart to go back. Then she decided that if something was wrong, maybe it was an injured animal and it might need help. On she walked, not afraid but alert. Not alert enough.

She heard the menacing click of a rifle being cocked.

"Far enough, kid. Stop. Hands high."

She turned to see a greasy haired, bearded man in a checked shirt emerge from a thicket with two other men, all carrying shiny Winchesters.

She took off the hat, shaking her hair free. She looked like a woman now and not a little girl. "Whoever you are, you are making a mistake. I am Caledonia MacReynolds, my father is over there. I insist that you put down the guns and leave me alone."

It was a tone of command learned from years of listening. It wasn't working. The lead gunman leaned over and whispered to one of his partners. They chuckled. Cal seethed. He turned back to her with what could have passed for a smile. "We ain't seen a white woman in months, girl. Now, how about being nice to some hard-workin' boys who been ridin' the range?"

"No filthy range bum is going to tell me what to do!" She told them exactly what she thought of them. She started to turn and walk away. One of the men moved and cut off her escape.

"Talk like that is not sociable at all, even for Wyoming manners," he growled. "Maybe you want to apologize with a little kiss, pretty girl." He made a face that might have been ludicrous under different circumstances. Cal was not smiling. She was lining up which one to kick first.

"Enough." One word. But fear was stark on their faces as they looked at each other and then at the figure of Rourke, standing by a pine with his pistol aimed.

"Rourke," said the man who had done the group's talking.

"Lloyd, how do?" replied Rourke. "You boys graduated to hurting young women?"

Lloyd's arms flailed at his side. "No harm intended," said the leader. "We was havin' some fun. Just get a kiss, friend. Just fun with the lady. Never touched her. We don't touch ladies." The three range bums' heads swiveled as they saw O'Toole with a rifle covering them from behind.

"We'll see what the lady says," replied Rourke. "Cal. Cal!"

"Rourke?"

"You hurt?"

"I'll be fine. They were more talk than action."

"Didn't mean nothin'," said Lloyd. "Got a tongue like a school teacher on her, she does! Didn't know she was a friend of yours, Rourke."

"She is that. Very much that, Lloyd."

"Sorry, miss," said Lloyd, stammering. "We stopped for water and there you was. We come down from the North Platte. We ain't seen a white man in days and not a white woman in weeks."

"You boys are lucky she didn't shoot first and ask questions later," Rourke said. "What were you doin' up by the North Platte?"

"There was a roundup. Big Ed Stephenson up on the Double J. Horses. Army loses them in raids then they turn wild. Sold 'em up by Fort Phil Kearny. More work than it was worth. Headin' down to the railroad camps. Easier work there, they say. Range talk is you met up with Red Jim."

"I did."

Lloyd swallowed.

"You drive branded stock up at the North Platte?"

"Some," Lloyd replied. "Mostly wild. You know how it is, Rourke. Ranchers always lose a few head. Someone else gets theirs; they get someone else's. Way it is. Not rustlin'. Just the way it is."

Cal lifted an eyebrow, "These friends of yours, Rourke?"

Rourke thought a minute of how to explain it to Cal. "Man rides as much as I do, he sees a lot of men, Cal. As long as we drift by, no sense in trying to settle differences that don't matter most of the time. Maybe not friends, probably not enemies, Cal. Think the boys know they crossed the line today. There's worse on the range, if there's better, too."

Cal thought the answer over. All over the West there were men who had parts of good and bad in them. Which side was on top might depend on which day it was. Now that she had a look at them, they looked more defeated than dangerous. They actually hadn't touched her. Who knew what they were thinking? Men were so often stupid around women it was hard to tell. Well, they had had worse around the fire over the years, that was certain. "Tell you what, Rourke, Pa had about enough coffee for everybody, so they can get down and come by the fire a minute if that's what you want."

Rourke thought about it. Lloyd Jeffries and his cousins were not a lot worse than most of the men who drifted from this to that around the Territory. He knew that by their standards, they probably meant what they said. Men being stupid drifted to men bein' bad so fast that the line was pretty hazy on the best of days. No sense giving anyone a shove. "Boys?"

"Thank you, miss," said Lloyd, looking slightly ridiculous as he took off his hat in what passed for a bow. "More than we deserve, and thank you."

Zeke and the Jeffries boys had seen each other here and there. They were not much different than many of the men Rourke and O'Toole rode with in the war. The coffee disappeared fast, and the Jeffries boys drifted away, calling out a mixture of thanks and apologies along with hopes to meet again on the trail.

When they were gone, O'Toole saddled up to ride back to the fort. He said he'd ride out in a few days and head to Green Hills, where Zeke and Cal would be. "The life of a scout, sir. Always riding," remarked O'Toole.

"Always out of sight of your officers, you mean," corrected Rourke. They laughed. O'Toole galloped off in a cloud of dust and Irish melody.

When they were all gone, Rourke stood by Star idly, looking across the prairie lands of Wyoming.

"Want to talk about it, cowboy?" Cal asked.

"Those boys, O'Toole, me. All of us kicked loose by the war. Sometimes, Cal, I wonder. What makes those boys act like they do? Mean as a snake one minute, polite as pie the next. Good? Bad? Don't know how to define those words sometimes, Cal, because people have so much of both in them." The words were true, but they were also the tip of his thoughts. He wondered how long it might be before a bounty hunter became a range bum the day he could no longer ride and shoot, that is, if he even lived at all.

"You aren't like them, Rourke. Pa told me once a man can either give up on what he wants or keep fightin'. They gave up if they're riding and looking for work at places that aren't right. Me and Pa and you are still fightin'. You think too much on it, cowboy, you're gonna give your hat a headache."

Rourke thought over the words, gave Cal a half-smile, and rode back to Rawhide with his thoughts for company. He'd meet them at Green Hills in a day or two. He'd been thinking about some things he needed to do in town before he left and finally decided to get it over with. He was walking down the main street when he happened to see the rancher, Harwood. The man gave Rourke a big wave.

"Hear you might be helping my blacksmith with his shed," Harwood said, shaking hands with a big old smile as if he and Rourke had ridden together for years.

"Little early to head up north to winter," Rourke replied, once again liking the man instantly. "Fella and his girl been friends from the trail, and they can cook better'n me. You got good sources of information."

"People talk," replied Harwood. "While you're out there, come and talk. If you can help us stop the rustling, it will only help your friends. Changes are coming to Wyoming Territory, Rourke. The old ways people here talk about are going fast." A female voice calling something made Harwood stop. He waved toward someone by the hotel. It did not look to Rourke like his wife or daughter. It looked more like Andy Dickinson's wife. Whoever it was ducked out of sight. It didn't matter. When Eastern women wore their little silly disguises they called fashions, they all looked alike to him. "Well, I need to attend to my family," said Harwood. "Make sure you come to see me. Make sure you look around. And make sure you don't ride out until we have ourselves a good man-to-man talk." Harwood clapped Rourke on the shoulder with a grin and moved through the crowd, a powerful man filled with powerful energy.

As he watched the man divide the crowd like a knife passing through butter, Rourke wondered what it would be like to have goals and plans and the ability to carry them out. He guessed he might have had them awhile back, before the war. He and Lorraine had dreams, even if they were as substantial as the clouds. Now, though, every day was about walking through the things life threw at him. Every night was trying to stay a step ahead of whatever the past might dredge up for him to chew on while he slept. He looked again at Harwood, vaguely sensing that theirs were very different worlds. He wondered what life would have been like had he lived in Hardwood's world. Then he realized as he did that whatever might have been possible in some other time, all that mattered now was getting by. Eastern people lived in different ways. He had less and less interest in them as time went by. The land was all there was for a man like him. He looked over his shoulder one last time. Harwood was standing with some tough-looking men by the hotel doors. No ladies in sight. They went in together. Maybe it meant something. Maybe not. And maybe he had better things to do.

CHAPTER FIVE

Rawhide at night breathed sin. The raucous piano's off-key symphony seemed several times louder than during the daylight. It barely drowned out the hoots and laughter from the Last Chance Saloon's customers. The duckboards that fronted long-closed stores gave cover to groups of young men who lurked waiting for something—a drunk to rob, a chance to make a name, a fight that would prove their manhood, a woman. The reek of beer and the sharper scent of cheap booze came from the men sitting along the edges of the wood, the down-and-outers who were drifting like the dust from bottle to bottle.

Two men with stars walked the streets. The deputies were hired not to clean up the place, but to ensure that only the things that crossed an ill-defined hazy gray membrane of a line should ever be officially reported. Action to enforce the letter of the town's laws on wild, drunken cowboys would bring castigation from the rich and powerful of the town, who relied on drunks, fools, and desperation for their financial empires.

For the few who did not participate in the revels, nighttime, when the weather was anything except stone cold, meant hiding with windows closed, no matter what the heat, and keeping daughters close to home and locked away for fear of the cowboys coming to town for a night they would long remember and everyone else would try to forget.

Having completed his errands and feeling restless after a day of not doing much that was familiar, Rourke walked the main street. He soaked in the sounds and sights that changed little in the months between visits. He finally settled in at a table in the back corner of the Last Chance, plunking down a glass of beer that smelled almost as bad as creek water when a herd of cattle had passed through it. He recalled the days when he was young. He never would have tasted the drink, let alone smelled it. Young and stupid. Sometimes a miracle any of us gets out alive, he thought. For a time, liquor had driven away nightmares. Now, nothing did. Maybe nothing would or maybe even should. Scars were old wounds that had healed as best they were going to.

Anyhow, tonight was a night for being stone-cold sober so he could listen to the talk bouncing off the walls. Cowboys yelled their news, opinions, and challenges to one another like a gang of overgrown boys. Card sharps at the tables tried to gauge how much they could take a man for without paying the price. Older men who dotted the room either tried to be young again for a night or kept an eye on their riders to make sure they all came back home in one piece.

The talk was no surprise—a lot of criticism about the Army and the Indians, a lot of nothing about the weather and some talk about rustling. The morals of politicians came up for their usual discussions. The railroad they all talked about coming to central Wyoming would get there sooner or later, they assured themselves, even if it was a few years away. Rourke grimaced at that. He'd seen pristine prairies devastated by the filthy rails and the machines that rode them. Camps of toughs came to build and left destruction in their wake. Railroads might mean progress to the ranchers, but Rourke was starting to wonder if before he died, progress was going to wrap its filthy, greasy, grasping fat fingers over every bit of his West. He hoped he would never see the day when the West and the East looked alike.

He tried to focus on what he heard. The cowboys all knew who was doing the stealing, but none of them named the same names. Everyone knew the trails rustlers used. No one had actually seen an animal. In short, each rancher suspected all of his fellow ranchers. They were so focused on their missing stock, they could not see the pattern. Stealing would always go on, but every rancher was being hit. The rustling was more organized than a rancher here or there stealing an animal from somebody else. If nobody found the missing stock, then where was it? Horses didn't often sprout wings and fly away.

Rourke decided he'd had enough for one night and was about to return to the more pleasant atmosphere of the stable when Steve Owens pushed through the batwing doors of the saloon. He walked through the barroom, ignoring all around him. He climbed the stairs to the rooms on the upper floors with the practiced ease of a man who had done this a thousand times. Rourke was curious and troubled. Owens talked about settling down with a steady woman, but Rourke had never actually seen her. A man did what a man did, but something didn't set right. Rourke couldn't help but get his itch scratched. He left the untouched glass of watery beer and drifted through the clouds of noise and smoke until he reached the cool, redeeming quiet of the night. He sauntered down the street like a man with nothing on his mind, then came back up the far side of the street, beyond the light thrown by the saloon's lamps. He found a place where he could see the door and the stairs that led down from the second floor to the ground outside the saloon. He was not surprised when he saw Owens walking down them with a woman. He was, however, stunned when a glance at her face when she passed by the glow from the saloon revealed it to be the Harwoods' daughter. He watched their posture. They were not on a romantic interlude. They were acting more like conspirators. She kept her head low and away from passersby.

He ducked a lot, too. They talked with heads bent together as they walked. Rourke wondered what they were up to. They turned a corner. He was thinking about following.

Gunshots from the saloon changed that plan. Loud voices followed. It was instinct to run across the street and inside with his gun ready. A young man was standing in the middle of the saloon, smoke drifting from his Colt. A fancy vest man was slumped on the table.

"He was cheating me!" the young man proclaimed. Two burly men Rourke assumed were the gambler's intimidating partners were closing in. The gambler must be heeled, or the gunfighters would have been smoke in the wind. They were pulling guns. The young man, who looked drunk, scared, or both, stared with unfocused eyes. He held the gun as if it was a stranger to his hand.

"He cheated!" he yelled again, hoping one more declaration of innocence would stave off retribution.

"Murder," yelled one of the gunmen.

"Killer!" yelled the other.

Men were moving. The ones that wanted adventure were reaching for weapons. The older ones were sidling away to find cover. Rourke looked around for the law. He wondered if being a lawman in Rawhide meant you gave everybody time to shoot each other first. There was nobody coming through the doors. Well, he could only wait so long.

"Everybody freeze," he yelled in the voice that caused even his Texans to stop stealing during the war. "That means you boys, too," he added, eying the gunmen bearing down on the young man.

"We saw it all," yelled one, trying to whip up the crowd.

"Ought to hang him for killing an innocent man," yelled the other.

"Lynch him," called out a voice in the crowd that knew nothing, was plain drunk, or stupid.

Rourke strode to the young man. "Put the gun away, sonny," he said. "If you want to live, you watch my back and yell if they come."

He faced the crowd. "Hold on, boys," he called out, stilling the rumblings by holding up his hand as if he was really in charge. "Before you get all hot and bothered and hurt this fella, let's see what there is to see." He callously reached down and pushed the gambler off the table. The lifeless body lolled against the chair's back. Rourke hated the parasites who tricked fools out of their money. He reached into the gambler's vest, and threw an ace and a queen on the table. From a sleeve came another ace. The back of the dead man's shirt collar produced a king. Rourke spread the cards on the table.

"Man cheated, man paid," Rourke called out, staring them all down. "Anyone say something different?"

The gunmen were realists. They had lost. They would find another boss, another payday. In Wyoming Territory, a man learned when to fold his hand if he wanted to survive. Some in the crowd were turning their unfulfilled anger upon the gambler's friends. The gunmen knew the score. They held up their hands and drifted out. Rourke patted the gambler. The pants had a wad of greenbacks and a fistful of gold pieces. "Take your stake," he told the young man. "Then git and don't come back. Next time, you won't be so lucky."

The young man started to reach for the money, but was shoved out of the way by another man—a drunk who was bigger than Rourke. "I got cheated, too. All that's mine. Give it over."

"You forgot to say please," replied Rourke. He shoved the man back. He wanted to get away from them all. One of the saloon women hovered nearby—a woman with a head of long black hair all in curly ringlets. "This fool play poker with the dead fella?" Rourke asked her.

Before she could answer, the drunk grabbed her and held a knife to her throat. "The money or I cut her throat."

The woman's eyes were pleading. For a moment Rourke wondered who she was, how she had become a saloon woman in a place like Rawhide. Imagine dying here for nothing, he thought. Rourke shrugged. "Can't draw to that hand," he said, setting some money on the table and shoving it to the farthest side. "All yours."

The drunk was trying to plan how best to get the money while holding his hostage. He cast one glance at Rourke, then moved to reach across and scoop up the money. Not fast enough. Before the big man touched the pile, Rourke's fist caught him in the right shoulder. The knife fell. It skittered along the floor. The saloon girl ran and grabbed it, threatening all comers. Rourke ignored her and focused on the giant. The big drunk had pulled out another knife—this one a huge ol' Bowie knife—and waved it at Rourke.

"Gonna kill you. I'm gonna kill you slow. No one makes a fool outta me." Rourke waited. Not talking. Nothing to say. His enemy lunged, yelled, and swung the knife. Rourke brought up his left arm, deflecting the cut so that a long, red line opened, slowly dripping blood. The big man swung back and forth, missing most of the time, grazing Rourke's arms and face. The giant edged closer, swinging wildly, forcing Rourke to retreat. As Rourke moved backwards, he tripped on a raised floorboard. The giant leaped upon him, knife flashing, burying the blade in the wood of the sagging floor as Rourke dodged. The drunk struggled to pull it out, then grabbed Rourke by the throat and squeezed. Glass crashed. Shards and liquid rained on Rourke. The drunk lifted a hand to his head where the saloon woman had brained him with a bottle. Rourke barely noticed the saloon woman with the shattered glass in her hand as he rolled and stood. The giant wobbled to his feet. Rourke closed in. A left, right, left, right. Every punch drew a mist of blood. The blinded, reeling giant staggered. Even after Rourke stopped hitting, he was barely able to stand. Rourke took a step back, drew his gun, and swung it. The barrel connected with the giant's jaw. The man groaned, tumbled, and landed. Rourke's blood dripped to the floor. He gasped for air.

The town patrols rushed in. Rourke figured they had probably waited until the end of the fight. They were paid to see that drunks got home safely, not to risk their lives. They were visibly relieved that the situation was resolved. They were more than happy to oversee the removal of the gambler and the giant.

Rourke scooped up the money. He figured he had earned it. He saw the woman and handed her a thick handful of the greenbacks. "Obliged," he said. "You swing a mean bottle, ma'am. Take this and go find somethin' better. This ain't no way to die, miss. Whatever you left, it ain't worth livin' here. You ought to get out of here."

She replied with a smile and scorn. "And go where? Another Rawhide? Cowboy, when your man runs and you got no money, you got to do something. When the only thing you can do is wrong, you do it and deal with it. I don't want your sympathy. Right now you got your plate full saving yourself, so don't you worry about me. I know how to get by in a man's world. Not sure I want advice from a man dripping his blood all over the floor."

She handed him a wet bar rag. He dabbed at the oozing cuts on his arms. Nothing that wouldn't stop in time. He knew from experience. "Anything's better than this," he told her.

"Dyin' ain't, cowboy. Goin' back to my folks in Kansas ain't. I get me a stake, I can go to Denver and live with my sister, maybe."

Rourke shoved more greenbacks into her hands. "Then go!"

He turned and left. He didn't want to hear what she said in reply. She'd probably squander the money. Nobody ended up working in a saloon in Wyoming Territory unless life had backhanded them across the face. He didn't have the time to care. He wanted to get out of there.

Gratefully leaving human society behind, and a few gold pieces to the good for his trouble, he walked back to Star, to the stable. At least if he was going to be alone, he could be alone in good company. He'd seen enough of Rawhide to last awhile. In the morning, he and Star would ride out. They would leave all the trouble behind.

CHAPTER SIX

Rourke woke up early. The bar rag from the night before was covered with blood. His arms and face stung, but he was alive. The new shirt was ruined. Well, he still had one new one left. By the time the sun was fully up, he and Star were gone. He rode north first to get a look at Harrison's land. As he topped a rise he saw what had to be some of the last wagons of the year rolling westward on what the people back East knew as the Oregon Trail. It wasn't so much a real trail as the rough route wagons had been passing for years on the way to Oregon and California. Rourke saw people running. He heard yelling, even from a couple of hundred yards away. The wagons lurched to a stop. Everyone fanned out. Rourke knew that in fall, every day counted to get through the mountains before the snows. This had to be important. He nudged Star forward.

They were about 25 yards from the nearest searchers, who were calling a girl's name, when he heard the rustling in the tall grass behind a stand of oaks off to his right and behind him. He put his hand to his gun and turned Star fast.

He rounded the edge of the trees. A brown and white cow, chewing something, looked back placidly. Rourke relaxed and smiled. "C'mon, Star. Let's play cowboy."

Neither Star nor the cow took this decision very well, but in a minute the cow was heading back to the wagons and the kind of welcome Rourke assumed the Prodigal Son received. One man stood off from the rest with his hand to his eyes. Rourke waved and walked Star closer.

"Howdy," called the man. "See you found Daisy."

"Guess she approves of Wyoming grass," Rourke replied.

"Well, Emily and me got six kids so we need the milk," the farmer said. "You from around here?"

"More or less," Rourke nodded.

"This isn't much for farm country," the man said.

Rourke shook his head. "Grazing land, mister. Don't rain enough here."

As they talked, a woman and a flock of small children approached. The collection of boys and girls swarmed the cow and their pa. Their milk supply had been restored.

"Late in the year to be crossing the mountains," Rourke said. "It snows early in the passes. Hope you get where you're bound."

"This family never quits," said the man. "Illinois was not the place for us, no siree. No room to grow. It's been a journey, mister, but we're almost there. Bye, now!"

Rourke watched the talking cloud of family walk back to their wagons. For a moment, he could see the other side of the chasm that divided him from folks who had dreams. He wondered as he watched them what it would feel like to walk without the weight of a gun strapped to his hip, without checking the ridge line for riders, without looking for the dust of horsemen he was either chasing or fleeing. Cursing to himself and at himself for his foolishness, he turned Star away from the wagons. His world was rustlers and horses. But, as he rode off, he took one last look back.

Families. Rourke saw them all the time, but he never knew what they really were like. He'd been ten when his father killed a guard at Alyth in Perthshire in a fight over establishing a union at the mines. They fled Scotland for America. They had not been in Texas six months when Pa died of disease. Rourke grew up fast. Some people along the way had been kind. Most had not. Rourke had learned how to shoot and how to ride. He was a kid when the war with Mexico broke out. He scouted for the Army. He learned about death. When he got back home, he didn't fit anymore. He hired on for scouting mostly. Before the war, he'd ridden with the Texas-based Second U.S. Cavalry— John Bell Hood, Robert E. Lee, Albert Sidney Johnston, and some of the others who would later fight for the Confederacy. It was a natural transition from scouting for the Army to fighting in the Civil War. Then the fighting ended. All he knew was riding and shooting. He had come west for no good reason other than he could not stay where he was, like most folks. He stayed because it felt right. Even before Wyoming had been a territory, back when it was parts of Utah, Nebraska, and Colorado, he had come to love the land and the windy open freedom it brought him. Other people made plans and had tomorrows. Rourke just survived.

Gilbert Harrison's ranch was a mile north of the Oregon Trail. The house was set in a small valley, sheltered from the worst of the north winds. There were a couple of corrals for breaking horses. The bunkhouse was not that much bigger than the main house. Both were long, low buildings built for shelter, not for show. It was a working ranch–a man's world. Not much was painted. Stuff was dropped where it was.

"Hello, the house," he called.

A young man who had probably lost his left leg in the war hobbled out with a crutch under his left arm and a shotgun in his right. "Howdy," said the man. "You lost or lookin' for work?"

"Neither," said Rourke, describing his mission to investigate the rustling.

The ex-soldier grunted. "Gil and the boys went out yesterday to comb the coulees for strays," he said. "We're kind of spread out all over. Gil's not really hit as bad as it seems. Stray horses tend to wander to a meadow up north of the trail a ways. Usually ours, sometimes not. This year, the meadow was empty and Gil figgers someone got there ahead of him. He lost a valuable roan, and that's got him peeved.

"Pete Treadwell, now that's a man on a mission. He's got that family of his. To him, every horse helps feed another mouth. Pete gets Gil goin', partner, but, with all the strays running wild in Wyoming, it's pretty hard to tell where rustling starts and good luck ends. Army has lots of papers that ask lots of questions, but the officers forget to ask them sometimes, if you know what I mean. They got a man at the fort takes care of the officers, so I hear."

Rourke talked a bit. The man had been at Chattanooga. Rourke remembered the fight. Funny, now. Men who tried to kill each other usually swapped stories. The ones still fighting the war never did much during it. Rourke rode on, wondering if Harrison's ability to find strays meant he was inching over the line of the law. The man didn't act it, but when there was no law, it was hard to look like a criminal.

Rourke retraced his route to head south. It made sense that Treadwell would have troubles. North of the Oregon Trail, ranches were few. The Sioux liked to steal horses, but Red Cloud didn't want problems with the Army any more than the whites wanted war with the Indians. But south of Rawhide he was getting closer to the railroad and the line of towns that were rising and dying as the tracks inched westward. The railroad and those camps spewed out trouble and troublemakers like one of those geysers out to the west.

Treadwell's ranch was a lot neater than Harrison's. It didn't take long to figure out why. A woman and a couple of kids were on the porch of the place as Rourke rode up. Rourke noticed the woman sent the kids inside as he approached—either to get her a gun or get somebody to hold one. She had light brown hair that was tied mostly up except for the many stray strands that had escaped in the course of the day. Her apron was stained from use. She was about 35. Maybe pretty as a girl, he guessed, and now grown into a woman whose character had grown with the challenges of life. She was going to defend her man and his land. That was very clear.

"Ma'am," said Rourke, taking off his hat but not dismounting. "Name's Rourke. Pete and Gil Harrison and Bill Harwood asked me to poke around a bit on this rustling problem you all are having. I'm trying to get the lay of the range."

"I'm Abigail Treadwell, Mr. Rourke. Pete is out in the barn. He and his men are riding out in the morning. You can see them over there." She pointed.

He clucked at Star, who moved toward the barn. Rourke stopped and turned. "I gotta know, ma'am. That a shotgun or a Winchester under that blanket there?"

"A Winchester, Mr. Rourke. A shotgun is a little more kick than I can stand." She was smiling. "Most of the riders who come here never notice that."

"Like they don't see the cook with the rifle by the corner?"

"We protect ourselves, Mr. Rourke."

"Not arguin', ma'am. Don't want anything going off by accident." He rode to the barn and dismounted.

Pete Treadwell broke away from the riders he was addressing. "Rourke." He stuck out a hand. "Didn't think you'd show. Met the wife? She didn't shoot you so you must be honest. Zachariah, my oldest, is 12. He wants to shoot a rustler real bad, but I think she wants first shot. Find anything yet?"

"Still getting the range limits down in my head," Rourke replied. "You think rustling and the railroad towns are connected?"

"Rourke, I want to go to those railroad people and make them pay so bad I can smell it," Treadwell said. "Boys and I checked all the stock in their corrals the other week. A lot of brands, not a one of mine. By rights it ought to be them but it ain't. One of my riders heard some of the officers at the fort are buying their own horses and selling them to the Sioux at twice the price. Another one heard that there's a gang from Colorado that raids up here. I don't know what to believe. Gilbert gets strays up north. I don't find many down here. It will get worse now that Green Hills is going to be running."

"Hasn't Green Hills always been around?"

"Well, it was always a ranch, but there were a couple of old folks there. Ran a few horses. Kept a couple of riders. They died. It got sold to some Eastern outfit that sold it again. Now these Harwood people are fixin' to make big money. I know they are going to squeeze me. I can't afford to be squeezed. With the railroad coming at me from the south and Green Hills up north and west, I can't lose a single horse if I want this ranch to pay. Abby and the boys—well, I'm not losing my boys' inheritance without a fight!"

"Where's your worst weakness? Where you think a rustler would steal?"

"Easy. Toward Green Hills. There's flat land there where horses left to graze can drift. I know that spot. We ride out there all the time. Haven't caught a rustler yet."

Rourke thought that over. Treadwell was aggressive and smart. He knew the land. If he was losing horses and didn't know how, Rourke could not imagine what he could do better. Maybe Treadwell hadn't done everything, though. "Where's the least likely place to steal from you?"

"Due west. Hills make it hard to get through. Only a couple of passes. Why?"

"Well, Pete, seems to me you want to steal from someone you don't go where he's lookin', you go where he isn't. I got to ride out that way. When I see what's to see I'll let you know. You got your ranch to run. I'm supposed to poke my nose where it don't belong."

They talked for a few minutes about the land and the hills. Rourke mounted Star to leave. Abigail Treadwell was walking toward him. "Mr. Rourke. This land is Pete's life. You have to help him. He's a rancher, not a lawman or a gunfighter."

"I will, ma'am," he replied. "You raise them kids." He touched his boot to Star's flank. As he rode away, Rourke thought about Treadwell. It wasn't about horses and money. It was land and dreams and family. It was good people who didn't know how folks worked that were not so good. "Guess that means folks like me are good for something in this world, horse," he told Star. "Now c'mon. We got to get to Green Hills today."

Dan Wheeler watched Rourke and Star slowly leave Rawhide. He crossed to the hotel's dining room, the only place he had eaten in the three years since his wife had died. Louise Callahan came in, yawning. He knew that when she worked late at the Last Chance she might not be up, but he always looked for her. He stood up immediately and moved toward her as he saw the fresh new bruises on her face and neck.

She waved dismissively. "Another drunk, Dan."

"You should get out of that place."

"That's what he said."

"Who?"

"That bounty hunter." She related the episode. "Easiest $200 I ever earned."

Wheeler shook his head. A bounty hunter that gave money to a woman in a saloon? That wasn't how the breed worked. He remembered when Red Jim was the gunman for the movers and shakers who eventually became the people behind the territorial government. Then Red Jim branched out into killing on his own. Wheeler assumed Rourke was the next Red Jim. One day, another would ride in to kill Rourke for his master's pay. None of his affair.

"What are you going to do? You could make that trip to Denver."

"That what you think I should do, Dan?"

Martha Wheeler had been married to Dan for 28 years when she died. They'd been kids when they got married. Dan had never looked at another woman. He'd been eating with Louise about every day for six months. It was clear to everyone except him that she was special to him.

"Denver's safer."

She gave him a smile in return. "You want me safe?"

"Well, of course, Louise. I mean, not my, um, well, you know, Rawhide's no place for a decent woman."

"Not sure Denver's any better," she replied. "Denver's a big town with people who look at you as if they can buy and sell you. Oh, we got some wild cowboys here, Dan, but Bear Wallace lets me borrow a mare for nothing now and then. I ride out toward the hills. When I do, I feel free. I can feel the wind blow the cobwebs away. I can see eagles. I don't want to lose that. I don't want to go backward to whoever I used to be."

Wheeler understood. When Martha died, he had family in Kansas that invited him to stay. He never thought about it, even though it would have been a quieter, easier life. "Tell you what, Louise. Maybe it's safer for you to ride with me."

Louise smiled broadly. "I'd like that, Dan. I'd like that very much." Her breakfast finished, she stood up to leave. "A girl needs to sleep, Dan, before the cowboys ride in later."

"Maybe we can ride tomorrow?"

"That would be wonderful, Dan."

As she left, Wheeler saw Dickinson, the Territory man, come in. He looked Louise over far too carefully, as though she were a thing to be inspected. He looked at Wheeler, barely spared a nod, and went to the tiny back dining room, where a table was set with a fancy tablecloth. Wheeler, the fresh taste of the morning spoiled by a bitterness that he could barely conceal, left money for the food and went out to patrol his town.

He had not gone far when he came upon Caroline Dickinson, immaculately dressed as always. The woman had more clothes than anyone Wheeler knew. Wheeler looked at her, moving through Rawhide with something in her posture that said the place was not quite what she wanted to see. There was a set to her jaw and a purpose in her step. Every intense action looked like an important part of some all-fired important plan. Wheeler had never seen the woman smile.

"Mrs. Dickinson." Wheeler tipped his hat.

"Sheriff," she replied, stopping. Usually she passed without moving her eyes in his direction any longer than manners dictated. Today, she must want something.

"There are drunken cowboys near our house," she said.

"Yes, ma'am," he replied. For some reason, he could not quite avoid making her ask for what she wanted.

"Well? They should not be allowed to loiter in a stupor near the home of the assistant territorial administrator," she said. "We have important guests from the Army arriving later today and we do not want them to see that seamy side of this town. I also expect that when the major and the captain arrive with their escort that the troopers will not be allowed to drink and become intoxicated. I recall an incident this summer that was very unpleasant."

"Yes, ma'am," he replied. If he walked real, real slow and the sun stayed out full, those boys should wake up about the time he got there.

"That is all, Sheriff," she finished, walking toward the hotel with her eyes fixed straight ahead, ignoring everyone and everything as she strode toward breakfast with her husband.

Well, Wheeler thought, she's Dickinson's problem. If there's anyone who deserves her, he does. That gave him a small smile as he slowly moved toward where a few drunken cowboys had no idea how much trouble they could get in just by sleepin'.

Green Hills was located on a high table of land ten miles southwest of Rawhide. To the west, the jagged hills that ended the miles of flat lands rose gently—the first hint of the gradual change from the vastness of the Plains to the craggy strength of the Rockies farther to the South and West. Pine trees covered the slopes, standing out starkly in the whiteness of winter and even in the fall and summer, when much of the land burned brown if the rains didn't come. It was brown now, varied by patches of this or that shade, but mostly empty of all except tall grasses and bushes growing where they had always been until fire swept through and the cycle began again. The land was broken by winding streams and small hills. Wind had worn rock here and there. It was wild, barely touched by man.

From a point of rocks near the camp they had made by a blacksmith's shed that was a lot more dilapidated than she expected, Cal stood in the breeze and took it all in. Then she turned around and looked at the gleaming white scar of the ranch house half a mile or so away. It was out of place. Just like all Easterners! They had silly notions of what women should wear and do and how they should ride horses. Some of the ones she had met in her travels looked at her as though she was one step removed from a Sioux Indian. Eastern people mostly acted as if she shouldn't wear a proper sensible hat, or pants, or boots and should wear silly frilly things that would fly in her face when she galloped on a horse. Nonsense!

People traveling through from the East had told her about cities and paved streets and tall buildings. She thought about seeing eagles up high, and buffalo herds that dotted the Plains. She thought about the deer that could leap by the hundred when a fright took them, and the clumsy bears whose cubs looked playful but whose claws could be deadly.

She thought about last winter, when one day the sun came out and the world was unbroken white for fifteen miles in every direction from their camp and the sparkles were almost blinding. That was a moment she held deep in her soul. What kind of lights could anybody want to see that could be better than the stars? City people would never understand, could never understand, that all in the world anyone could ever want was right here. All a body had to do was stand still and enjoy it.

She had real doubts about this plan of her father's. He was the sweetest man God ever made, but he could lose money faster than a hawk could dive. She was afraid they'd given up their freedom to end up with nothing. She knew in the well-worn wisdom of those on the margins of life that people who dressed in fine clothes and lived in big houses and talked in big words about churches were the ones who turned families out penniless if they got in the way. The rich man who charmed Pa like the last one could have been as big a crook.

Staying still was just plain against her grain. Maybe it would be nice to be in a place if all the land was yours and nobody could tell you what to do on it. Not like living in a town where if you baked bread, they'd be putting a hand in the window to ask for a slice. It felt so wide open to stand here and see it all and let the wind blow clean on through your thoughts. Still, moving was what came natural. They'd been traveling most of her life. She'd never been a coddled princess. She couldn't imagine what women like that did when they met the gut-wrenching reality of scraping together a life on the Plains, or did chores with one hand while they birthed a baby with the other. Cal had held the dying so many times she could not count them. Out here, dying happened. What mattered was what you did until then.

A noise returned her to the present. She walked back from her vantage point to the camp. Pa was sitting by the fire, the battered coffee pot steaming. She hoped he didn't brew liquor with the coffee again. Everything out of the pot had tasted bad for a week. She loved him like she loved no one else. Pa doted on her. Every traveling man they met was an Uncle This or That. She never really knew what the word meant until she got older. She attached it to all the men who laughed with Pa at the fire. Ma had died when she was young. In the only picture Cal had of her, taken when Pa and Ma were young, she was a pretty woman with a dark dress and light hair. Family was what you made it. She never felt alone. Anyhow, she had the land. Her soul could roam free as long as the prairie wind blew.

She saw movement in the distance. She reached for her rifle. She believed in hospitality but also common sense, especially after the other day with the range loafers who had waylaid her. She looked. She squinted to be sure. Then she set the rifle down and waved the old brown leather cowboy hat that was stained from a thousand memories. The rider waved back. She could barely make out Rourke, but Star was plain to see. There could only be one like him around.

Rourke rode slowly across the meadows, clearly taking his time to look over the land, its features, its places for ambush and whatever else a mind trained for killing would need to know. Cal felt safe when he was near. She'd never really seen what went on the time they were attacked back in Kansas and this man with a huge gun had come along and saved them. She remembered the noise and the bodies. She remembered the panic in Pa's face when he'd told her to hide, and the relief when it was over.

She remembered Rourke looking much like he did now, more like a drifting range bum than a gunfighter. He had made protecting her a priority. For a man who was always somewhere else, he was in the nick of time more than once.

She wondered why he had come along. Maybe he was feeling the changes, too. She knew about Red Jim, of course. She wondered how long he was going to ride the territories killing people for money. Didn't he know that one day there would be a faster gun somewhere waiting for him?

There she was again, worrying about the future even though she kept telling herself it was pretty much a subject she didn't like thinking about these days. Pa's cough reminded her that he would not live forever. Once he was gone, she needed to have a life. Some of the boys she met were all right, but she hadn't been looking for a husband. All she ever really wanted was to ride around with Pa and enjoy the open places. They didn't have much as comforts went, but they were free and they had each other.

She could read and write—Pa had found books everywhere they went. She wasn't going to teach a school, or serve up drinks and show off her skin in a dance hall saloon. She could work for a newspaper, but she didn't want to spend her days up to her elbows in filthy ink. Well, she told herself again, the future would be there some other day. For the moment, Rourke was riding up the slope, a grin against the dark clothes he wore. He made a sweeping bow, taking off the flat-crowned black hat that was a relic of the war.

"Nice land."

"Too bad it's not ours," Cal pouted, contradicting her thoughts from a moment before. That was happening too often lately.

Rourke, knowing nothing of Cal's inner thoughts, shrugged. Having land meant doing things he was pretty sure he didn't do well. He'd done nothing much the past few years except ride horses and kill men. Most of the things that were part of the old life were part of someone else's history. He liked riding through the land and feeling the open space. Owning anything more than what he could carry was not something men like him did. The only other thing he did other than ride and scout and fight was carve wood, but carving toys and little things for Easterners wasn't going to ever feed a man. Cal looked serious. Growin' up is never fun.

One cure for that. He spoke to Star. The horse shoved Cal with his nose, getting the usual fuss and restoring a smile to her face. Then Rourke undid it all in typical male fashion.

"Them women Harwoods come out yet?" he asked Cal, wondering again what the girl and Owens were discussing and wondering how he could find out. "Didn't see sign of a wagon."

"You know them?" Cal asked, shortly.

He told her about meeting the mother and daughter. "Was she pretty?" Cal asked.

"Hard to tell under all that. Guess so," Rourke said, realizing he had said something wrong from Cal's grimace. "You know how Eastern people are. Fancy clothes and fancy hat stuff."

"No, I don't," Cal said, walking away to the fire where Zeke was waving a coffee cup at Rourke. "I don't know and I don't care. I didn't know you had so much interest in Eastern women."

"Cal!" A voice trained to command cavalry under fire could get very loud. It was echoing as Rourke called out her name. She turned back around. Rourke had climbed down and was motioning her toward him, one finger beckoning her. Not entirely sure why she was mad at him in the first place, she walked slowly back.

He was grumbling as he took something off the back of his saddle. He looked intently at her as he laid the bundle at her feet. "Maybe before you go off half-cocked about stuff that don't matter to nobody, you might want to give this a peek," Rourke said. "Might want to do that, Miss Caledonia Bad Temper."

An old Indian from Dakota Territory had called her that as a girl after one particularly loud outburst—nobody now remembered why. Pa never let it die. She didn't know Rourke knew that one, too. She blushed, feeling silly. Was there anything about her the man didn't know?

The bundle was bulky and heavy. It was wrapped in a new blanket that was a whole lot better than most of hers. She was starting to feel guilty for being rude, but she wondered why he was thinking about some Eastern girl who shouldn't be out here. She fussed with the string that tied the bundle. Those people belonged back in their cities and not out here ruining the Territory.

"Am I supposed to be able to untie it or is this a trick?" she asked, having lost track of what her fingers were doing while her mind snarled thoughts about Eastern women. Rourke threw her his pocket knife.

She cut the rope. The blanket wrapping the bundle fell away to reveal a beautiful buckskin fringed jacket. She stared at the jacket then and looked a question at him.

"Maybe you might want to look at it, put it on, see if you like it, see if it fits you, something like that," he suggested.

Her old jacket had so many stains that they had all blended together into a deep brown, obliterating whatever lighter color it had once been. She had been growing out of it, but there was no money to buy another one. She shrugged it off and put on the gift. It fit perfectly.

"Thought maybe that old one was being held together by stains," he said, casually. " 'Fraid the wind might blow it in the fire and the smell would attract wolves and bears and such."

Cal could not return his smile. She was without words for a minute. She knew how much a coat like this cost. There had been one a Fort Laramie sutler sold for $40. She and Pa could never have bought one. He bought it for her, just like that. She took a step toward him.

"This is wonderful. I love it. Thank you!" she said.

"Probably something else in there," he said, nodding at the bundle. There was no expression on his face.

She bent down, loving the smell of the new leather from the jacket. She never had felt the lack of anything, but it was so wonderfully wonderful to have something no one had worn before, that was all new and all hers! She sliced the string holding together the brown paper that was wrapped around something heavy. She threw the knife back.

"You're supposed to close it, Cal."

"Now you tell me, tenderfoot," she replied, getting a laugh for her efforts. Inside the paper wrapping that seemed endless as she dug through it was a gleaming Colt, smaller than the Remington cannon Rourke carried, or the old Colt revolver that she had inherited from Pa. There were also boxes of ammunition. The gun was lighter than the gun she had been carrying— one that was so heavy she left it behind a lot more than she should have.

"Figgered you need somethin' to have if you're gonna be around people now that you are in the blacksmith business," he said lamely, wondering in the back of his mind what kind of man gives a woman a pistol as a present and if he should have gotten her some silly woman thing.

This time, she did not hesitate, but crossed the distance between them in a leap and a step. She wrapped her arms around him. "I needed that because that old thing is so heavy. I looked at one last spring but it cost too much," she said. "Did Pa tell you? How did you know? Thank you, thank you, thank you!"

"Just guessed," he said, with a smile bright in his eyes as he saw her radiate happiness. It had not really occurred to him until then how much it mattered that the girl was happy. His arms had snaked around her as she talked.

"I don't know how to thank you, so there!" she said, before planting a big kiss that was aimed for his cheek, but when he turned, it ended up below his mouth. She flushed, unsure whether it was worse to be bold at kissing or bad at it. Rourke solved the problem for her by putting a hand under her chin and tilting her face up to his. The kiss might not have ended any time soon if not for the voice that erupted in glee from behind Rourke and made them both leap.

" 'Bout time she kissed somebody good and proper," Ezekiel said with a racking, cackling laugh of unmeasured delight. "Wondered when you two were ever gonna get 'round to it. Sick of watchin' the two of you watch each other like what you were thinkin' was a secret. Eeesh! Was a time this summer I thought that boy down near the Cheyenne lands was gonna get the gumption to go after her, back at that barn dance, but she wasn't of a mind. Thought I was gonna be an old man before I saw my grandkids. Hee! Well, there's hope in these old bones at last! Coffee's ready and there are biscuits—that is, if anybody here has the time for eatin' and drinkin'. Don't matter none to me if nobody ever comes up for air. I'm gonna eat while I can."

They had broken apart as Pa spoke. Cal looked at Rourke. He didn't seem embarrassed.

Cal herself was as red as a summer sunset, but she was smiling over her shoulder as she walked ahead. Rourke followed, holding Star's reins as he tied him with the other horses, wondering again what horses talked about when the people weren't around or if animals had more sense than to waste it talking. Then he took off the gun belt, this once, and sat real close to Cal, ignoring Zeke's conspiratorial grin. Together, they settled around the fire as if the only clouds hanging over their lives were the giant white buffaloes chasing each other playfully across the deep blue Wyoming sky.

CHAPTER SEVEN

Rourke slept little. Every time he looked, Cal was looking back. Finally, they built the fire back up a bit and sat watching stars move across the sky. They weren't quiet so much out of respect for Zeke as that neither of them was much at talk. Rourke knew there were things words were too small to hold properly. The night sky in Wyoming was one of them. Another was what a man felt inside for a woman. After a while, he held out his hand. Cal took it. She set her head on his shoulder a while later. Eventually, her rhythmic breathing told him that she was sleeping. He threw a blanket over her, and let her rest while he drifted the way soldiers do on night watch, a few minutes here, then listen to the noises, then a few more minutes until the first streaks of light showed in the East and it was safe to shut his eyes.

Zeke was sleeping when he woke up. Cal had cakes cooking. She winked when he rose and stretched. She was smiling. Didn't matter why or about what, he told himself. Human critters take smiling days and muck them all up with words. Not this one, he told himself. Not today.

Cal brought him a steaming cup of coffee. It cost a little kiss. The smile he got was warmer than the coffee. He could get used to that sort of thing.

He checked on Star; he checked the Plains. He looked again and then again. Right then and there, there was something more important than time with Cal. He could see a lot of movement in the early shadowy grayness. He could hear the telltale noises: a lot of horses were out there. That was odd. Treadwell's place was too far to the southeast; Harrison's too far north. If that was as big a herd as it sounded, it wasn't somebody digging out strays from the canyons and coulees where they would gather.

Full daylight allowed Rourke to see better. The herd was visible for miles. Rourke recalled both Dickinson's talk about Harwood making his ranch a big business and the concerns of other ranchers about rustling. He could guess where they were heading from his recollection of the ride he had taken the day before. There was a natural pasture northeast of Green Hills, toward Rawhide. Thick pine woods lined most of a vast meadow, making it easy for a small number of riders to control a large herd. The horses were being driven in that direction. Rourke followed the cloud of dust. It stopped, indicating the horses had reached their destination.

He also caught another dot of movement. Along the smoother part of the trail, a wagon jostled along. He could tell there were two women in the wagon along with two men; must be the Harwoods. He was more curious about the horses than the people. He knew from experience that rich people were best left alone because they expected poor folks to do their work for them. He let Cal and Ezekiel know that the Harwoods were coming—and got a mixed reaction as if Cal was still bothered by something. He said he had to ride out to look at something out on the Plains. No one asked for details. Cal could see he had his serious face on. That meant whatever it was it wouldn't be involving a pretty Eastern girl. Pa kept saying they had to meet the Harwoods, but she was in no hurry. They had work to do. The hole in the roof was patched, but they still needed to do a lot of work to stop the little leaks. She wondered what was bothering Rourke, but she figured he'd tell them if it mattered. He wasn't a talker, and he didn't ask permission, but he kept looking at Cal as though he expected her to say something. She wasn't quite sure what to do, so she did what seemed natural.

"Sure, ride out and play, cowboy," she told him. "Maybe there'll be a potato left in the stew when you get back. Just don't complain if after a full day of real work for me and Pa, you get the cold leavings of the pot."

Their normal banter resumed, Rourke laughed and mounted Star. He picked his way down the gentle slope, keeping to the woods to avoid being seen. He was acting on instinct: Never be seen until you know who is looking at you. The horse herd might be made up of horses with legitimate bills of sale. It might not. He'd know soon enough.

Dan Wheeler was smiling as he and Louise slowly rode up the hill to the west of Rawhide. They hadn't talked much. There wasn't a lot to say. Louise had her hair down and was hatless in the wind, enjoying the sun and the feel of the freshness as the west wind gusted. In the distance, there was a faint cloud of dust. It could have meant anything. Whatever it was, Wheeler wasn't in the town limits and none of it was going to interfere today. They had the Plains to themselves.

Then he frowned. Wheeler smelled the cigar. He looked down below where the trail to Green Hills met the one to the fort. Harwood, the mover and shaker, was talking with Dickinson. Talking? Arguing more like. The picture didn't make sense. Dickinson was clearly the one giving orders. Harwood was nodding yes. Wheeler could not hear the words, but there was no mistaking the anger, or the dominance Dickinson had over Harwood. Something to wonder about.

"Are you going to sit like a statue or ride, Dan?" Louise touched the spurs to her mount. Harwood became the last thing on Wheeler's mind.

★ ★ ★ ★ ★

Star slowly made his way through the trees. Rourke was not scratching Star in order to hurry. Soon, any semblance of a path petered out. He looped Star's reins around a low branch and went the rest of the way on foot, boots crunching through dead pine needles as he moved through the trees. He could feel the heat of the sun increase as the dimness brightened and he neared the edge of the woods. He drew his gun from habit. No man went spying on another without being ready for the consequences.

Screened by the low branches and the scrub growth along the edge of the meadow, he looked out at the herd. The horses didn't draw his attention the most. The riders did. They were heavily armed, without the carefree attitude of cowboys relaxing now that a herd was bottled in a safe place. They reminded him of the irregular cavalry outfits he'd run into back in Tennessee during the war—the bottom pickings of the barrel, men who called themselves soldiers but were barely one step better than thieves. They were dispersed around the herd. One sat his horse not ten feet from where Rourke was hiding. Each had a rifle loosely held across his saddle, as if they were planning to shoot first and ask questions later. Rourke waited. He was in the shade; they were in the sun. Nobody could sit still and bake forever. Sure enough, the man near him moved a few feet closer to the creeping shade of the trees. With the man and horse no longer a barrier, Rourke moved a few feet closer to the edge of the trees for a better look at the animals. A quick look confirmed his suspicions. There were more than a few different brands in there. He would bet his bottom dollar that the riders had no bills of sale, only lead for anyone who dared to ask.

Outnumbered, it was time to pull back. Dickinson was in Fort Laramie or some other place for a while anyhow. There might not even be time for him to tell his friend about what he had found. Horses needed to graze. If these were bunched here, the meadow would only hold them a few days. But these men looked like they planned to stay. Nothing much he could do for the moment. He'd get back to the shed and bide his time, maybe see if O'Toole had found out anything and look in on the horses now and again. He was sure this was Green Hills land from the natural boundaries that shaped the ones drawn on paper. This must be an outfit that didn't know Green Hills had a new owner. If there was no one to defend a piece of land, there was no right of ownership, regardless of what some paper might say. He was wondering if he should tell Harwood right off; the man might not like rustlers using his land.

Behind him the underbrush came alive. A deer was being chased by a wolf. The deer was making a clean getaway. The wolf tried to leap through a patch of underbrush to head off his quarry. The deer veered right, moving almost into Rourke and then out into the meadow. Heads turned at the commotion. Riders were galloping over almost before the deer fully emerged from the shadows. Rourke needed to move fast to avoid being seen by the many eyes now peering into the dappled light of the woods. Too late!

"Stop you!" called a voice.

"Somebody in the woods," called out another voice. "We got a spy in the woods."

Another voice yelled louder. "Forget the spy. Mind the horses, mind the horses! Get back to the horses!"

The deer had spooked a few horses. The riders had their hands full containing them before they could spread panic and start a full-fledged stampede. Rourke could hear the yelling and cussing behind him as he ran back to Star. He stopped before mounting. There were no sounds of pursuit. The woods were too dense. He moved through the last stretch of trees as before, slowly and carefully. He didn't want to attract attention. They had their hands full and would worry about the animals more than a stray rider.

He guessed wrong.

As he left behind the noise of the herd and its chaos, the pounding of one set of hooves became louder off to his left. One rider was throwing caution aside and galloping through the trees on some pathway Rourke hadn't discovered. Soon, the rider would be catching up or heading him off. Rourke thought about his options. During the war, running worked most of the time. When it didn't, the next best thing was surprise.

A weather-scarred man riding a brown stallion careened around the bend in the thin trail that led to a small open space among the trees. As if surprised, he pulled back on the reins, hard. Dirt flew from under the hooves of the horse as the animal tried to obey the command. The rider was scanning the open space. He could see the path through the grass left by the rider ahead of him. The silence of the meadow was a warning that the horse he was chasing might have stopped. He might now be riding into an ambush. Keeping his gun ready in his hand, the rider spurred his horse. The animal responded, jerking as it went from trying to stop to trying to run. The rider pulled on the reins to control the horse.

He barely looked up in time. Coming across the meadow at a steady run was a giant black horse with a white blaze on his forehead, and a rider low in the saddle. Surprise cost him precious seconds as the realization sunk in that the hunted had become the hunter. The rider jammed his Colt back into its holster and pulled the Winchester from his scabbard. He'd done it before. He moved swiftly to take aim.

The rider never fired. Rourke had been firing guns from horseback for most of his life. All he needed was his Remington. His first bullet caught the rider in the center of his chest; the second at the base of his neck. The man toppled in the saddle, folding up like a sack of potatoes somebody dropped. By the time Star and Rourke reached him, there was blood in the dirt and not a breath of life left in the rider.

Rourke dismounted. He calmed the dead man's horse. He pulled the man's legs from the stirrups, allowing the corpse to topple to the ground. Rourke checked the saddlebags. He found some shells that would fit the Remington; no papers. The man's pockets had some tobacco, some silver dollars, and a few gold coins. Rourke guessed the money would do more good in his pocket. At first, he left enough to cover the cost of a grave. Then he decided to leave nothing. Rustlers got what they got. The money might be handy if Cal and Zeke needed anything after he rode north for the winter. He took the guns as well. Whoever found the man might assume the rider was shot during a robbery. He slapped the horse on the rear end, pointing it back down the trail. Mounting up, he looked back. No one else seemed to be following him. He turned Star deeper into the forest, knowing that sooner or later they could find a route back to Cal and Zeke. Right now, he had to stay out of sight. As he rode, he found a small pond, where he disposed of the guns. They were nice guns, but they were also links connecting him to a killing. Even though he had killed nothing but a rustler, he'd had enough experience with killings to know that life was simpler if he could avoid getting blamed for one.

"Get lost?" Cal quipped when he rode out of the early evening shadows. "Or did you figure the work all got done and it was finally safe to show yourself? Don't expect me to warm up what got cold waiting. In my book, a man who doesn't work is a man who doesn't eat."

"Well if that don't beat all for the way to talk to a man at the end of a hard day," Rourke replied. "Had to ride to Texas and back and it took a while to find a tornado goin' my way.

Anybody come by while I was gone?"

Ezekiel replied that no one had stopped. He said there were some riders far down the valley. Once he thought he heard a gunshot—most likely somebody out hunting. Cal's expression told Rourke she could smell some kind of trouble. He was glad she didn't press it. Sooner or later someone would ask about a dead rider and when they did, she needed to be able to know nothing about it. She didn't know how badly she lied and he wasn't going to be the one to tell her.

"Are you going to stand there all night, simpleton?" she challenged. "There's a plate by the log that I've been trying to keep warm and it isn't for Star."

Zeke's laughter rolled across the liquid night. Cal fumed and fussed and plopped next to him leg to leg as he ate half-warm beans with a little meat mixed in and felt like the king of the world.

CHAPTER EIGHT

A thin band of lighter blue was wedged between the darkness of the hills and the star-dotted black of the sky. Rourke sat by the charred and glowing sticks that marked the remnant of the evening's fire. Food was long gone, the coffee, too. Zeke was telling tales about Mexico again. Cal was clearly enchanted with what Rourke knew were mostly lies. Then he heard it. Hooves walking. Not one horse. Many. Moving steadily closer. Maybe friendly, maybe not. They were fanning out. They knew how to be ready for a fight. Rourke needed to be ready, too.

"Do not move," he muttered to Cal. Raising his voice louder he said, "I'm getting it, woman, I'm getting it." He moved away from the fire's light toward the blankets where his rifle was kept. Whatever was out there, he didn't want to be blinded when he had to face it. He checked his pistol as well. Ready, if he needed to be.

"Hello, the camp! Want to come in and talk." The young man's voice, not unfriendly, came from beyond the fire's glow.

Ezekiel called out the well-worn greeting: "Get down. I'd invite you to come in, but the roof ain't much more than a thought."

Six men moved closer and dismounted. Four more stayed on their horses. By the time the dismounted men walked up to Cal and Ezekiel, Rourke was on their flank. He could hit them but they would be hard-pressed to fire without hitting one another. If they were friendly, there would be no problem. If not, he could protect Cal and Zeke. Once they had moved into the circle of flickering, dim light, he moved forward so they could see him.

The leader of the group watched Rourke's final approach, which any fighting man would recognize as somewhere between a challenge and a warning. The man turned back to Zeke and Cal with a mild, coaxing tone in his voice. "Not meaning any harm here, folks. Name's Rick Gallagher. Me 'n' my men got a horse herd down below. One of our riders got killed today by somebody that robbed him. We was a-wonderin' if any stray riders came by. Guess from up here you can see a long ways. Maybe you saw somethin'?"

Gallagher was young, much younger than Rourke. He took his hat off when he spoke. The firelight showed a clean-shaven face with strong features, dark eyes, and black hair. His eyes lingered over Cal for a moment longer than Rourke thought was necessary. He was built like a rider, lean, with broad shoulders. He exuded an air of confidence and leadership. If he felt concern for the armed man watching him, he didn't reflect it. He looked like any one of a thousand cowboys in Wyoming Territory living in a hard world filled with hard lessons that were learned fast by those who survived. Rourke figured he was more than he said, but that was true for a lot of men—good as well as bad.

Ezekiel spoke for the group. "Nope. Been working on this here shed all day. Saw some dust. Thought we heard some guns maybe about the middle of the afternoon, but nobody rode this way so we didn't put our noses into anyone else's troubles," he said. "Maybe them Eastern people what own the land saw something. House is just over the rise there. Might not help much. Want coffee? Maybe got some leftover biscuits."

Gallagher declined the hospitality, offered in a tradition that cared little for whether a traveler was on one side of the law or the other. Out here, man could be on one side today, the other side tomorrow, depending on who drew the lines.

"Like sure enough to stay, but my men back with the horses are short-handed. We saw the fire a ways off and figgered if there was anything that came this way, you folks would have seen it." Gallagher studied Rourke a moment, as if recognizing something different in this man from Cal and Zeke. "You don't look like a homesteader or a ranch hand."

"Not," said Rourke. Cal flushed. Rourke could be so rude, as if the rules of hospitality didn't include him. Gallagher nodded, like a man who found out what he wanted to know.

"Me'n the boys will be around a week or so to rest our herd and move on," he said, turning back to Cal and Zeke. "Down about a mile off the north and toward the east, there's a pasture, sort of a natural-like corral. You see riders or trouble, ride down and we'll come and help. I know a pretty young woman like yourself, miss, out here might need help, even with these fellas around you."

"We'll do that," said Ezekiel, standing up beside Cal protectively. "Ride straight."

Gallagher smiled in a broad, engaging grin that focused on Cal. "Maybe we'll see you folks again." He tipped his hat toward her, then turned to Rourke. "I'll see you around, too, cowboy." He walked back to his horse. The other dismounted riders, who had fanned out behind him as he talked, mounted up and left, without ever having spoken. The four who had not dismounted followed. Rourke stood rooted, listening until he was sure they were gone.

"Did you learn your manners in a Texas horse barn?" Cal said angrily. "Pa and I are hospitable to everyone, and if you don't like it maybe you should . . . well, you should change your ways."

"Man like that," Rourke said thoughtfully, "is used to taking whatever he wants, Cal. Reckon he is. And he knows I'm likely to get in his way. I think I'll stand guard awhile just to see what there is to see."

With that, Rourke walked away to the small rocky ledge that was a slightly higher vantage point than their camp. Cal watched him, fuming. Just because a man smiled at her once was no reason for Rourke to go off half-cocked. Maybe he could learn to try smiling and talking nice like that Gallagher fella sometime, instead of being bossy and rude to people.

Rourke sat on the rocks, looking over the darkness. The riders had long since gone. He was finally sure they were not coming back—at least not this night. If he did not know what he knew, they could have been what Cal thought they were. He had seen the man look at Cal and her look at him. He wondered if what he was feeling was something akin to jealousy. He didn't like the man looking at Cal that way. A lot of men looked at Cal, no doubt, while he was off chasing Red Jim or any of the rest of them. Cal could take care of herself, and she knew what she wanted. Then, as he looked out over the night, he could hear in the quiet the disquieting thought from his mind: Was what Cal wanted what he wanted, and even if it was, did he need to figure all this out real quick before somebody else came along and took her?

The big house at Green Hills had been built by someone who knew the land and its seasons, even if it was so new that the white paint on it all but hurt Cal's eyes when she looked at it. It was circled by trees for shade in summer. A double row of pines stood between the white, wood-frame house and the north winds. The house rose two stories high, a rarity on the High Plains of Wyoming, with red shutters next to glass paned windows, an even greater rarity because between hail, rocks, and bullets, there always seemed to be something flying that was sure to break glass all to pieces. A porch encircled the house. Hitching rails flanked the main door. The place had an air of grandeur, as if it was home to someone a bit better than most.

Cal and Zeke rode in the wagon; Rourke rode Star. He could see a bunkhouse, some outbuildings, and a small corral. Everything looked as if someone had painted the scene. Too neat. No men idling around in between chores, no piles of stray stuff lazy hands tossed aside. It looked like something from a play actor set and not like a working ranch. He was uneasy. Then again, he had been uneasy since the night the riders came by. Rustlers camping on the range of a ranch wasn't a good sign. They knew that spot and drove the horses right to it. The riders who came to their camp had new guns, not the usual lot of weapons range bums would have. To Rourke, they had the feel of an outfit, not strays coming together for one rustling job. An organized gang of rustlers would be serious, because most of the farmers who bred and raised horses lived by a code that assumed all men could be trusted. That's why rustlers were hung. They tore out the heart of what living in the West was all about.

Rourke's sour mood wasn't helped by the fact that he wanted to be anywhere else. Zeke had been adamant that he needed to say hello to his boss and wanted Rourke to be with him. Zeke was nervous. Rourke understood having a boss changed everything. He hadn't had one since the war. The windy unbridled freedom to ride out of any place at any time if he didn't like something had become ingrained in his way of life. He reminded himself to behave the way Cal would expect. He remembered Lorraine telling him that time in Richmond not to wipe his muddy boots on the legs of the silly little wooden chairs that could barely hold a real man. He didn't know how she knew he was thinking of it. It must have been some kind of special woman sense. He had enjoyed doing it anyhow, even though she knew he did.

"Behave," Cal called out to him threateningly, as if she knew what he was thinking. Cal had been barely less rebellious than Rourke about the visit because she knew Pa wouldn't let her avoid it.

"I been good all morning," he replied.

"You've been talking to your horse all morning," she shot back. "You have been alone too long. It's time to remember you are supposed to be civilized when you meet these silly, stupid, simpering Eastern people. We can't act like Wyoming range bums around Eastern people, Rourke. This job matters to Pa."

He realized wryly that Cal, who could defy armed men and shrug off tornadoes, was fretting over the judgment of a couple of Eastern women who could not hold a candle to her on their best day. How could she not know that? For her sake, he would try. He tried to recall what people talked about other than horses and guns and work. He didn't remember much. Well, he'd keep his mouth shut and listen. Zeke was good at talking. He'd just stay out of the way.

The Harwoods were waiting on the porch as they drew up to the house. A few men stood by a barn watching, acting more like guards than hired hands. There were some rifles propped against fences. He hadn't seen them before. Somebody wanted to be sure they could get to them if they needed them. Against an old man, a cowboy, and a girl? Nope. Had to be the way that outfit worked. An outfit that was ready for trouble meant trouble followed it.

The Harwoods were warm and welcoming. The women made polite remarks to the men, but mostly they talked to Cal. Cal was talking back in a chirpy kind of voice Rourke didn't know she had. The Harwoods led the way around the porch to show the view of the hills. Cal walked next to Rourke and hissed, "You stare at me any longer, cowboy, I am going to shoot your ears off when we get out of here, if I let you live that long!" Rourke wanted to laugh, because she said it with a phony smile plastered on her face, but settled for coughing instead to hide his smile behind his hand.

Rourke hated remembering names. Elizabeth was the daughter and Mary was the wife. Well, those were simple enough. Now that he had moved beyond the stage of first impressions, having seen them close up at Andy's house for dinner and now in the harsher light of day, he was not impressed. He'd seen all kinds during the war. There was a difference between the real thing and the imitation. The women had wary eyes and an overall demeanor that told him they were used to something other than refined ways of living. Mary Harwood's teeth were yellow like men got from smoking too much. But Eastern women didn't smoke, he knew, and barely tolerated men that did. Elizabeth Harwood was harder to read.

The Harwood women talked on and on about this and that piece of furniture as they went into the house itself. Rourke was jiggered if they didn't look a lot closer in age than a mother and daughter were likely to be. But they soon disappeared in a cloud of conversation that enveloped Cal and whisked her away with an urgent need to show off the house. Rourke figured Cal would get a handle on them. She could tell him her impressions later.

Harwood showed Zeke and Rourke into a room he called a study. It had big paintings and big chairs. Zeke was clearly in awe of it all. Harwood offered them drinks from crystal glasses while the meal was being prepared. He exuded confidence. Once he started running 200 horses in his herd, Ezekiel would have more work than he could handle. They were going to start with about half that, roughly the size of the herd Rourke had discovered. Ezekiel was clearly happy he was in at the start of a growing spread, so he could have work for a while. Rourke's doubts were growing, but he stuck to his plan of keeping his mouth shut.

The women took Cal for a tour. She'd never been in a house this big. One room seemed as big as the bar in the Rawhide saloon. She said so, then flushed as the Eastern women raised their eyebrows at one another. Cal mentioned the girl's run-in with the drunken miner in Rawhide, and laughed about her own run-in with the range bums.

"Men get wilder'n the critters out here, don't they?" she said.

"I suppose you know about men like that," said Elizabeth Harwood.

Cal was taken aback. She'd been in saloons as a little girl with Pa, but as she got older he stopped taking her and then stopped going himself. She knew right and wrong as well as anyone. No Eastern woman was going to talk to her that way. She wondered whether asking the women why they had to have faces the color of whey would be considered rude and decided it was. The question was on the tip of her tongue when the burly man they said was the cook came up behind her and announced that dinner was ready. She fumed wordlessly and followed.

Rourke went outside to a pump and washed the grime off of his hands. He hoped Cal would notice. He was curious and walked around. Something was not right. It didn't fit. He'd only seen three or four men. There was not enough activity for a place that was going to raise horses. Nowhere near enough corrals. He peered into a bunkhouse that was clearly empty.

"Spying, Rourke?" asked a voice behind him.

Rourke spun around.

"Lloyd, how do? You and the boys catch on here? Don't look like much of a crew for a spread this size." The other two Jeffries boys had fanned out behind their cousin.

"Boss' business, not mine," replied Lloyd. "Why you pokin' around?"

"Harwood invited me with his blacksmith. Remember that girl who might have shot you if I hadn't rescued you?"

Jeffries smiled to cover embarrassment. "Boys and I were a little wild that day, Rourke. Didn't mean no harm."

"Yup." Rourke let it lay there a minute. "Harwood talked about a job."

"You? You ridin' for *him*?" Lloyd's incredulous tone told Rourke more about the Harwoods and the outfit than he was likely to have found out himself. "Trails run funny, don't they, Rourke? I better git. Foreman said when the boss has company the hired folks should stay out of sight. You might think on things before you decide, Rourke. You might just do that."

Rourke watched Lloyd saunter toward the barn, with the two cousins behind him as always. When an outfit added men who lived on the edge of the law, but usually never quite put their toes over that edge—at least when anyone was looking—it meant they were either a desperate outfit or one that wanted desperate men. Which one was Green Hills?

The Harwoods were rounding up their guests as Rourke walked back inside. He sat next to Cal and across from Elizabeth Harwood, who kept glancing at Rourke throughout the meal in that funny way she had, but said nothing beyond stray remarks as the talk turned to the weather. The dinner and the conversation afterwards flowed smoothly. The Harwoods were, Rourke thought, very smooth.

Harwood asked Rourke to stay behind when Cal and Zeke made ready to leave—Cal certainly more than ready to do so the minute they finished eating. Pa was more inclined to sit and smoke and maybe have another drink. She shot Rourke a look that meant some level of displeasure, but since they were all being so all-fired polite, it was hard to know what was going on behind this façade Cal was wearing instead of her usual face.

Harwood walked Rourke back into the study. The women

disappeared someplace. The rancher offered a drink from a fancy-cut glass bottle. Rourke declined.

"I want to repeat our discussion from the other day. I need a rider who knows how to use a gun and knows how to get a job done," Harwood said. "If you can't defend what you own, somebody takes it. I beat the people on Wall Street back in New York City at their own game. I can do the same out here. Are you interested in a job? You can finish helping your friends. I pay top dollar and even though you don't need a horse today, you could have pick of the herd. Why, I could even stake you to the start of your own spread. There's enough of it out here for the taking. Green Hills is going to grow. Rawhide is going to grow. This is your chance to grow, too. It would be good for you, and good for your friends."

Rourke said he wasn't quite sure, which he wasn't. He was still trying to sort out what was really going on with the horses, with Harwood, and above all with Cal. He had a feeling if he told Cal he was going to have land so he could maybe settle down that the girl would be happy. He was not going to get it in a way that made his teeth grind, though.

"You never did say. Where you gonna get your herd?" Rourke asked with as little concern in his voice as he could muster. He hadn't planned to bring this up, but curiosity had long since got the better of him.

"Got some boys driving a herd from Colorado. Some buyers in the East are obtaining some top stock for breeding," Harwood said. "They should be here in a week."

"Funny thing," said Rourke. "There's a herd not far from here that looks like it's got about a dozen or two brands in it. Hope if that's yours, you get a bill of sale from them boys to make it legal. Fellow running the outfit, name of Gallagher, came to Zeke's fire. Man said they got in a fight with somebody and got a man killed. Sounds pretty shady to me, sir. Hate to see a man like yourself new to all this get mixed up in something bad. In these parts, no one wants anything to do with a man with a whiff of being tainted as a rustler."

The poker-faced rancher raised his fancy glass of amber liquid to his lips and pretended to take a swallow. He studied Rourke over the glass. Rourke had that feeling again that he had in the war when things were getting bad. Talk always got a man in trouble, he reminded himself. Tell the man what he wants to hear and ride out, he told himself.

"What would you do about this if you were ridin' for me?" Harwood asked. "I don't know how you handle these things."

Rourke tried to evade the question, but Harwood kept asking until Rourke threw caution to the winds. "If I didn't see bills of sale from the owners of any branded stock, I wouldn't take the horses," Rourke said. "I might also let the Territory men and them folks from the Army who are supposed to keep the peace know who is out here selling horses without the right kind of papers. Might settle some of the cases of missing stock from the ranchers around here."

"What if I take the horses?" Harwood said. "I'm a business-man. I can't be chasing all over Wyoming—and Colorado and Utah and Nebraska for all I know—to find out which ranch might match up with whichever brand might be on an animal. If someone can't hold onto their own stock, what business is it of mine? There are far too many careless ranchers out here. I certainly understand that Green Hills stock drifted before I came out here. It's the cost of doing business. When you do it badly, the cost is high. Taking what others lose is good busi-ness."

Rourke was puzzled. Harwood seemed not to understand the perils of dealing in stolen horses. "Horse thieves hang," he said. "Ranchers whose stock gets stolen wind up as vigilantes, sooner or later."

"If that were true, I will have even greater need for protection. Legally, there is no claim to return property someone carelessly loses. If this came before a territorial court, no one in the territorial administration would find against me, I can assure you. Are you with me?"

Rourke had a terrible feeling that there was more to this than horses. Something was wrong. Every instinct he had from the war said a trap was being laid through whatever Harwood was up to. He looked over his shoulder. Elizabeth Harwood was walking toward them with her hands gripped together in the funny way Eastern women walked. She would be the interruption he wanted. He could leave and be a mile away before he talked himself into real trouble.

Rourke tried explaining that there were some things no one could justify. Stealing a horse when a man needed a ride was as much a hanging crime as stealing them for profit. The Easterner didn't get it. Rourke didn't realize he was getting loud until he heard himself.

"Don't mean to preach," he concluded lamely, nodding at Harwood's daughter, who had come up behind him. "Guess I better go. We're ridin' different roads, sir. No hard feelin's if I said anything that offended you?"

Harwood shook his head. "We wish you could have joined us. I think it would have been the best decision for everyone, including your friends. However, we cannot always guess correctly." There seemed to be real regret in his voice.

Rourke was focused on Harwood's face. He saw it reacting to something. He turned and saw the gun in Elizabeth Harwood's hand slashing down toward his head. He tried to avoid it. Then he saw nothing at all.

"What do you want me to do with him?" asked Gallagher, taking his gun back from Elizabeth Harwood and looking at the sprawled figure of Rourke lying flat on the fancy rug.

"Kill him, you fool!" exclaimed Harwood. "Do not do it here! In the morning, I want you to gather a few of the horses together that came from local ranches. Take them down near Treadwell's place. Rourke's body should be found with them. Then they can blame him. We would have had to do this sooner or later. When we bring in more riders, we can tell them it was for our own protection. If the old man and the girl ask too many questions, we can get rid of them, too. Nobody in Rawhide is going to miss these three nobodies."

Gallagher nodded and called out. "Jeffries, Calhoun! Get in here and throw this guy in the bunkhouse. Tie him up. Take the gun away but keep it handy. We'll kill him in the morning so it looks good. Ride to the herd. Weed out those horses we took from Harrison and Treadwell. Meet me around dawn about a mile north of Treadwell's place by the bend in the creek."

Gallagher hooked arms with Elizabeth Harwood. She smiled back at him as they walked toward the stairs. He spoke as he walked away. "Get him out of here. I got me some plans for the night. We'll finish it in the morning."

The two men dragged the unconscious Rourke to the bunkhouse, past Star, who watched impassively. They tied his hands and tossed him on the floor, where he could keep until it was time to kill him in the morning.

CHAPTER NINE

Cal was worried. Hours after she and Pa had returned home, Rourke had not yet appeared. No conversation could take this long, especially not with pasty-faced Eastern women who had tongues like rattlesnakes. Pa was snoring so loudly anyone approaching would think there were six men sawing wood in the camp. Dinner at the Green Hills big house had been upsetting. She didn't like those women. She didn't like that mousy little thing batting her eyes at Rourke. She didn't like Rourke not being back from a place none of them should have ever set foot in. She didn't like any of it. And she wasn't a little Eastern woman who sat around and did nothing.

She rode out toward the big house. There were lights on that were too bright for candles. Star was hitched and saddled. That was not like Rourke. He never left the saddle on Star when the horse would have to stand all night. Something was not right.

She walked softly over the hard-packed dirt and the trampled grass around the house. She heard voices in the back room. It was the only one where there were lights. She saw the oil lamps on the long table where they had eaten earlier. Harwood was there with his wife. Two other men sat there. Cal thought she might have recalled seeing them, but she could not remember where. For a minute, she thought her eyes were playing tricks, because she saw Mary Harwood smoking a cigar like a man. For certain there was a bottle in her hand that looked like the fancy one Harwood used to pour liquor. Mary Harwood held it up to her mouth and took a swig. Then she put the cigar to her mouth and blew a smoke ring. Cal was shocked. Was this what Eastern people were like under that layer of fancy clothes?

Cal crept closer, out of sight, and listened. She had heard all kinds of conversations, and she knew from the conspiratorial tone, even when she could not hear the words, that they were discussing something that was evil.

"Elizabeth will keep him in line," she heard Harwood's voice say. There was a muttered feminine response. "Mary, he's a man, isn't he? Elizabeth knows how to handle men, don't you think?"

As a chorus of evil laughter roiled through the room, Cal moved away from the house, softly, wondering where Rourke could be. Then she froze. Boots were crunching dirt. She heard a man's voice. In the darkness, there was a flash. Someone was lighting a cigarette. She could smell the tobacco. The man stood by the house a moment, then walked back the way he had come. Cal tiptoed away. She was afraid of getting caught but Rourke had to be there, somewhere. If Star was here, then Rourke was here. And if he wasn't anyplace else, there was only one place for him to be—in the arms of that Eastern girl. He must have been the one they were laughing about! How could he do that to her?

Cal felt tears in her eyes as she half-ran back to her horse, then rode away.

Waves of nausea passed over Rourke. He had no idea where he was. It was a floor. His head was throbbing. There was no light. He tried to remember where he was. Harwood! He tried to sit up and almost fainted. Then he realized his arms were not numb, but tied. His feet were not. They just didn't work. After multiple tries and falls, he inched himself successfully to his feet along the wooden post of a bunk. His eyes had finally adjusted to the dimness. He was in the Green Hills bunkhouse. He wobbled. At last he could stand on his own. He looked out a window. Star was there, still hitched, forgotten. In his youth, he might have been able to leap on Star's back the way he was, but not tonight. Not with his head throbbing.

He could see a light on in the house. He had no idea of time. He could have been out five minutes or five hours. He needed time, but he had no idea when whoever had dropped him here was coming back. He strained to reach his boot. There. He could feel the edge of the knife handle. His hands were numb. The fingers were clumsy. He flexed his thumb and forefinger. Over and over. The blood started flowing. He hoped he had time. He could not worry about that. He tried again. At last! He could grip the knife handle. Awkwardly, he tried to free the knife from its sheath. Now his hands were sweating and slick. The knife clattered to the floor.

When the door to the bunkhouse opened, Rourke dove and rolled toward the knife. Boots clumped on the wooden floor. They kicked the knife Rourke had dropped. A hand roughly turned Rourke over. Lloyd Jeffries looked down at him. Jeffries put a finger to his lips. Rourke nodded. Lloyd grabbed the knife and cut the ropes. He handed Rourke the knife. Rourke rubbed his hands and arms together.

"Rourke, we don't ride the same trail, but I don't like seein' a man murdered for horses," Lloyd said softly. "I ride for the man that pays me, but some things I don't do, Rourke. Mess with my payday and you get what you get, but this ain't what I get paid to do. You and that girl and her pa ought to git. Don't cross this outfit again. You can't win."

"If you hate this outfit so much, Lloyd, come with me."

"Naw, Rourke. Earl and Clyde and I, we got nobody but each other. Not many places take all three. I've ridden for worse. When it blows to Kingdom Come, we'll ride on to somewhere else. Now git, before someone hears and I got to shoot you." He held out Rourke's Remington pistol. "Take it, Rourke, and git out of here!"

Rourke thought about going after the Harwoods. Whatever the odds were, they were against him. He was in no condition to take on however many men there were. He was not even in a condition to take on the women! He took the pistol from Jeffries.

"Obliged, Lloyd. I'm in your debt."

"Go!" Rourke looked at the man's face, hearing the agitation in his voice. There was nothing he could say or do but take what he was given. He hoped Jeffries could face whatever this gesture would cost. For a second, he wondered if it was a trap. He checked his gun. Loaded. If it was a trap, he would take someone with him.

He slowly opened the door. His heart pounded after one hinge squeaked loud enough, in his ears, to raise the dead. He took one last look at Jeffries, whose face was an unreadable mask. Then he was outside. He moved as fast as he could to Star. He needed to get away quietly before they knew he was gone. He untied Star, whose noises told him that the horse had missed him. They walked slowly until he thought he was far enough away that no one would hear the hoofbeats of a lone horse. He mounted up, swaying in the saddle as his head reminded him of its injuries. Then he clucked once, and Star started walking. The motion was dizzying, but he held on. He tapped Star once with the stirrups, and the horse moved along at a slow canter. He let that be their pace. It would take a little longer, but he would be less likely to fall out of the saddle.

Cal didn't try to sleep. She built the fire back up to have something to stare at, and passed the time by feeding it sticks. She had gone through a thousand conversations with Rourke while she waited for dawn. She was hoping he was dead somewhere. She wished he was calling for her.

She hung her head, arms wrapped around her legs. The wind sighed. Pa had told her when she was little to feel comforted when she heard that noise. He had said the breath of angels was moving through the treetops to protect her. She could use some protection now, mostly from her thoughts and her emotions.

The sky started to lighten. She heard a noise. A hoof. Another. Moving slowly. Rourke must have known what was waiting for him. She picked up her rifle. He was going to see that she meant business. The only way to show a man that was to have a gun in your hand. The horse came closer. The white on his forehead was distinctive. It was Star. No one was sitting in the saddle. She called Star by name, and talked as she moved closer. She led the animal back to the campfire. The saddle was warm, as if someone had just been riding it. Her hand touched something wet. She sniffed it. Blood! Her first impulse was to panic. She very carefully felt Star for cuts. None. Maybe when it got light she could find something. She unsaddled Star and led him over beneath the trees where the other horses were tied. She was no less angry as she returned to the fire, but she was also puzzled. There was a growing sense of unease and dread that inexorably filled her mind even as dawn turned the world first a faint, black-shot gray, then a rosy pink, then the deep, rich blue of the clear Wyoming sky.

Cal woke her pa with a torrent of words. "Star's got blood on his saddle and Rourke never came back. We got to look for him." Her voice shook. "He might be hurt. We got to look for him. I don't know what those Eastern people did. I could kill him but we have to find him first! Get up, Pa, we got to find him!"

Zeke was less excitable and a lot sleepier. If the Civil War hadn't killed Rourke, dinner with some Eastern people was not likely to do it either. He wanted coffee and food. If Rourke was really up to something stupid with that Eastern girl, he might need all the time Zeke could buy him to come to his senses. The man didn't seem the type, but Ezekiel knew that men could fall off of their good intentions easier than falling off a horse. Then he took a closer look at his daughter as he came fully awake. Cal had been crying and hadn't slept much. Soft words had never been a part of his life. He didn't know what to say or how to say it. He gruffly told her they could look for Rourke.

Cal had the horses saddled and they were getting ready to mount when hard-riding horses pounded into view. Cal saw it was Gallagher—the rider from the other night—with a group of armed men. Gone was the superficial politeness of their first encounter.

"Where is he?" Gallagher snarled.

"Who?" replied Ezekiel, trying to remember where he had left his shotgun. Cal watched Zeke and worried. She could see what he was thinking. If she could, they could. She wished she had strapped on the gun Rourke had given her. It was sitting under her new jacket where she had left it by the fire in case she wanted to burn Rourke's present.

"Your partner," Gallagher replied. "Man who shoots cowboys."

"Haven't seen him," Ezekiel replied. "Went to Green Hills house last night. Probably still there with a big head or something. My daughter and I came home without him. Ask the Harwood people if you don't believe me."

"He's not there," Gallagher declared. "That horse of his is here. We followed his tracks. Where is he?"

"Son, I spent the night sleepin' and not worryin' about a man who kin take care of hisself," Ezekiel said. "We got some food and coffee and if you want to talk to him so powerful much, come on down and set a spell and wait. Can't say I've ever known the man to go far without his horse, so if the horse come back then the man'll follow."

"He killed one of my men, old man."

Ezekiel shrugged. "Man's killed lots of men. He's a bounty hunter. Not my affair, none of it. Now, my daughter and I got work to do here. If you got no objection, we'll go about our business." Ezekiel moved toward the shed, where the shotgun was propped against the anvil. He walked slowly.

The click of the hammer of a .45 stopped him. "You make one false move, old man, and I will kill you and your daughter." Gallagher ordered the other riders to search the brush, then find places to wait. They found positions to ambush Rourke, whichever path he chose.

Gallagher watched Ezekiel and Cal move into the shade of the building, toward a pile of tools. He followed.

"Girl, when I tell you, duck," whispered Pa.

"Pa, you can't fight all of them! They're killers. Don't do something stupid! They'll kill you."

She saw Gallagher watching. She was chilled by two thoughts that came together—first, that the man had caught the urgency in her tone, if not her words. He must know they were planning something. She also realized the man who boldly looked her over once before might be thinking of taking advantage of her. This time, Rourke would not be around to protect her. She wondered what had happened to him. He might be lying dead somewhere, or wounded.

Pa's face looked both sad and resolute. "Daughter, I ain't never been what you might call a proper pa. Maybe it wasn't much of a life bein' broke and ridin' all over God's green Earth. Every time I look at you I see your ma. I don't know how you are gonna remember your old man. You ain't gonna remember me as someone who didn't stand up for you. Now do what you are told when I tell you."

Cal wanted to tell him that she was afraid. She had no idea

how life would work if she lost Pa. She bit back her words. There was a time when a man had to be a man.

"What are you two talking about?" Gallagher's voice cut into her thoughts. He was gesturing with the .45 in his right hand. She saw the look in Pa's eyes. She picked up a small piece of wood. She could at least throw it at him.

"Man's got a right to talk to his daughter, ain't he?" argued Ezekiel. "Got some problem with that?"

Gallagher's eyes shot from one to the other. Surely, Cal thought, the man could see Pa's hand reaching down to the shotgun that was parked by the anvil, right behind his leg.

"Boss!" called one rider. Gallagher turned his head. Ezekiel moved faster than Cal had ever seen him. She threw the small board at Gallagher's head. Pa pulled the shotgun's two triggers in a simultaneous explosion that deafened Cal as she dove for such shelter as the anvil could provide.

More gunfire rang out from the woods. Men were screaming. Gallagher's reflexes had seen the wood hurtling toward him. He hit the floor of the shed. The lead from the shotgun passed over his head harmlessly. Gallagher rolled over and came up in a sitting position with the .45 pointed at Pa. Cal screamed. More explosions came one after the other after the other. She closed her eyes and screamed some more.

Then the shooting stopped.

"Pa? Pa!"

Ezekiel was moaning on the floor. A man pushed past her. She grabbed his leg to knock him down. He pulled free. She grabbed again. No one was going to get to Pa. She could gouge his eyes out. She could bite him. She could kick. If Pa was gone they could get her, too. A pistol lay a few feet away. She grabbed again at a pair of boots to pull the man down so she could get to the .45.

"Let me go, Cal," snarled Rourke, jerking his leg and looking down on her with annoyance until her surprised hands let go. "Cal! Cal! What ails you, girl? Zeke's shot, now let me see to him."

She let go. Rourke? How and when did he get there? Showing up when it was all over! Just like a man. She got up from the floor.

Rourke rolled Zeke over. One bullet hit him in the neck. Close call, but the blood wasn't spurting. Men had ridden away with worse in the war. They needed to patch him up.

"Cal, get me something to put on this. Move, girl! Move! We ain't got all day to sit around here."

She had a retort ready about his Eastern woman, but what mattered was Pa. Rourke had been giving orders so long she felt bound to obey first and argue later. Trained in the violent ways of the territories, she had clean things ready for wounds. She ran to the wagon, where she hid her box of cloth, whiskey, and that salve the Indians swore could heal anything.

As she reached the sun-drenched campsite, she stopped. Four lumps. All dead. Rourke. She'd heard about what he did, but she'd never seen it up close.

She grabbed the bandages and ran back to the shed. There she saw Gallagher, face down with two bloody holes in his back. Rourke had saved them. She realized they would have been dead without him. Her legs went weak and she stumbled, then picked herself up. Pa needed her. Her hands were shaking. Pa lay on the floor. Rourke told her that Zeke would live, but he needed to be very still for a while. She needed to sit with him. When Rourke started to put the bandages on Pa, she came out of it.

"I can do that."

"You hit?" he asked.

She shook her head. "What about that woman? That Eastern woman? At the house? The one you were with?"

Rourke's brow was clearly furrowed, reflecting his confusion over her words. "Cal, I haven't been with any woman. Eastern women don't mean nothing more than trouble and spite in ribbons, and we don't got time for that stuff right now. If you mean them Harwood people, only thing I want to do is kill 'em all. We got to get out of here before more of these riders come around. You get hit on the head? That why you're talking funny?"

"You mean it?"

"Cal! We got to bandage your pa. Can we talk this through later once I'm sure we're all gonna be alive come sunset? Cal! Snap out of it, girl! I need your help with Zeke or we're all gonna end up like Gallagher here."

She nodded. Relief, shame, and curiosity flowed through her like fire. Her eyes started doing that wet thing she hated when she was going to cry. She started blinking. Rourke touched her shoulder. He looked into her eyes as if he could read her soul. He bent down, issuing a small groan, and kissed the top of her head. "Be strong. Everything is going to be peaches, runt."

He had always called her that—even after she grew almost as tall as he was. She gave him the smile she knew he expected. Rourke dragged Gallagher away, leaving a trail of red behind.

Pa mumbled something. "Shush, Pa, I'm fine. We're safe. Let me put this on you." She felt the tears; she thought she saw one in Pa's eyes. Then she focused on what her hands were doing. Out West, what was going on inside had to wait until after you were sure you could survive to think about it later. She thought for a minute about God. It seemed the only time she thought about Him was when she was alone with the land and when Pa was hurt. How many times had she asked God to care for him? A thousand? She asked again. Rourke once told her God loved people with nothing more than anyone else in the world. Maybe He would listen this time again.

She kept pressure on the wound. The bandage filled with the

red stain of her father's blood. "Don't you dare die, Pa." The second bandage stayed white longer. The third one she wrapped around him, coating it with the salve that she had traded about a foot of her hair to get. She tied the bandage around his neck carefully.

Zeke was drifting in and out of consciousness. She knew he could hear her, so she talked. She could hear him breathing evenly, not like men did when they were dying. After a while, she ran out of things to say. She simply sat next to him, holding his hand, dividing her time between watching him and watching Rourke.

Rourke's head had dried blood on it. He didn't have on a hat; he always wore that old thing she figured was from the war. It looked that worn. She noticed his wound, his pallor, and the way he walked like every bone hurt. She tried to recall what she had seen. Four men down and Gallagher shot to rags. He still needed to explain. Last night, the Harwoods were their friends. Today, he wanted them as dead as the men she could see him dragging into the woods. If he was in love with that Eastern woman it sure didn't show. She watched him carry a pile of guns to the wagon. He turned the riders' horses loose. She could hear that. Then he was back in the doorway, a dark silhouette, breathing hard.

"How is he?" he asked.

"Sleeping," she replied. "Rourke, what is going on?"

He chuckled a grim mirthless laugh. "Was about to ask you the same thing. Want to tell me what you think I was doing last night? It's got to be a better story than mine."

She dipped her head. She didn't really want to explain. He settled next to her. "You got upset over somethin', Cal. Maybe you think I was entertainin' the Harwood girl? Whatever the poison, let's get it out and deal with it."

She told him everything. She didn't tell him everything she

wanted to say to him, but she figured that he could guess. He waved his hand when she got to the part about Gallagher arriving at their camp.

"Saw them," he said. "I got worried when you and Zeke came in here because he was the fastest. I was afraid I couldn't get them all before one of them got you two. Guess Zeke had his own plan."

"Where were you and what happened to you?" she said. "If you weren't with that woman, why did you stay so late? I looked and looked for you."

He told her of Harwood's apparent offer and then being knocked unconscious and taken captive. He told her that the women were probably not Harwood's wife or daughter, but his partners. "Richmond had women like them in '65," he told Cal. "Drink, smoke, skin a man for a dollar. Harwood ain't an Eastern fella looking to start a happy life. He's a criminal or rich man who found New York City or some other place too hot for him. He came out here to build himself an empire by whatever means he can. He fooled me, and I feel pretty stupid right about now except for when it hurts too much."

He had fallen off of Star not far from the camp, but had no idea where he was until it was fully light. By the time he arrived, he had heard riders and kept to the trees to avoid being seen.

"You killed them all?" she asked.

He nodded. "Didn't see any other way out. They're all rustlers anyhow. They were gonna kill you, Cal. I don't tolerate that sort of thing, girl."

"Now what?" she said. "We can't wait here."

"I want Zeke to rest a little, then we'll put him in the wagon and move to the hills out there," he said. "I don't know the country well, but we got to find a safe place for you two, then I got to go find Andy and the Army and stop all this."

"All what?"

"I don't really know, Cal. Harwood is rustling big time. These little ranchers don't know what they're up against. I got to get Andy to call out somebody to stop this, or there won't be anyone else here but Harwood sellin' and raisin' horses. Something Harwood said made me wonder if Andy knew more than he told me. I just can't remember what it was."

He was quiet a moment. Then he took off a hat he had taken off of one of the dead outlaws and ran his fingers through his hair, grunting when he came to the part sticky with blood.

"Let me clean it off," said Cal. "It's going to hurt worse. If you don't do something, you're going to stink."

"No shortage of nice things you have to say to a man, Cal," responded Rourke, the lopsided smile he wore around her back in place, as if they were around a fire like on any one of a thousand normal days and not where five men had been killed.

"Maybe I should have told you to soak your head," she shot back, leaving him with a grin as she went to the stream for water.

She took a cloth and wiped away the blood, telling him over and over not to move as she stood over him and tried to clean the wound. "Men!" she finally exploded. "Get yourselves hurt and then whimper like puppies when someone tries to fix you up. We women should let you all shoot each other until you get it out of your system." She stood back. "He cut you pretty deep. You got headaches? Can you see all right?"

"I don't rightly know," he said. "It is kind of dark in here. Let me look at your face."

She sat down on the floor of the shed. "Are your eyes blurry?" She was concerned. A gunman who could not see well would not last long.

"I don't rightly know," he said once again, sounding weak and uncertain. "Maybe you need to move closer. I guess I can see far off but I don't know about near up."

She moved closer. She could see his eyes moving over her face. "How's this?" she said, swallowing hard. "If I moved any closer, I'd be behind you."

"Just about right," he said, squinting and moving his head. He could see her brow furrow. "I think I see something . . ." His voice trailed off as his right hand softly touched the left side of her face. He could read a question in her eyes as he looked into them until eyes no longer mattered and their lips softly touched, lingering in a longer, gentler kiss than anything Cal had ever experienced.

"Nobody else, Cal," he said when it ended. "Can't tell you what's ahead, and I hate making promises. Words are cheap and easy. I promised Lorraine the world. It never came true. I live with that every day. She died knowing I failed her. But there ain't no one like you anywhere, so stop thinkin' about Eastern women or any other kind of women because they don't make but one kind that matters—you. Ain't gonna lose you. Understand? Rustlers or nothin' is gonna get in the way. You want to walk away you do that, but I ain't a-gonna. Understand, woman?"

Cal wanted to cry. Rourke was almost never serious like this. She'd never heard him talk about his wife before. She didn't know what to say. "I thought . . . you know . . . when me and Pa were gonna go up against those men that nobody in the world was gonna help us. 'Cuz I was mad at you and you had left us. But I knew, deep down, that if I was in trouble you'd be there if you were still alive. And I don't make fancy talk like ladies, but I don't want to lose you either, Rourke. Not now and not ever."

He put his arms around her and they held each other; a flower of hope in a landscape of violence. They stayed that way for what seemed forever. Rourke broke the embrace. "We'd best move, Cal. Somebody will be looking soon. That wagon can't move fast and it'll be days before Zeke can ride a horse."

Cal grabbed on for one more kiss. "Cowboy, I never felt like this in my life. Whatever it is, I'm with you. You don't have to promise nothin' comes out right. I'm not a silly little girl. Just be there. Got that?"

"Got it, Cal. Now we better ride before all this talk don't mean nothin'."

CHAPTER TEN

Cal picked up every piece of Ezekiel's hardware she could find, despite Rourke's impatience. "Rourke, everything we have is here and in the wagon. I can't leave anything behind because we can't replace what we lose."

"We're gonna lose Zeke pretty soon, Cal, if we don't get a move on."

"Then quit talking and if it looks useful, throw it in." She flashed a smile. "If I knew you were all talk, cowboy, and no work, I might have thought things through a little more."

In a few minutes, they had everything of use loaded, including every extra gun the riders had brought. They were slowly rolling away from the place where Zeke's dreams of a peaceful life had come to a shattering conclusion. Every time, Cal thought. Every time something comes along to make life better, life gets worse.

She took one last look back. Riders!

"Rourke!" she yelled, pointing.

There was no way short of a miracle that the wagon with its precious cargo could out-race horsemen. They were out in a wide meadow, without cover, and with the next ridge that could provide any shelter far on the horizon. The pursuers were rounding a rocky bend they had barely left behind. It would have to be a fight.

Six men fanned out, galloping hard. Rourke knew wagons were easy prey for hard riders who knew how to shoot. He also knew that surprise won battles.

He moved Star close to the wagon. "Get to that tree!" he yelled at Cal, who was driving the team. He pointed toward a lone stunted oak about a hundred yards away.

"Rourke!" she screamed back.

In the last second he saw her face contorted in misery, the thought passed through his head that this might be their last words. "Go!" he ordered.

Rourke drew his rifle, moving away from the wagon to draw their fire. He fired blindly. One saddle emptied. The remaining five turned to catch Rourke, the wagon forgotten until they could dispatch Rourke first. Rifles crackled. Rourke heard bullets fly past his face. So far, he was lucky.

Rourke pulled hard on the reins and sharply pulled Star to the left, then kicked the horse to top speed again, putting more space between himself and his pursuers, who could not turn as quickly. They fanned out more—like a net. Rourke had played this game before with Yankee cavalry. Again he pulled on the reins. This time, he turned Start completely around and galloped straight at the riders. By now, the riders on the edges of the group were too far away to do more than fire wide. The rider in the middle was sighting Rourke along the barrel of his rifle when Rourke's bullet caught him somewhere in the body. The man sagged over the neck of his horse, who reared and ran at the unaccustomed weight of the rider landing on his neck.

Something nicked his left arm. A shot from the flank. Rourke felt the panic with the pain. He kicked Star hard. Four men closed in as Rourke rode for the tree where he had told Cal to seek shelter. One rider rode down upon him, pistol raised at the end of his arm the way artists made it look. Rourke heard the rifle before he saw the flash, then the rider was gone. A puff of smoke showed where Cal had taken up her position by the tree. Rourke pushed Star as fast as he could run. Only two riders followed him. Cal downed another one, then Rourke fired over his shoulder. The last cowboy chasing Rourke tumbled into the dirt, clutching his side as he disappeared, screaming under the hooves of his horse. Rourke rode until he reached the tree and the wagon.

"You get lost in thought there, Cal?"

"Just wanted to see how fast Star could really run," she replied deadpan. "If this was how you fought the war I guess I know why the Yankees won. A girl saving your hide, Rourke. Wait until they hear about this!"

"Think maybe a girl could focus on getting back on that wagon so we can get out of here?" He grinned at her. They had survived a close call.

"Let me check on Pa."

"I'll see if these fine fellas want to donate their guns to us," Rourke said. "You keep shooting wild we're gonna need every bullet we can get."

"Just keep it up, Rourke. Next time I won't be so quick to pull the trigger!" She grinned back. Being alive when the people who tried to kill you were dead made a girl giddy. But seeing her father in the back of a wagon made it all serious once again. "He don't look good, Rourke."

"One minute, Cal. I'll be right there and we'll find a place."

Rourke hurried over to grab what he could from the riders. There was no telling how many more were coming. They would need every gun and bullet he could find. He moved fast, going from one to the other. Maybe too fast.

"Drop it." Rourke turned at the voice. A bearded man was pointing a gun at Rourke. Rourke moved to his right and dove. The gun fired once. Something burned Rourke's face. The gun clicked on a used round. The bearded man threw the gun at Rourke, who ducked. The rider tackled Rourke hard, slamming him to the ground. A powerful fist crashed into Rourke's jaw.

Rourke rolled and broke free, facing his opponent. Grabbing his knife, the cowboy charged. The knife sliced Rourke's face. Wetness ran down. Rourke moved left as the man missed his next wild swing, stumbling on an injured leg. Rourke feinted left, then right, and as the big man tried to get a bead on him, Rourke turned and charged the cowboy. The element of surprise stunned the man long enough. Rourke hit him hard on the left side of the face. The man went down. Rourke pulled out his .45 and fired. The bullet could not miss at that range. The man's face registered shock from the impact of the slug in his chest. Rourke fired one last time. When the stakes were life and death, the only mercy to give the loser was to end it quickly.

Hoofbeats. He pointed the gun at the sound. His vision was hazy. He heard a familiar voice. O'Toole.

"Cap'n?"

Rourke nodded, weak, but too proud to show it. Blood from the cowboy was staining the dirt. Wonder if anyone will ever find him, Rourke wondered. O'Toole was talking as if it was important that Rourke hear something instead of trying to breathe. O'Toole repeated his message. "Unless you plan on me eloping with the lass and leaving you behind, boyo, we need to move. The wagon is now rolling with your lass, who seems to know her way around a Winchester. Remind me to mind me manners when she has it in her hands. We need to be riding. Can ye ride, Your Worship? We need to go, Rourke, laddie!"

Wordlessly, gasping for breath, Rourke nodded. O'Toole dismounted and helped Rourke mount up. Rourke held onto the saddle, but barely. O'Toole grabbed the reins to lead Star to catch up with the slow-moving wagon and its precious cargo.

Cal said nothing as they rode into sight. She credited O'Toole's arrival as a miracle, and his explanation that he was planning to reach Green Hills that day all along could not dispel her conviction that something had saved them other than themselves. Rourke looked battered and wounded, but he waved and pointed toward the line of hills about 15 miles distant. She understood. They were now hunted. If they didn't reach cover soon, none of it would matter.

O'Toole kept talking, but Rourke didn't seem to hear. "Sir!" he exclaimed. "Allow your obedient servant to remind you that should a flock of lambs surprise you, in your current condition, you could not escape without a beating. Stay with the lass; she can look out for you, and let me find a place to hide this contraption and ourselves. Sure it is your head is hard and you have proven it. Need you risk all?"

Rourke knew O'Toole was right. As the soldier-turned-scout rode off toward the hills, he dropped back to ride by the wagon until Cal stopped the team and pointed to the seat next to her. Rourke obediently tied Star to the back and sat next to Cal as she drove.

"Are you going to be all right?" she asked. She was glad he had climbed off of Star. The way he was swaying, she had to watch him and the rocks. Now, all she had to worry about was the wagon. She waited for an answer. None came. She looked at the man next to her, so important to her and yet a stranger for all of it. They rode in silence. "You say something?" he asked at last.

" 'Bout five miles back," she said. "If you die, can I have Star?"

He heard that one. He smiled. "Sure, but not today. It was close, though, Cal. It was close." He slouched in the wagon seat, and despite the bouncing over rough ground, was asleep in moments. Gunfire woke him with a start. Two shots—then silence—then two more. "Ride for the noise," he told Cal. "It's Thomas. We used that signal in the war."

O'Toole had found an old miner's shack. The rickety shack was dirty, but it was shelter. There was a creek nearby that would be a barrier to riders trying to attack. The hills sloped gently away to the north. The rugged part of the hills was about a mile away. If things got too bad, they could make a run for it. Otherwise, the ground was all open—which meant the shack was the only cover anyone would have in case they had to fight. They were worn and wounded. It would have to do. They settled Zeke inside and used wood from an outbuilding to start a fire.

O'Toole explained that he had been riding from ranch to ranch to hear who had what to say about rustling. He was on his way back to Fort Laramie when he heard the gunfire. "Rather assuming, sir, that when there is this level of festivities your worshipful self would be in the middle of it, I decided to forbear the rest I deserved." He asked how they had come to be on their own, and reflected surprise at the response. "The Army of these Yankees, sir, has great faith in this Harwood man, because they talk about him the way people do when someone is important. A man of great respect. Perhaps there was a misunderstanding?"

Rourke could understand how people could be fooled—even the Army. Then he thought of the horses. Especially the Army. If the Army could buy horses cheaply from Harwood, officers could make money re-selling them to the Indians through the trading posts that the Army controlled. Other ranchers could not compete and no one would buy their horses. He mentioned this to O'Toole.

" 'Tis a poor head I have for the world of business, sir. Even the Yankee Army, sir, requires horses that are not stolen. Perhaps something he said you did not understand?"

Rourke felt a flash of irritation at O'Toole. That was twice his friend had implied Rourke didn't know what was going on under his nose. He was going to say something when O'Toole spoke. "What do I tell the Army about your predicament, sir? And what should I say to your friend at the Territory?"

"Nothing, Thomas. Nothing for now. I don't know what's happening. First, we have to care for Zeke. That's what matters. Then we'll see what to do about the Harwoods."

"This is not the war, laddie. Men who have powerful friends can make deadly enemies," O'Toole remarked. "If there's nothing holding you here to fight this battle, does it make sense to fight people you cannot defeat?"

With that valediction, O'Toole rode off, promising to be back as soon as possible.

O'Toole's eyebrows had done a dance when Rourke told him that if he saw Dickinson, to deny ever having seen them. "Tell him what you know we did, things any rider would know who can read the signs, but that we disappeared and you went back to the fort," Rourke said. "I do not want anyone to know where we are and to know how weak we are."

When O'Toole was gone, Cal braced Rourke. "I thought you wanted them to know about Harwood, but you didn't tell him everything. What's going on Rourke?"

"I rode with Thomas a long time, Cal. Thomas has a way with rules that is a mite more flexible than most people. If the Army has a shady deal, and Harwood is in the middle of it, and if officers there are in the middle of it, Thomas might be on the edges of it somehow. I don't know. Something is off, Cal, and I can't explain it."

O'Toole's dust was slowly fading away in the late-day sun as Rourke mounted Star to patrol. Dust far off appeared almost as the sun was going down, but no riders ever came in sight.

Caroline Dickinson was used to men arriving at all hours of the day and night. She hated it when they pounded enough to break down the door. "I'm coming," she yelled. Andrew was a step ahead of her, having put on his jacket, and he rushed from the back of the house where he had been enjoying a cigar.

"Are you expecting trouble?" she asked.

"Right now, darling, when everything we worked for is so close to its culmination, I am ready for any trouble at any time." He was smooth and unruffled.

Caroline offered the expected smile and let Andrew answer the door.

Three cowboys entered. They identified themselves as Green Hills riders. They had names, but Caroline never cared with those people. Saddle tramps came and went. She had long stopped remembering their faces.

The lead cowboy was watching Caroline as he spoke to Andrew.

"You can speak in front of my wife," Dickinson barked. "Now, out with it, man."

Lloyd Jeffries told the tale, haltingly. Rourke had escaped to parts unknown after killing several Green Hills hands. Harwood had sent him with the message that Rourke was to be hunted as the rustler they had been looking for.

Andrew was frowning, Caroline saw. That meant his plan was not running smoothly.

"You could not find him or track him?" Dickinson asked incredulously.

"Nope," replied Jeffries diffidently.

"A cowboy, an old man, and a girl and you can't find them?"

"Guess they know the country, Mr. Dickinson," said Jeffries. "Mr. Harwood wanted to know something about a sale with the Army moving forward as soon as possible. He said to tell you that it needed to be wrapped up soon. Those were his words."

"All right," snapped Dickinson. "There's a man at the fort. Not an officer. He's a scout named O'Toole. Find him. Tell him what you told me. And on your way back, get more men to look for those fugitives! Harwood has plenty of men on his payroll for this!"

After they left, Andrew poured a drink. Caroline knew the danger signals.

"This man is not what you thought, is he, Andrew? I fear also that your partner is planning something of his own. Which is the greater concern, Andrew, Rourke or Harwood?"

He looked her dead in the eye. "Both."

"Then let me help you figure this out. You need a woman's touch. We cannot afford any more mistakes!"

The door was being assaulted again. This time, Caroline answered it.

"Andrew, look who I have here—a man who wants to talk about some horses," she said with a smile, ushering in one of the few men she found charming in Wyoming—Army Scout Thomas O'Toole.

Cal came out of the shack as Rourke returned from scouting. "Pa's not looking very good. He needs to rest." She dug into the wagon and emerged with a brown glass bottle. She made a face. "I don't know if I should give this to him, if it helps him or kills him, but since he has some every day, maybe it will help."

Rourke shrugged. Zeke's ways with a bottle were a mystery to him. "Cal, it don't matter if he drinks a bit. It matters if he lives." She nodded and went inside.

Rourke stayed outside. Cal had made some flatcakes that were enough to keep him fed. He didn't want a fire outside at night. If they were careful and lucky, they could stay a few days, if no one came looking. They were about a day's ride south of Rawhide, pretty well off any trail that connected the town with any of the ranches or the railroad camps. They had a dozen long guns and several extra pistols, as well as enough shells to stand off a small army. He hated waiting, but right now it was all they could do.

The next few days were mostly spent bandaging Zeke, feeding him what they could, and watching him survive past the fever and chills until he was clearly going to live. Rourke went hunting a couple of times. At night, Rourke would sit outside with Cal, watching the last days of the moon as it sailed through clouds and sank behind the hills. There wasn't much talking. He usually held her hand. A few nights, she went to sleep on his shoulder. They were alive and together. The world was far away. Rourke was not going to muddy up the time with words that didn't ever express what he felt anyhow.

Finally, on a day when the itch to act was more than he could bear, Rourke told Cal he was going scouting. They needed information. "We have no idea what's going on. It would be silly to leave here in a wagon if there's an army waiting for you over the hills. We can't stay here forever. We need to know who's doing what out there. Maybe Andy's back and can help me if he wants to. Maybe we go straight for the Army. I have to figure they have forgotten about us, gotten rid of that horse herd, and it will be safe. Rawhide and back is about a day away. If I leave well before dawn I'll be back around sundown. You and Zeke should be safe that long. If you get a hint of trouble, girl, get to those hills."

Cal didn't want him to go. It had been a pleasant interlude. At night they would sit by the tiny fire she begged him to have until it died. She would drift off to sleep on his shoulder, waking up with a blanket over her, the fire out, and the memory of a pleasant comfort in her dreams. She wondered what he felt. He never said. She wanted to ask about his past. She knew he rode from the Texas plains to scout for the old Army all over the West, and then came the Civil War. Well, she thought, a man is what he is, not what he used to be. A body could ruin everything with too many questions that shouldn't matter anyhow. Rourke was hers, because he was. All the reasons and words didn't make a hill of difference, not compared to the way it felt. They sat quietly as the night wore on. Rourke knew it was time to go. He'd never been much on goodbyes and had no idea what to do. Cal solved that. She wrapped her arms around him.

"Come back, cowboy. I almost lost Pa. I'm not losing you. Hear?"

As he rode out, he waved to the darkness, knowing she was watching and would see. He hoped the next time he saw her he'd be there to take her to someplace safe, if there was such a place in Wyoming Territory when a rich, powerful man was set on being the King of the Horse Thieves. He figured if things went wrong, she could last there awhile. She knew how to shoot. Anything that could hold water was filled, so she would need to leave the shack as little as possible. She wouldn't be alone. Zeke's fever had broken and he was awake more. They had to go somewhere before trouble found them, but one false step could mean the end of their luck.

CHAPTER ELEVEN

Star was full of energy, but Rourke paced him for the first few miles. The line of hills that separated their hideout from Rawhide was enough of a barrier that the main trails went around it. Rourke and Star easily picked their way through a twisting path until they found open ground. It was still early when he reached the town.

He led Star into Bear Wallace's stable. No sense in advertising his presence until he was sure what his reception might be. Wallace was the same as always. Not much for talk. He grunted, took a couple of coins, and then left the stable for his lady friend. Rawhide could have been overrun by Indians and Wallace would act the same if they never came to the stable.

Rawhide in the morning was still sleeping off the night before. The main street was empty. He heard the door shut before he saw it. Coming out of the hotel dining room was Sheriff Dan Wheeler. Their eyes locked. Wheeler walked in Rourke's direction, thrusting his hands very deliberately into his pants pockets. Rourke met the man partway. Wheeler moved down a short alley by the general store. Rourke followed, intrigued.

"Hear talk about you, Rourke. That I do," Wheeler began enigmatically.

"What kind?" asked Rourke.

"All kinds. Good. Bad. Lot of bad lately, come to think of it."

"Want to tell me what this is about, Sheriff? I'm not in much mood for games."

Wheeler's eyes bored in to Rourke's. "Word comin' out from the folks who are s'posed to know what's goin' on is that you done killed a bunch of Harwood's men. Seems they caught you rustling. Then you kidnapped that girl there. Somethin' else. Yup, that little Harwood woman there, the daughter, says you tried to take advantage of her."

"Want the truth, Sheriff?"

"Funny thing about the truth, son. It tends to change depending upon who tells it and what you get paid to believe. Now, even if you done every last thing they said you did, you're gonna tell me it's not so. But what I told the fine folks from the Territory who were gettin' an earful from Harwood is that as the sheriff of this here fine community, whoever shoots or steals outside this town is nothin' I can do a lick about, since I only get paid to enforce the law inside the town. You understand me, son?"

"They told you all this?"

"That Harwood fella told the Territory men. That young Territory man who likes women and liquor was the one who told me. The slick one don't get his hands dirty."

"Where are they now?"

"Harwood and that Owens boy went to the fort, son. Since I got no jurisdiction and the Territory men don't quite seem to know what to make of everything, it's the only place they could go. Now, I know you said you went back a ways with the Territory men, but maybe it ain't quite as far as it seems in your mind, son. I won't say they were tellin' me ride out after you, but they weren't telling this man Harwood that what he was saying wasn't so."

Rourke was mystified. Harwood was after him. That was clear. Owens probably was as weak as the judge always feared, and was not going to stand up to Harwood. After all, Rourke and Owens rarely saw each other. And there wasn't a soul who could tell Rourke's side of the story except Rourke himself. Only he and Harwood knew what they said to each other. "Andy Dickinson go along with all this?" he asked at last, trying to work through the puzzle in his mind.

"He wasn't here," Wheeler said. "He rode off to the fort in the night even before the others. Some Army scout showed up. Some big deal."

"The scout?" asked Rourke, not wanting to know but needing to know. "Irishman? The kind that could charm the Sioux out of their buffalo?"

"Sounds like the man to me," replied Wheeler. "He's the one that usually comes to see them. Not to tell you things you don't want to hear, but they have either been cooking up something that may have been a hair on the shady side, or maybe they just always do their business at night."

Rourke was confused. O'Toole had promised not to say anything. Maybe it was coincidence. Dickinson had been going to the fort the day Rourke left, though. He didn't think the man went there that often. Then again, he didn't really know what Andy did most of the time either. Maybe everybody changed while he was out riding. If Thomas O'Toole was up to some kind of skullduggery, it would be the same old Thomas he always knew. It would not be linked to his predicament. Or would it?

"Sheriff, I didn't do anything like what they said. Harwood thinks rustling is the way to build an empire, I wasn't having any part of it, and some of his boys tried to threaten Cal and her pa. The Harwood woman is mean as a snake. Self-defense is still self-defense around here, isn't it?"

"Well, it is, son, but you might have to argue the law with Harwood's riders. Big bunch came through yesterday. If I got their thinkin' right, they figger you went either up north to Harrison or down south to Treadwell if you didn't hide at the fort.

I'm kind of surprised you even made it here. They were scoutin' the roads for you. Might not be too long at all before they come by, in case you might want to know."

"Guess I better ride then, Sheriff. Obliged."

"I'll let them know you were seen headin' toward the fort, then, son." Eyes met eyes once again. "Heard of you. Don't see you for a rustler, Rourke. Men that like to push people around make my bunions hurt. That's why I spent the mornin' in my office not seein' nothin'. I should prob'ly be there now."

Wheeler walked up the alley and down the street, taking his hat off to a passing woman and acting unconcerned. Rourke took the route behind the buildings to the stable. He mounted Star and walked the horse out of Rawhide, heading east toward the fort until he reached a trail he knew that led back south. He rode back west then along the foothills, staying off the main trails. There was a spot about three miles west of Rawhide where the main trail south toward the railroad met the east-west trail that ran from Green Hills to Rawhide and then on to Fort Laramie.

Sure enough, there were riders camped out and waiting. If they were here, they would be camped toward the fort as well. The only way out would be to go through the hills and take the rough country's backtrails toward the fort. With a taste of defeat in his mouth and bitterness at his plight, Rourke turned Star back to the hills. He had a few hours left to ride, and Cal and Zeke were all alone.

Cal was glum when Rourke finished explaining their plight. "We're trapped," she said. He shrugged. It was about right. The riders were pretty poor fighters, but there were a lot of them. They knew a wagon could not outrun horsemen.

"Mebbe we ought to leave the wagon here, girl, and ride out the best we can," Zeke said after a long silence. "Don't know that we can put this blacksmith shop idea back together. Maybe all this is God's way of telling us to start fresh, daughter."

Cal was shocked. Their entire lives were in that wagon. Then again, stuff wasn't much good to dead people. With what they had left behind at Green Hills, and everything else that happened, going back to their old life was probably not an option for the future. "I'll do what you say, Pa," she said with a meekness that was at war with her nature. Cal was born to fight, not run.

Rourke felt guilty, without exactly knowing why. It wasn't right that the innocent suffered while the guilty got rich, even though it was the way the world went 'round. He wondered if he hadn't run into Cal and her pa if the blacksmith shop would have worked out, or if it would have been another one of Zeke's busted dreams.

"Not your fault, son," Zeke told Rourke, clearly reading his face. "Man who settles down when he was born to keep moving asks for what happens after that. Mebbe we'll find something to set up shop with again when we get out of this. Got me some ideas, son. Always got me some ideas."

Zeke's words did little to lift the mood. Cal was silent. Rourke said they would leave the next night to give Zeke one more day of rest and give Cal time to take the things she wanted to save from the wagon, in case it wasn't there when they got back.

She was in a temper, he could see, as she stuffed things into a sack when he went down to see if she needed his assistance.

"Need a hand?" he offered.

"No," came the reply.

"Something I can carry?"

"Don't trouble yourself."

"Cal, you want to explain to me what you are upset about?"

She slammed down the bag she was holding on the wood of the wagon. "You want to hear it, cowboy? I'll tell you. I'm mad because in about two days everything I ever had is gone, and it isn't because of that Harwood man. I want to kill him and all of them—bad. You ain't much better sometimes! Did you have to tell that man you were going to go against him? No! Do you ever, ever, ever think about the price that other people pay? Ever? People stole horses before we got here. They will steal them when we are dead, Rourke. Why should I care? What good came of any of this? Tell me! You think me or Pa cared what horse we were going to shoe, or if it was gonna be rode by a nice man or some worthless miserable rustler? We could have eaten every day and not wonder if tomorrow there would be Indians or the day after there would be cowboys on a spree! All the world manages to do what they want for themselves and not worry, but you got to fight these people for some notion that don't mean a thing. Why? What you got to show for it is nothing! You got no home, no family, no nothing, Rourke, and I'm going to end up with the same thing! Now let me alone!"

There wasn't much to say. Fancy words about right and wrong didn't mean a hill of beans to a woman losing everything she ever had in the world. Maybe because there was so little, losing it cost her so terribly. "Cal, I . . ." he began lamely, without really a clue of what to say.

"Just leave me alone!" she yelled.

Rourke slunk away. It didn't matter whether he got them into this mess or whether life its own self was to blame. He had to get her and Zeke out of it. It was awhile before things started to clear up in his head. If the riders chasing them had a good-sized distraction, maybe they would be so busy they would not get in the way of Cal and her pa reaching the fort. Maybe that distraction could solve everybody's problems. The long odds made him grin at the audacity of it. It was so simple and foolish, it had to work.

He called Zeke for a private talk, and drew out a rough map

on the dirt. "You two start without me. I'm going to scout a side trail—over here, see? To make sure nobody surprises you. Once you hit the wide trail, it's straight to the fort. Got that?" Rourke added a lie. "I'll meet you at the fort."

Zeke nodded. His right arm was weak, but otherwise he was as good as an old man got. He could ride but not shoot. "She'll come around, Rourke," he said, nodding at Cal. "You know she's got a temper."

Rourke shook his head. "Maybe, Zeke, maybe not. You rest a little longer. We go tonight after dark."

Rourke tended to Star, cleaned his guns, and stayed out of Cal's way until sunset.

"Time," he told Zeke as he entered the shack, not looking at Cal. "Like we planned." Cal looked at Zeke, not Rourke.

"We got to go, girl," was all he said. They mounted wordlessly. Zeke moved easier than Rourke had hoped. They rode in silence for about a mile.

As the hills grew nearer, Rourke reined in. "Gonna scout that trail I told you 'bout Zeke. See you 'n' Cal in a couple hours."

Cal, still silent, was sitting her horse next to Zeke. Her face was in the shadows of the brim of her hat as the moonlight picked out the highlights in the hair spilling down her shoulders. Her eyes were unreadable. He had no idea if he would see her again outside of his dreams, but there were no words that would matter now. He swallowed hard. He nodded and rode away quickly, turning once to see them moving along the edge of the trees, barely visible in the dappled moonlight. Then they were gone. Lost and gone forever, like the song said. Well, a man was what a man did. Not what a man dreamed. Time for a man to act like it.

Rourke could feel his heart racing as he rode closer to the meadow where the stolen horses were kept. In the dark, he might accomplish what he could not dare to try in the daylight.

But at night, shots fired wild could kill anyone. Ask old Stonewall Jackson back in the war. But if he could carry this off, the riders would be too busy to think about Cal and Zeke.

The moon was a little too bright for his purpose. He stopped and put some river mud over the white mark on the forehead of his protesting horse. Now, they would blend a little easier. Nice and slow. He tried to will the tension in his shoulders to ease. He slumped down, flopped in the saddle, and looked relaxed, like it was another night shift and he was barely awake.

He was almost to the herd when a voice came from behind him. "Samuels, what are you doing out here? You come on with the next shift. You up to something, fella? You drunk? You got warned same as the rest you get fired if you get drunk."

Rourke had no idea what Samuels sounded like, but the rider challenging him would know. Time to open the ball! He turned and pulled the Remington. One shot rang like thunder. One saddle was empty. Men were shouting up ahead. The drowsy were now wide awake. The wakeful ones were focusing on the muzzle flash and the sound of the gun.

Rourke charged the herd, the Remington in one hand and Cal's old Colt in the other. He fired and screamed the way they did when he and his Texas scouts charged the Yankees. In a moment he and Star were in the thick of the herd. He fired until the hammer clicked on an empty shell. He stuffed Cal's old gun in his belt and reloaded the Remington. Someone was firing. Someone was yelling not to fire. He fired six more shots. He concentrated on controlling Star. Panicked horses collided as they fled his path. At the edges, like a whirlpool, horses were running faster than a man could stop. He could see the lead animals making their way out of the natural corral and onto the wide open plateau. Where one horse went, others would follow. He could see lines of horses running at least three separate ways. Soon, they would be scattered like wheat in a tornado.

The rustlers would be lucky if they saw half of them again. Anyone watching roads should soon be chasing horses.

The whining of a bullet past his head reminded him that he might not see any of them again either. He hung low in the saddle and rode with the herd, hoping one more horse in a stampede could get away unnoticed. The riders were too sharp to be fooled that easily. Although their shots went overhead, they kept following as he rode with the herd out onto the grasslands. He jerked the reins. Star cut right. One rider was almost on top of him. The guns fired together. Rourke felt himself lifted in the saddle. He'd been shot in the war. He felt it once again as the bullet went into his side and out. Aiming through the pain, he emptied the gun, not knowing whether the shots were hits or misses. He kicked Star's flanks with his boots and the horse responded, leaving Rourke to hang on.

When Star's charge slowed, Rourke looked around the moonlit landscape. He had no idea where he was. The moon didn't seem to be where he thought it should be. His side hurt. Blood was leaking all over that new shirt he had bought to please Cal only a few days ago. Well, he got to wear a red one at the end, anyhow. He wanted to rest, but he knew if he slid off of Star, he would never have the strength to sit the saddle again. He loaded his gun. That mattered. It was quiet. Wherever he was. Far off there was noise. Lots of noise. It seemed very far away, though.

He looked again at the moon. It was getting hazy. Maybe it would rain. He sure was thirsty. He didn't remember being that thirsty before. He made a noise that came out sounding like a man choking, and pulled. Star started walking in what Rourke hoped was the right direction. He hoped Cal wasn't still mad. He hoped so. Then he hung on to Star's mane. If his mind had any more thoughts, he never knew what they were.

★ ★ ★ ★ ★

Gunshots carry forever across the great open spaces of Wyoming, even more so at night. Cal and Zeke heard gunfire and something that sounded like thunder as they reached the Fort Laramie trail a couple of hours after leaving Rourke behind. There were no riders, no patrols. Cal stood still, listening.

"This way, girl," Zeke said, pointing the nose of his horse toward the fort. "Whatever the man did, we got to get to the Army. If he bought us some time, daughter, we can't go a-wasting it." When she did not reply, he rode to where she sat her horse. "Girl? Come on, girl, we need to tell the Army about the doin's here."

The moonlight reflected the wetness under Cal's eyes. "I said horrible things to him, Pa. I told him to leave me and us alone. I wanted something to go right, Pa. I wanted to have a house and a home and something and not always run, Pa. I don't mean that the way it sounds, Pa. I don't know what I want, Pa." Now she was really crying.

Zeke sighed. He reckoned this was not the time to tell his daughter the things that her mother had told him in anger; words that didn't mean a thing in the long run of the short time they had together. The girl had her mother's temper for certain sure.

"Caledonia," he said, making a rare full use of her name, "Rourke is a man who takes a risk every day because it's the way he survives. He is what he is, girl. We can't ride around in the night all over Wyoming Territory to find him. He knows we're heading to the Army. He's sure got to have a place in mind to hole up until light. He didn't do what he did so we could throw our lives away, girl. He did what he did to make sure you got away. Now you have to come with me, daughter!"

Zeke's talent for making things worse with women had not

deserted him. Cal was crying full bore now and holding onto him. "He went to go get killed to protect us and all I did was yell at him."

Zeke took the reins of her horse. "Daughter, there's nothing we can do now but go. We have to ride!"

"I will not!"

Ezekiel sighed the way only one person in the world could make him sigh. "Girl, be sensible . . ."

"Are you coming?" she asked, pulling the reins back into her hands and turning the head of her horse the opposite direction from the fort.

"Girl, you can't find him in the dark."

"I'll figure it out, Pa."

Zeke bowed his head to the inevitable. His choice was either to agree or to ride looking back at her to see when she broke away. He half wanted to smile for the way she reminded him of her mother—strong-willed in everything including loving a man no one thought was any good. Well, they'd been happy until the sickness took her. Now, their daughter had grown up. He was hoping the stories the preachers told about people in Heaven knowing everything that happened on Earth were true. She'd be getting a kick out of this one.

"Daughter, you boss me around almost as good as your ma," he said. "We'll do what you want."

They rode. They thought they found a trail at one point, but then lost it. Darkness gave way to dawn without a sight of Rourke. Signs of his work were all over, as horses galloped in twos and threes, heading nowhere and everywhere. A massive stampede had scattered horses in all directions, obscuring any hope of reading signs. Cal was frustrated. They were no closer to finding Rourke than when they turned back from the Fort Laramie trail. She had made a mistake to turn back. Rourke was either dead, had disappeared, or had gone on by some route she could not find in the dark. They would need to go to ground and wait. Pa needed to rest, and she could not ride around alone in daylight without being found sooner or later. She looked out at the night and spoke in a quivering whisper. "You get yourself killed, Rourke, and I ain't never gonna forgive you!" Then she turned to find a place for Pa to rest. She was not going to lose them both.

Chapter Twelve

Sheriff Dan Wheeler never liked being summoned to the home of Territorial Administrator Andrew Dickinson. He liked it even less when his breakfast with Louise Callahan was interrupted by the summons, delivered by the woman who was the Dickinsons' maid.

"Oh, go be the big, bad sheriff for a while," she had told him. "I need to sleep anyhow. I will meet you here for lunch?"

Wheeler took his time making the walk. A man's life shouldn't be at the beck and call of another man's whims. Caroline Dickinson answered the door. She didn't even try putting on a phony smile. This must be big trouble, Wheeler thought. Bigger trouble. Bill Harwood was there as well, looking ominous.

"My major horse herd has been rustled," he said without preamble as soon as Wheeler entered the room. "I want them found. I want the rustler Rourke hunted down, along with his confederates."

"As I told Mr. Dickinson some time ago, sir, my authority is limited to the town of Rawhide. Somebody shows me something like proof of all the tales going 'round, I'm certain sure to stop this Rourke fella the next time he comes into town. But until I get that, with all kinds of respect, sir, I can't do anything."

"The Army needs those horses, Sheriff," Harwood retorted, his face reddening. Wheeler wondered if the man had been drinking already. "The safety of the people of Wyoming is being undermined by this rustling! My future as a major rancher here is being attacked. For all I know, this Rourke is in cahoots with those small ranchers who should have been out of business years ago. I want a posse and I want it now!"

"Really, Sheriff," chimed in Dickinson. "The town would be nothing without a prosperous rancher like Mr. Harwood. You can't stand by and do nothing!"

"Are you too busy with your personal pursuits, Sheriff?" sniped Caroline Dickinson, twisting the words like a knife. "Should we talk to the mayor about a new sheriff who can do the work the town requires?"

The powerful waited for the sheriff's expected capitulation. He smiled instead. For the first time in years, Dan Wheeler felt that wonderful freedom he had known when he and Martha were out on that small Dakota ranch, before she took sick, before they needed to live closer to a town.

"I will give this important matter due consideration," he said, rising and walking to the door. "That I will. I thank you, all of you, for bringing this to my attention. I'll form a posse as soon as I have had time to think about it, maybe next year."

"Wheeler!" Dickinson was angry. "I will have your badge."

"Well, sir, you have a nice conversation, sir, with the mayor, sir, if you can find him sober, sir, and a good day to you all." Wheeler lifted his hat, whistling as he closed the door. He smiled. He hoped Louise wanted to go into ranching, because the law business had just about gone belly-up—and a good thing, too.

Rourke was swimming deep under the surface of the lake. The water was cold and clear. He had not been in that lake since he was a boy. There was nothing there; no fish, no anything. Then there was something at the surface, something dark. Something looking down through the water. It was talking indistinctly. Maybe it was a talking fish. The only way to hear was to surface.

He didn't want to, but he had to. His head broke the surface. He opened his eyes.

When the wetness covering his vision cleared, he could see he was in a tiny shack, lying on a rough-hewn bed. It was dark. There were no windows. A dim glow from a fire barely lit the room. He moved. Pain lanced through him. He groaned.

"Young man, rest," said a gentle, kind voice. "You lost a lot of blood but you're going to live. Hear? You need to rest first."

Rourke wanted to ask where he was, but his throat was parched. He made croaking noises. A canteen was pressed to his lips. He drank, spilling the water onto strips of cloth around his chest. There was more cloth around his left arm. He didn't remember getting shot there. When he finished swallowing, he looked at the man standing over him. He was a short, roundish man with white hair and a flowing beard. The man's face was weathered from the sun, but his hands had been soft.

"Where am I? Where's Star?"

The man smiled. "Your horse is outside. I don't think he approves of you in here while he's out there, but it's a bit too small for both of you," the man said, good-naturedly. "We are a couple of miles outside of Rawhide. You almost made it here the other night, when that tremendous stampede took place, but you fell off your animal. Your horse stayed with you. I thought you were one of the men with the horses, but no one came by looking for you. I can help you get back to that outfit if you need to. My name is Gabriel Evans. I am now a minister by trade. I have been many things, including a doctor during the war and a merchant before that, as well as things best forgotten. I came out here to preach the Christian religion to the Indians, but I have come to reconsider. Many of the white men I see are far more in need of religion and faith than many of the Indians."

Rourke could understand. Indians who lived on the edge of survival worshipped what they knew—the earth and the sky.

"How long have I been here?"

"Two days."

Two days. Cal and Zeke should be at Fort Laramie by now, he thought. He probably needed to get moving as well. All he needed was a rider looking for a stray horse to come by. He started to get up. The room went a little sideways, but he grabbed onto Evans, who made disapproving noises but held on. He helped Rourke walk to the door. He opened it as Rourke stood in the doorway.

Star was there, the prettiest sight Rourke could imagine, well, except for Cal. There was a hint of light in the east. He'd lived through it; he could feel the renewal in his body. Maybe he'd stay one last day, rest, and then head toward Fort Laramie by night. Evans led Rourke back inside. Rourke sat on the bed and grabbed the bread Evans handed him. He needed food. He needed strength.

While they ate, he told Evans the story. In case riders came by, and he asked the man to lie, the preacher needed to understand what was going on. Evans shook his head in sorrow at the end of the tale. "Rustling is always a curse out here, but this is making it into a business," he said. "It is odd, is it not? When someone steals a horse, they are a thief. When a man like this steals hundreds of them, it sounds like a business, the way they do business in the East. I wondered about you because I thought I had seen most of the rustlers riding by, and you didn't have saddlebags filled with whiskey bottles. Of course I can help you. There is a road toward the hills that will avoid most of the riders who come past. It is rough, but your horse is rested. You should rest, but I met men like you in the war. I know when it is useless to preach a sermon."

The preacher fixed stew, lots of it. He and Rourke were eating when they heard the riders approach.

"Hello in there." The voice calling out was in no way friendly.

Evans opened the door, as he did to every rider. Four men in a line, widely spaced, sat their horses. They waited beyond the hitching rail where Star was tied.

"Your horse?" asked the lead rider.

"He came into the yard. No one claimed him, so I'm going to sell him in Rawhide. He looks like I could fetch a good price. I am preaching the Gospel to the Indians. My mission needs every spare dollar I can turn."

"We're looking for his rider. He's a thief."

"There is no one here but me, gentlemen. There were many horses around here the other night, perhaps the man you seek is out in the brush that way." Evans pointed the opposite direction from the one Rourke would take. "Now, if you will excuse me, I need to return to my prayers."

Evans went to close the door.

"Stop old man. I think I'll come in and take advantage of the hospitality you ought to give a man." The rider reached for a rifle and lifted a leg out of the stirrup.

Evans swallowed. He had no weapons and no training in using them. Rourke could not defend himself. "I can assure you . . ." he began.

A gun barked from indoors. The rider dismounting his horse landed in the dirt. Evans slammed the door shut as bullets thunked into the wood.

Gunfire echoed over the small hill where Cal and Zeke were riding slowly, trying to find some sign to tell them which way Rourke had gone. They had been looking for two days. Every time Zeke suggested going to the fort, Cal got angry. They had found a mark in the dust that looked like dried blood and were looking for more drops when the gunshots sounded.

Cal and Pa exchanged wordless looks and rode faster in that direction. They topped a rise and could see several men with rifles firing at a rundown farmhouse. Only a couple of shots came in return. The shack was small. No paint, not much of anything. One shutter was open. Cal could see a gun barrel poking out. "Look, daughter," Zeke said, pointing. Star was loose off to the side of the shack, reins trailing.

Cal saw men rushing the shack, running low. They threw torches at the doors of the house and retreated while their comrades provided covering fire. That made up her mind. Rourke had to be in there. She and Pa rode closer. They were close enough now to hear the men.

". . . and I will guarantee your protection if that man surrenders to the duly constituted authorities here," one rider was calling toward the house.

"Throw down them guns and we'll talk." It was Rourke's voice.

"Be a shame if the whole house burns down and you in it," the rider was yelling, amusement creeping into his voice. The riders outside were laughing.

Cal whispered to Pa, "You go around behind that big tree. When I start, ride in. I'll take 'em this way." Pa nodded.

The torches had caught something. Bits of smoke rose from the rear of the shack. The men in front gathered and waited. The men inside had no choice. All they had to do now was wait. The sounds of coughing came from inside the house. The rustlers peered toward it. It would not be much longer now.

"Drop those guns, boys." Cal was twenty feet behind them, the new Colt ready and steady. She could see Pa moving into position. When they turned to her, he would have their flank.

One rustler turned, looked her up and down, and appeared to dismiss her as a threat. "Catchin' a dangerous horse thief, ma'am," he said. "Nothin' that should concern a girl. Now sit this one out and you won't get hurt, little lady." He turned his back.

Her pistol shot kicked up the dirt at the speaker's feet. "I said to drop them guns."

The speaker muttered something she could not hear, but she could make a guess. One—two—. . .

The line of gunmen turned in her direction. Cal fired into the middle of the group. Pa joined in, galloping and firing from horseback as if he was a *Harper's Weekly* woodcut. He missed his first shot, but not the next. In a moment, all but one of the riders were down. The remaining one started to run toward his horse. One gun from the house boomed. The last rider was slammed to the ground.

The door to the shack opened. Two coughing men emerged. One wrapped in white went back in and started throwing out objects. The flames licking up the side of the shack gathered momentum. The other man, a white-bearded man, turned back in as well. Finally, carrying one last load, both men dumped a collection of pots, pans, guns, and provisions into the dirt, gasping for breath and grinning like a pair of fools. The bandaged man looked up at the woman on the horse.

"Hey, Cal!"

"This new toy gun here that I got shoots a mite to the left, you know, Rourke," she said coolly, ignoring the feelings within her and hoping that her voice did not shake the way her hands wanted to. "You should tell a girl things like that, you know, in case she needs to rescue your sorry hide someday without the time for real target practice."

"Girl should practice with a new gun once she gets to someplace safe instead of riding around Wyoming Territory looking for trouble when she's supposed to be in Fort Laramie," he responded.

"If a girl was in Fort Laramie, there's a fella who would be steak about now," she observed. "Course, maybe he was ready to be cooked and that's why he came out to see his woman without a shirt on." She laughed as Rourke flushed. She was sure it was the first time she had seen him embarrassed. She had noticed huge patches of skin on his shoulders and back that were white with old scars. They reminded her of how little she really knew about Rourke's past.

"You people know each other?" asked Evans, trying to make sense of the bantering as well as the gunplay.

Rourke explained that the woman and old man were the ones he had told the minister about.

"I think from watching you that the rustlers should be worried about you instead of you worrying about them," the minister observed. He turned to Cal. "I have served in the war, miss, and I have seen many men fail to shoot as well as you." He bowed slightly.

"I had to," she replied. "I had to catch up with this crazy man before he got himself killed by somebody else because I haven't decided yet if I want to do the job myself to make sure it gets done right." The words were a joke, but the look in her eyes was not. Rourke caught the meaning, but there was no time for private talk. Instead, all four sat under the tree to plan their survival—but only after Zeke and Rourke rummaged the dead for the guns and ammunition they had on them.

"Smoke went way high, preacher," observed Rourke. "You're going to have company, and I don't figure it's friendly. We got extra horses. You can pick one and ride with us, or ride out on your own way. Don't know how safe it might be on your own 'cuz I don't rightly know quite where we are, so's if you want to ride with us, you're welcome."

Evans knew he had little choice. "I know some people in Rawhide who will let me stay there for a while," he said. "It took me months to build that cabin. I don't think I have time to build another one before winter sets in, if it is everything they say it is out here."

"It is," replied Rourke. "Snow covers it all, Preacher. Snows so hard and so much out on the Plains that all the ugly things get buried and you can get a bit of peace."

While Evans and Zeke were loading supplies onto the animals, Cal and Rourke moved off alone.

"You were supposed to get out and be safe, Cal," reproved Rourke. "Now, we're kind of back where we started."

She told him about hearing the gunfire from his stampede. "Do you really think I could let you die here and ride off to Laramie like a scared little coward Eastern woman? Whatever you think ladies are and ladies like, I'm not afraid of being out here. I can get mad at you when you do stupid things. It doesn't mean you have to do more stupid things. Pa threatens to fry eggs on my forehead when I get mad at him. That's what happens when my menfolk do dumb things. I'm not a little girl anymore."

"That little girl part. That much I noticed."

She blushed, and there was a smile that interrupted her thoughts. "We don't split up again; you don't protect me again without telling me; you don't do things for my own good without telling me; and you don't ride off on any stunts like that without telling me. If we don't do this as partners, then we don't do this at all. Is that clear?"

She ended up jabbing a finger at him, poking him in the middle of a bandage that was sodden with blood from a reopened wound. She looked at the blood on her finger. At first she gasped, then when she saw the laughter in his face, she joined in.

Rourke had not been lectured by a woman in years. He thought, as she spoke, that she had never looked prettier. He grinned loosely in the happiness of living when he knew he should have been dead. "What you mean is that you don't want to miss the fun?"

She started to explain to him what she did mean, but then the eyes gave it away. She slapped him in the arm, then winced even more than he did. "I'm sorry!"

"Now I understand. You want to beat me to death and you don't want anyone else doing the job for you. C'mon. Move closer. I still got one arm that mostly works."

She laid her head on his shoulder. "I don't want to find out you got killed, Rourke. If you're gonna do something that gets us killed, I'm going with you. Or I'm keeping you alive until you learn to do what I tell you."

"Do I get a choice?"

"No." It was the last word either of them said for a long time as his arm pulled her close; she held him both tightly and gingerly, and a sunset that filled the width of the endless sky with reds and oranges washed away everything else from their minds as they watched it blossom, flower, and finally fade. As the light dimmed, and the cover of darkness spread its protection from pursuing eyes, it was time to ride.

Evans, who knew the area best, led the way.

"There was a miner who gave up his claim this summer," Evans said. "He was digging near an old cave. That can give us shelter for now. Nobody goes there."

It was another moonlit night. They took it slowly. By dawn, they had reached the cave. Rourke took the first watch as the others tried to rest in the cool of the cave. They still needed a plan. Fight or run. That was never a choice. Not with Cal. Not with him. He looked around at the sleeping forms of his army—a girl and two old men. A grin split his face. Yup. He was onto the right idea when every good, solid thought in his head said it was impossible.

Later in the day, Cal looked at Rourke as he rested. They had slept away much of the day, exhausted. He looked like he might fall down from a stiff breeze. She had noticed how thin he was when she had seen him earlier—just bones, far less substantial than he usually seemed. There were rings under his eyes. He had the kind of pallor people only got when they were leaving this life behind. He had been too tired to josh her about anything, and had fallen asleep about as soon as his head hit the ground. He had slept through every noise from the pots and pans falling over to Pa and Preacher Evans playing cards. Her father swore again.

"Pa!" she scolded out of habit, knowing that he would never quite be civilized but knowing also that he would be far worse if she gave up trying.

"It's not fair!" Zeke exclaimed. "I'm being cheated."

Evans had a beatific smile on his face. Cal wondered if preachers cheated at cards like everybody else, or if God didn't care about breaking the rules in the Devil's business. "It's only a card game, Pa," she said.

"Only a card game! Daughter, we been playing for how many drinks a day I can have, and now we're down to two whole days without a drop of anything but water or that coffee you make for Rourke. Why, it's not fair."

"Come on, Ezekiel," coaxed Evans, with a broad wink at Cal. "Double or nothing?"

Cal turned away not to laugh. A preacher cheating at cards so her pa would not drink. Now she had seen everything. Rourke was still asleep. A thought hit her. She wondered if he was dead. He had not moved in hours. He could have died right there and no one would know. She could not tell from the blanket she had tossed over him if his chest was moving and he was breathing. She looked around. She felt foolish, but she got up close to his face so that she could feel any breath. She almost screamed when the eyes an inch from hers popped open.

"Lookin' for something, Cal?"

"You fool!" she exclaimed, noble thoughts forgotten in the

shame of being caught. "I wanted to see if you were dead."

"Well, I might be if some woman doesn't walk so loud so's a man can't sleep, and if that same woman doesn't figure out how to make food so that the men don't start gnawing on each other."

"You're getting griddle cakes because we have flour and not much else," she said. "And you . . . you!"

He moved too fast for someone who looked so ill, she told herself, as an arm snaked out of the blanket and went around her. "Just set a minute. Zeke's so busy trying to win back his liquor that he won't know if he eats or not. Anyhow, ol' preacher there was a card sharp back East, along with his other things he came out here to forget, so I figger by the time they finish, Zeke will be dry as the desert the rest of his life."

Cal cast an amused eye at the two older men as they intently played cards and talked like old friends. She relaxed in Rourke's grip as he sat up and threw aside the blanket. "Are you going to live?" she asked.

"Been shot worse. Lived then. Not worried. A mite tired, but it passes." His eyes scanned the ground below. They froze. She turned to see what caught his eye, but it was a deer. "I'm more worried about you. You been through a lot. You aren't used to this. Pa, me, all of it." He took her hand in his. "If I knew a way to keep you safe I would, but I think we have to play it through."

"I told you, Rourke, I don't want to run and hide. Me 'n' Pa been through a lot. I know he got chased a few times, but those were folks who got mad and got over it. This is different. I don't know how we end this. I don't know what happens. I'm scared, Rourke."

He had no soothing lies to offer. What he was thinking would do nothing to ease her fears. He put his arm tighter around her. They waited with fear, with uncertainty, knowing that whatever came next, at least for now they would face it together.

"Rourke?"

"Present."

"Um, cowboy, you know about everything there is about me and I really don't know a thing about you. You think you might want to tell a girl who it is that she's kissing?"

Rourke hated talking. Cal deserved to know. "I was born back on a farm over in Scotland. Town called Alyth in Perth-shire. My mom died young. My pa was mixed up in some kind of union trouble. We left, ended up in Texas. He died, and I was on my own. I knew horses real good. I got work on a horse ranch. There was some trouble, and I had to leave. I—oh truth is, Cal, I killed a fella in a gunfight and he had friends and I didn't. Fair fight. Army needed scouts, not particular about the age, and I joined them awhile. Second Cavalry down in Texas. Lots of Confederates there. War came. I went with some boys from Texas through Shiloh and Atlanta and all them battles. I met Lorraine in Nashville, in '61. We got married. She died in '64 in Richmond while I was in Georgia. I never knew for months except letters stopped coming. When it ended, I come out here. Andy and I had met in the war; you know soldiers only hated each other when it was time for a battle, rest of the time we got on fine—them Yanks and us Rebs. His outfit and mine took turns guarding the same place from each other in early '64, got along like brothers for weeks until we all had to march and fight again. Well, I run into him in late '65. I was at loose ends after Thomas went back in the Arm. Guess that's it. Not much to tell, Cal. Past is dust. Not much clings."

"That doesn't sound like a very happy life, Rourke."

"Never thought much on it, Cal, not until Lorraine. After, I figured I had what I was gonna have and I might as well do what I pleased until I got called to cross the river. Livin', dyin', all the same."

She swallowed hard. "You still think that way?"

174

"No, Cal. Livin' matters now. Some days it matters so much that I get you out of this, sweetheart. I . . . well . . . Cal, I was thinkin' that maybe, after, all this, uh . . ."

"Ain't interruptin' somethin', am I?" Zeke was standing with a smirk on his face. "Preacher cheats at cards almost as good as I do. Daughter, we got anything for a man to eat?"

"Flatcakes is it until somebody gets me something better," she said. "You two! You drag a girl all over Wyoming and expect she's got food when there's nothing to cook!"

Zeke dropped a sack at her feet. "Couple pans and some flour and such. Preacher's stash from his shack. While you was doin' other things, I figured you'd want these sooner or later."

Rourke volunteered to go hunting but Cal would have none of it. She had tossed dried meat into her saddlebags, so they had something that was very much like stew, without most of the ingredients. But they ate. As they sat around the fire, Rourke voiced the thought he had not been able to answer.

"Now what? We got four against the Harwoods, and for all I know the Army and maybe the Territory."

Evans spoke up. "Won't those small ranchers you spoke to me about be on your side? Even if they only have a hand or two, you would have someone to back you up."

Rourke felt guilty. He had forgotten Harrison and Treadwell. How long ago was it that Wheeler told him there were riders looking for him at the other ranches? He had another dilemma. One was north, one was south. He had promised Cal they wouldn't split up, but that seemed to be the only way to check on each ranch.

Cal had a different idea. Evans had told her that the old shack where they had left the wagon, which had food in it, was about three miles southwest of where they were holed up. "We go get that, then swing south to check on that Treadwell family," she told Rourke. "We can be there by sundown. If they're

175

fine, Pa and the preacher will stay there and you and I can ride north."

Rourke had not taken many orders since the war, and no matter how nice Cal said it, this was one. It went against the grain, but he gave in. "We'll do it your way, Cal," he replied. "But if there's trouble, you do what you get told to do. Hear?"

Cal saluted. "Yes sir," she said in a gruff impersonation of a soldier's voice. Then she smiled at Rourke. "I know you like to do these things on your own, Rourke, but you don't have to do that anymore."

Zeke cackled. "Like to see someone else bossed around now and then," he remarked.

"And you!" Cal exclaimed. "I know where to look if I want to practice shooting and use a full bottle!"

Zeke grinned back. He was alive. His daughter had found a man. Nothing hurt much today. Life maybe could be better, but it wasn't likely.

The wagon was where they had left it, near the dilapidated shack. Two horses were grazing about 100 feet away. One horse whinnied. Rourke looked out at the broken landscape of brush, scrubby trees, and tall grass.

"Hey!" Cal exclaimed when Rourke cut her off from leading the way down the slope to the flat plain where the shack was waiting, door open invitingly.

"My play. You wait," he said in a tone that brooked no argument. He pulled the Winchester from its scabbard. He could not see any fresh tracks in the dirt. He stopped 50 yards from the shack and looked at it. The door to the shack moved fractionally.

Rourke fired three times, blasting holes in the door. Wood flew. From the doorway, a large rabbit dashed around the shack and off into the grasslands. Behind him, Rourke could hear whoops of laughter from Cal, Zeke, and the preacher. Feeling the blood rush to his face, he lowered the rifle.

"Shame on you, Rourke, for scaring that poor rabbit," Cal called out, riding up to him.

He started to look toward her and replace the rifle in its scabbard. A creaking hinge turned back to the shack. The door opened wide. Two men with rifles filled the space.

Rourke pulled hard on Star's reins. The horse bumped into Cal's mount. Rourke and Star screened Cal from the first bullets that flew harmlessly overhead. Rourke grabbed the rifle as he vaulted out of the saddle and ran toward a patch of knee-high brush. He landed hard. He could feel the wound on his arm pop open. He stayed on his belly and fired at the shack.

He looked back. Cal had dropped from the saddle and was lying on her belly. She had a gun in her hand. He hoped she was not hit. Evans and Zeke had dismounted. They were firing long range. Neither were likely to hit anyone, but they could distract the two men. Rourke poked his head up. Mistake! The two bushwhackers were on either side of the doorway, using its cover to fire at him. Well, if they wanted him they were going to get him! He leaped up and ran farther around to his right, almost to the side of the shack, then ducked down behind an old dusty trough. It was quiet. They must be waiting. The sun felt hotter than he remembered it. He was thirsty. Nothing changed. The feeling in the belly right before a charge was the same. Half fear, half anxiety. The men in the shack only had a couple of options. He hoped he was guessing right.

He jumped out from his cover and ran straight for the side of the shack. A rifle poking out of the window told him he had guessed right. It fired and missed. Rourke fired the Remington until he had used up all six shells. Another gun fired from the front of shack, the distant rifles replied. Cal's pistol barked. Then it was quiet.

"One down in the doorway, Rourke." It was Cal.

Rourke reloaded. He moved cautiously closer. The thin slats of board that made up the wall of the shack were shattered where he had fired. He looked through the glassless window. A man was lying on his back, with at least two holes in him.

Cal, Evans, and Zeke moved closer with their guns trained on the man slumped in the doorway. He was not pretending. He was dead as well.

"You knew?" asked Cal. Her heart was pounding. She was short of breath; almost dizzy. Rourke was nonplussed. Did she even know this man?

"I shut the door when we left, Cal. Somebody had opened it. We don't have a lot of friends in this part of the country right now. Whoever found the place and waited wasn't likely to be makin' coffee for us."

The two dead men were dragged into the shack to avoid attracting the attention of anyone on their trail. Knowing how sound carried on the Plains, they hitched up the team and rode south toward the Treadwell ranch.

"You did what?" Louise Callahan was incredulous. Dan Wheeler had been an unchanging rock in all the time she'd known him—since she landed in Rawhide.

"Something wrong in all of it, Louise," he replied. "If I have to do wrong to wear the badge, somebody else can wear it. I got my eye on a little bit of land off toward Dakota. Might raise me a few head of cattle. Might make enough money to get by. Might be a good new start. Guess I've had about enough of town life."

"I thought that land cost money."

"Well, I got a little. No sense savin' for after I'm dead. Um, Louise?"

"Yes, Dan."

"You ever think about bein' a rancher's wife? I know we ain't talked about that sort of stuff, but I'm not gettin' younger and since you don't seem to be in as much a hurry to get to Denver as I thought you were, maybe you might want to stay in Wyoming. Try ranchin'."

Louise had tears in her eyes. "Dan, you are a wonderful man. But I can't be your wife. I came here because, well, because when the man I thought would be my husband forever took up with another woman and left me, I did things that I'm not proud of, and I had a terrible time with drinking, Dan. I . . .."

"Louise, it don't matter. Look at this place. Look at these people. Whatever they were, whatever they been, they're who they are right now. The past don't matter unless you make it so. This is Wyoming Territory. If an old buck like me can start over, a young girl like you can do the same."

"But you can't quit. The Territory men are mad at you. Is it safe?"

"It will all blow over, like a dusty day. I want to get this done. There's a fella named Evans. Preacher. Comes by every so often. Next time he comes by, you'll be ready?"

Louise Callahan had imagined several ways Dan Wheeler might take their relationship. This had never been one of them. In surprise and happiness, she replied, "It seems I don't have a choice."

"Good. That's settled." He stood up and plunked his hat on his head. "Now I got to go see what all this horse nonsense is all about."

"Dan?" There was a tone in her voice he had never heard before. "You know, you could kiss the woman you plan to marry, unless those horses won't wait."

"They will," he said, setting down his hat. "They will indeed."

Rourke was riding out in front, with Zeke and Evans back by the wagon. Cal drove. He'd been wondering what had happened to the Treadwell ranch. More than once he'd thought about the woman and her kids. Cal could read tension in his every movement. Then a smile started to break across his face as they rounded a bend about a mile from the ranch. Still holding Star's reins he moved his hands well out from his hips and pulled up to a halt.

"We ain't out to kill anybody today," he called to the rocks off to his left. "You're a good watchman up there, son. Put the rifle down and let's talk. I'm a friend of your pa's."

"I know how to shoot and we've had enough of your kind! Keep those hands up," came a thin, high voice from the rocks. Rourke spotted the boy in a pile of rocks nature had tumbled together. Great cover, but the shooter could only fire for a short spell until, from what Rourke could see, the rocks would block his aim.

"Name's Rourke. Got a preacher and a couple friends. Here to see your pa. Been here before."

"No tricks."

"No tricks, son." He turned to Cal and the two men. "Keep it real slow and real easy. This is how folks get shot by accident. The boy up there is ready to go off half-cocked. Must be one of his first days guarding the ranch."

Rourke watched the boy climb over the rocks to keep a bead on the four visitors. Only a kid could climb over all that so quickly, he thought. Treadwell ought to be real proud of his boy. Rourke would tell him so.

The ranch was transformed, for the worse. Order had given way to chaos. There was a corral full of horses. The house had its shutters closed, except for the barrels of two rifles poking out.

Rourke dismounted and walked toward the house with his hands up. "Name's Rourke," he called. "Been here before. Abigail, you got to remember me. Had some scrapes with folks ridin' for Green Hills. Tryin' to help."

He stood there with his hands in the air, feeling slightly ridiculous as time stretched out. He started to sense that something was very wrong. He watched the house for a sign of movement.

The door opened. Holding a shotgun with steady hands, Abigail Treadwell took a step outside.

"Gun on the ground," she said. "Any of the rest of you got iron, do the same."

Rourke dropped the Remington. He heard thuds behind him.

"Miz Treadwell, we're not here to hurt nobody."

"I should kill you."

"Miz Treadwell . . ."

"Did you tell them everything you could? Do you feel happy with the job they did? Are you here to finish us off?"

"Miz Treadwell, look at us. I got me a preacher and a girl and her pa and we been on the run from the Green Hills people these last days. I don't know nothin' about anythin'. Let me explain." He took a step forward.

She put the gun to her shoulder.

"Rourke." It was Cal. "Rourke, before you go off half-crazy and do something stupid, I think there's something you ought to see over by your left there."

Rourke tried to move his eyes as far as he could while still keeping an eye on Abigail Treadwell. By a tree, where there was grass that was green and not brown, was a cross made out of sticks and some fresh dirt. Somebody had tried to put some whitewash on the sticks.

"Boys and I dug that," Abigail Treadwell said. "The ones he killed we left for the buzzards then dragged off to feed the hogs. You can join them."

"Mrs. Treadwell," Cal began, "we have been on the run from those people for days. Please believe us. We don't want to hurt you. We came to try to help. We . . . we didn't know we would be too late." Cal had gotten down off the wagon and was walking slowly toward the Treadwell woman. "We won't hurt you. I don't know if we can help or not, but we are here as friends. My pa was shot, Rourke was shot. We lost almost everything we had." Cal and Abigail Treadwell seemed locked in silent conversation.

Treadwell's widow lowered the gun a little. "Pete brought in some stock from the hills," she said. "He told me there were rustlers. He was going to protect what he could. Then one day they showed up—the Green Hills riders. There must have been twenty of them. They told Pete they were taking his herd. He got a couple of them before they got him. Our boys have been firing guns since they could walk. The men who ride for us came back and there was a lot of shooting. The riders left. They killed Pete and Fred Johnson, one of our men. The last riders we had went out the next day to see about the herd, but they haven't come back. Before they left, we buried Pete." She looked at Rourke, eyes wet. She finally lowered the shotgun to the ground. "Pete never hurt anyone, mister. He was a good man. Why did they have to kill him?"

Rourke had no answer. Treadwell had been a man with a dream. He lived for it. He died for it. Cold comfort for the widow.

Cal and the preacher went inside with Abby Treadwell. Zeke checked on the horses, and moved the wagon to the barn. Rourke walked over to the dead man's grave. He could feel it again—the unreasoning anger when innocent people had been crushed. In the war, it was simple. He could take it out on the nearest Yankees. Maybe it was that simple here in Wyoming Territory. If the folks at Green Hills were the root of all this misery, and they were sending riders to kill a rancher who wanted nothing more than a small slice of land for his family, then it would be only justice to let them taste a little of their own medicine.

CHAPTER THIRTEEN

Cal was foot-stomping angry at Rourke's plan. "I thought we were going to stay together!"

"Cal, you know this is somethin' I can do best alone. I don't know what's there, who's there, or what I'm walkin' into. If I take you with me, I'm gonna worry about you. This is the only way I can do this, woman! I ain't plannin' on another widow or another grave, 'ceptin' for the Harwoods. They killed a good man. Are you gonna tell me I can walk away?"

There was no answer. "You get killed and I . . . I . . . I'm never gonna forgive you, cowboy."

"I'll be back, Cal."

She looked at him. "I wonder how many times Pete Tread-well said that to Abby." She walked back into the house. The door slammed shut.

Rourke had explained to Zeke and the preacher how to defend the house and ranch until they were sick of the details. "We wasn't born yesterday, Rourke," chided Zeke. "Get your business done and get back here pronto before someone comes after you."

The Green Hills house was standing just as he recalled it. Then again it had only been a few days since he rode up to it the first time, unaware of what it concealed. From a hill overlooking the ranch, he could see the land stretch on forever. There was a stiff breeze that cleared a man's head. The sun's warmth made the day seem like one made for happier things than dealing with rustlers. How could such evil exist in a paradise like this? People brought it with them, like a disease.

The house seemed still. He wondered if the Harwoods were even home. He waited. Easterners never waited. They were in a hurry to be rich in a day, to build in a day. Indians knew about time. Cal was right—he was getting more like them as civilization got closer and closer.

He left Star under the trees, in the shade, and moved down toward the house, slowly, trying not to make noise. He scanned the place through the scope he'd gotten in the war for long-range killing. The bunkhouse and cookhouse were deserted. There were no telltale trails of blue smoke from a wood fire. Wherever Green Hills' riders were, they were not guarding their own ranch.

The sun was high in the sky as riders came down the trail. He saw the uniforms and gold braid. The Army! For a minute, his heart soared. The Army had found out what the Harwoods were up to. The rustlers were getting what they deserved! He could ride back to Cal and maybe they could figure out what life held next.

He was wrong. Only two men rode down the trail. They dismounted to effusive greetings from Harwood and his wife. Rourke looked through the scope. There was no mistaking the friendly smiles being exchanged before they all went inside. Rourke considered his options. He could hardly start shooting with the Army there. He had no way of knowing who was in the house. He kept his distance. He worked his way to where there was a view of a window from the tall grass. Through the scope he could make out shapes within, but nothing more.

Impatiently, he waited. The sun was about halfway down its descent toward the hills when the officers emerged. Everyone was still smiling. Rourke thought that through the scope, the

Army officers—a captain and a major if he read the ranks correctly—looked a little drunk. They mounted, waved, and galloped down the trail.

The man and woman watched them go. The man lit a cigar. Their voices ebbed and flowed as they walked along the porch. Rourke took advantage of the late afternoon shadows to move closer to within hearing range.

The door opened. Elizabeth Harwood, a cigar between her teeth, appeared. "Are you two crazy?" she called across at them. "What on earth made you tell them about Rourke? Would you obey orders for once and not try to think? Neither of you have ever been any good at that or we would have been set in Washington and never have had to leave it for New York City in the first place. We know how well you two did there!"

"Well, if you and Mr. Smart Britches are so high and mighty smart, how come you let this guy get in the way at all and didn't kill him?" Harwood said in reply. Rourke wondered who he meant.

"You still don't get it! The guy was a range bum, a gunfighter who drifted. The way it was supposed to work, he would be in all the places where the horses were taken so that if we needed to make him responsible, we could do that. Who would argue against the Territory if we needed a quick hanging to cover the tracks? When we planned all of this, we expected there might be a rancher who would fight back, but this was something different. The last thing we needed to tell the Army was that this cowboy was still out there riding around! If they pull out, we're out of business."

"They already knew!" the older woman argued back. "Their own man told them. Didn't you get that? They don't care what some lone rider knows. The deal is going through. The hands recovered a lot of the herd and got what they could from Treadwell and Harrison. They can't resell as many as they thought, but everyone still makes money and we have cleared away everything that was in the way. If that Rourke cowhand shows up at the fort and talks to the wrong person, this could still fall apart and there go all of our plans for this land. Now we know no one will hear him except those we want him to!"

The young woman threw the cigar from the porch onto the hard-packed dirt in front of the house. One end sent a thin trail of blue smoke upward. "They are scared of what's coming. Everyone knows Grant will get elected. When that happens, everything in the Army will be changed because he knows how they work and will want a cut. You made it sound like we had no idea how to deal with him."

"Well, did lover-boy tell you anything?"

"Of course. Maybe he didn't tell either of you because you drink too much and talk too much. If you don't like it, go back to New York and face the law there. You didn't mind getting out of New York when we planned this. Maybe you two are too old for this. Now shut up from now on except to play your parts. Don't ever change the script again or I will shoot you both."

She slammed the door behind her.

The older man and woman remained on the porch. They talked in tones too low for Rourke to hear. He waited until they went inside. Then he scrambled from his hiding place, walking stiff-legged to Star. They galloped away as the sun started to hover over the horizon.

Cal was sitting on the steps of Abigail Treadwell's house when the woman came out.

"Worried about your friend?"

Cal nodded.

"Men never understand, do they?" Abigail said. "You'd think they want to get killed the way they go about things. Then they whine like puppies if they get hurt!"

"I'm sorry about your husband."

"Pete had a short fuse. Always did. Half the reason we left Illinois was that he couldn't get along with anyone. He was a good man, though. He didn't like factories and towns and places where the people in charge treated everyone else like dirt. He didn't want his children going to work in some filthy place for the rest of their lives. That's most of why we came. When Zachariah, the eldest, got offered a job at the factory, I thought Pete was going to punch the foreman. We sold what we had, what there was. We were gone in a week. He wanted the boys to have something they could own, something no one would take away from them."

"So you're going to stay on?"

"Can't do much else," she said with a shrug. Her eyes misted. "Pete died to give the boys a home. If I left here, I'd be giving up what he died to hold. Got nowhere else to be. Pete's here. Not in the ground, but in every fence rail and every board of the house. He told me one day he'd buy me glass windows. I told Pete I wanted the boys to grow up strong. You and your man got kids?"

Cal blushed. "We're not married."

Abigail laughed. "Well, girl, don't wait too long. The trail only goes so long. Me and Pete, we didn't waste a day. I don't have much to take as comfort, but I know that there's nothing I would go back and change. Everybody dies. But you ought to grab your dream before you do." She stood up. "I better get back in. Your man will come back. He don't look like the kind that kills easy."

Cal wondered what was going on when Rourke returned tight-lipped about the Harwoods. When she asked one too many times, his retort that they didn't matter left her puzzled. They were the people behind all this, weren't they?

"I don't like being on the outside, Rourke," she said when everyone else had gone inside or into the barn to sleep.

"Cal, you ever been in the dark so deep that you don't know which way is up or down and you can't even trust your instincts because those might be wrong?"

"Rourke, you ever gonna talk in straight lines?"

He summarized the Green Hills conversations and their meaning. The Army was buying from the Harwoods, but there was a bigger game. Someone else was controlling the Harwoods. He wondered where the plan was made—Wyoming or back East. Steve Owens, the judge's son, had made a long trip there to supposedly collect the judge's inheritance. At last, he blurted out the part that he had chewed on all the way back to the Treadwell ranch. He had questions that were more important than rustling.

"The Army has its own man watching and reporting on this," he said.

"Who?"

"Cal, who knew we were at that shack?"

"You, me, Pa, and your friend, O'Toole." She looked back. Then it hit. "Oh, no!" She covered her mouth with her hands, eyes wide. "No, Rourke, it can't be. He's your friend!"

"Wheeler said something when I was in Rawhide that made me wonder. I got no proof of anything, Cal. But the way things look, Thomas might either be ordered to keep an eye on us, and he's fooling them, or he's fooling me. If the Territory is involved in this at all, that's either Andy and the judge's son, or somebody above them. Either that, or the Army is up to something and no one wants to get in their way. Then there's the railroad, and there's nothing more corrupt than the railroad."

"So you don't really know anything."

"Nope. But when I see this world, Cal, and I see all the people changing, I think maybe I see people the way they used to be and not the way they are."

"Any exceptions to that, mister?"

He had to smile. "Maybe one. And your pa."

"Right answer, cowboy. Now can we forget all this for a few minutes? For once we don't have to hide. It's a clear night and we got a nice fire. Just sit with me."

He intertwined his fingers with hers.

Then the hoofbeats pounded. "Down!" he yelled, pushing her flat as he drew the Remington.

"Halt or die!" he called to the riders, knowing that if Green Hills' raiders were coming, it would be one of the last things he ever said.

He could hear the horses reining in as the lead riders came within the faint glow of the fire. "Ain't you that Rourke fella?"

"Harrison? Gil Harrison?"

"Me and what's left of my outfit. Where's Pete?"

Rourke was silent. Abigail Treadwell and her sons came out of the house. Zeke and Evans emerged from the barn with rifles at the ready. Rourke turned to them. "Friends," he called.

He moved closer to Harrison. "Pete's dead. Green Hills came through a few days ago."

"They must have hit him first. They got us two days ago. We were out gathering strays. They rode in, killed Colby, the cook fella, and then went after the stock. We were outnumbered so we came down here, figuring maybe we could get to Pete in time to help him save something." Harrison dismounted and walked toward the house. He took Treadwell's widow's hands in his. "Abby, I'm mighty sorry. Pete was a fine man."

She invited Harrison and his men in for something to eat. Before he went in, Harrison had a message for Rourke.

"We stopped in Rawhide on the way. Nothing Wheeler could do to help out here on the range. He wanted us to tell you, if we found you, there was gonna be a posse forming together to scour the range for you. He also said there were three fellas coming into Rawhide hired by the Harwood people—with the name of Nestor. Thought that would mean something to you."

Rourke kept his face impassive. Inside, his spirits sank. The Nestor brothers were guns for hire. Not bounty hunters, but plain killers for hire. They were good at what they did. Real good. He had met them once, a year or so ago. There was an instant antagonism. They were not sure how good he was. He was pretty sure with three of them they were better than he was, so it was allowed to pass. Now, they would meet again.

News of a posse was not good, either. Even if they picked the bottom of Rawhide's barrel, when anyone put enough men on horses to scour the land, sooner or later someone was bound to get lucky. If the Territory was forming a posse, then somehow either Owens or Andy believed he had gone bad. Or, he told himself at the end of his thinking, there was something going on that he didn't actually want to admit to himself.

The first thought he had was that no one else should suffer. If the posse found them at Treadwell's ranch, a widow and her sons would be put in more danger. Now that Harrison and his men were here, they could protect the family. The shack was a trap, but Evans insisted the mine and cave were hardly known to anyone. "Then we go back there," Rourke said. "A few of us can hold off a lot of anybody else."

They rolled out of the Treadwell ranch in the early light of dawn. By midday, they had reached the cave, where they unloaded all the supplies they had from the wagon. Between the mine up the slope and the cave, they had two hiding places. The wagon went in one, with brush covering the entrance to hide it from casual riders.

"When it gets dark tonight, I'll go hunt," Rourke told Cal. Whatever else he was going to say was cut off by two quick shots in succession from the valley below. Silence followed. Two more shots.

Rourke looked Cal in the eye steadily. "O'Toole. That was our sign."

"What are you going to do?"

"See my friend. Ask him about horses."

He scrambled down from the cave and fired twice, waited, then fired twice again.

"Could ye not at least leave a map for a poor man?" bewailed O'Toole. " 'Tis lucky I am not to have been eaten whole by the heathen savages. I have ridden this forsaken land over twice waiting to find you."

"Why, what did you steal?" responded Rourke.

"Laddie, laddie, laddie. How many times would ye have starved to death without the services of Thomas O'Toole?"

They bantered as they unloaded the supplies O'Toole had loaded on his packhorse. Then Cal, with a nod at Rourke, moved back into the cave with Zeke and Evans. O'Toole and Rourke were alone. Rourke plunged ahead.

"Tell me about stolen horses and the Army, Thomas. Not what you want me to know, but all of it. The Harwoods are in this up to their necks, but they are not in it alone. There are too many dead men for secrets, Thomas. You are in this, somewhere. I need to know. We were friends a long time, Thomas."

O'Toole gazed back at Rourke. "There is that." He spat in the dirt. "The Army, God bless it, is as corrupt as the day is long, sir. The fort pays $40 per horse for nags worth next to nothing, but the War Department says they can only do business with someone who has the Army's license to sell to the Army. So, the officers, sir, found ways around the rules. I made my contribution to the cause, as ye might expect. Yon Harwood man made them a bigger offer. He would sell at half the price, as long as no questions were asked about where the horses came from. There was a legal bill of sale, but it was about as ac-

curate as the numbers we reported at roll call after Chicka-
mauga, sir. The officers were going to sell what they bought to
the other forts. I was getting a wee bit of the take, sir, for making sure the thieves outside the Army were not stealing from the
Army and that the horses got moved so's no one who might be
suspicious was the wiser.

"Breaking Army regulations, sir, is not like breaking the law.
We both know that! Captain Ross and Major Roberts, sir, were
the leaders, but Colonel Kilpatrick is sadly deficient as a com-
mander. Well, sir, something went wrong. The Harwood people
were late gathering stock. When you showed up, sir, they thought
that you might be spying for someone higher who was not in on
the business, or even the War Department. They didn't want
you to know what was going on. The truth, sir! I told the Army
you were not interested, but by then the Harwood man and his
cronies were in this pretty deep. I tried to go back to the shack
there and warn you, but you had left it and some unpleasant
folks were there instead. For days I've been hearing about riders
and horses and gunfights, but it was only now that I was free to
ride on my own."

Everything O'Toole said fit with the facts. After all, the man
had been the unofficial regimental thief when they were scouting for Cleburne in the war. He was never going to change. But
O'Toole had talked himself out of every punishment the
Confederate Army had to offer, and Rourke knew he could be
fooled by his friend.

"Green Hills men killed Pete Treadwell," he told O'Toole.
"They chased Harrison off of his land. There's something more
in this, Thomas. Something you aren't telling me."

"I told you what I know, laddie. I don't know how Harwood
got the horses. The rest is guessing. The Territory was a silent
partner. Your friend Dickinson knew about the Army's deal, but
I don't know if he was bribed to look the other way or ordered

to by someone above him, or what. The young man who is the son of that judge is an unsteady rod that is easily bent and may be in league with Harwood. He, I know, is very deep into this. The other man, I don't know, sir. Truth it is that, Rourke. But this there is: Ever since you hunted down Red Jim, there was talk that said the outlaw was once very close with powerful men, until they decided he was too unsteady and found you to silence him. Perhaps things are not what you wish them to be, Rourke."

Rourke was disappointed, but not surprised. Steve Owens lacked the character that defined the judge, which he suspected the old man knew. Rourke was far more concerned whether Owens was responding as Andy's assistant or as a feckless man making wrong judgments. As for Andy, he had to admit he did not know.

"Jamie?" Rourke looked back at O'Toole. He never heard his first name used. Almost no one knew it.

"Thomas?"

"I'll steal what I want and live the way I want, laddie, but the sun never held a day I would betray you. That's for those new people from the East, Jamie, not me."

Rourke felt ashamed.

"Now, now," O'Toole went on with a grin. "For sure when there's stealin', if you didn't suspect me, I'd feel I lost me touch."

He threw an arm over Rourke, and for a moment, all was well.

Rourke told the rest of the group the gist of O'Toole's information.

"You know," said Evans, "I know a lot of people in Rawhide. Maybe if I went there I could learn more than the rest of you. No one is out to shoot me. Then I can let you know the lay of the land. If your friend is there, Rourke, I can find him and ask him to help you."

Rourke agreed. Evans was most likely not going to be an as-
set when it came to shooting. If the man wanted to be out of
the way, it was fine with Rourke. He didn't exactly want to see
Andy right about then. Maybe it would all blow over, as it had
with Thomas. Maybe it would rain in a clear blue sky. Well, he'd
worry about that later. He took Cal aside with trepidation.

"We got two things to do, Cal. We got to deal with the
gunfighters in Rawhide, and we got to deal with the posse
because they are going to swarm out here until they find us. I
do one, you do the other. This is the best natural defensive position I have seen, so I think staying here makes the most sense. I
don't want you and Zeke out on the prairie when they find you.
Let Thomas have some of the fun, too."

She knew it was good sense, but she didn't like splitting up
again. She started to tell him, but Zeke walked over, a self-
satisfied smirk on his face. "Well, it's a good thing you two
aren't responsible for me, because I think you'd about kill me."

Rourke waited. Zeke liked winding up for a good story. This
ought to be a good one, from the start of it. "That Irish fella
and I, we don't like bein' boxed in, you know, the way we are
here. We found an old entrance that was filled in and cleared
it."

Rourke was elated. Now, Cal could escape. Rourke led the
horses around to the far side, and let them graze loose. When
the posse showed up, Cal, Zeke, and O'Toole would hold them
off as long as possible, then give themselves a good head start
and ride to Rawhide.

"You'll be in Rawhide?" Cal asked.

Rourke nodded. He didn't tell her the part about not being
sure if he would be dead or alive, but that wasn't part of the
bargain. Anyhow he had the confidence that he used to feel in
the war when a fool plan that should not have made sense was
going to work out. Cal and Rourke were finally alone for now,

Zeke having hauled away the clueless O'Toole, who had never seen his former captain have any connection to a woman.

Cal came close. Rourke held her in his arms. "You really think this is gonna work, cowpoke?" she asked him. "We could light out for Texas right now and never look back. Pa wouldn't care. This would blow over in time. I guess that would make me an outlaw's woman or something but we could change our names. No one would look for us since all this is about making sure we are dead so these people here can steal until they gorge themselves to death."

"You *really* want to let them win?" he asked.

She looked him in the eye. "No," she replied. "I don't want to bury you, either."

"Fair enough," he replied. "I promise not to get buried and you promise to cook some of that stew I like. Maybe when this is over, and there ain't nobody shooting at us for a spell, it would be a good time to talk about things."

"What things?"

"Um, marrying things."

Cal's laugh sounded like bells to Rourke. "Rourke, is that how you are trying to ask me to marry you? Your horse could make more sense!" She was smiling and laughing and there was a tear in her eye. "I guess I have to say that I will so that you don't do anything man-foolish but I've got some things we need to discuss."

"Such as?"

"I'll let you know later," she replied. "You can hardly expect a girl to be asked to shoot her way out of some scrape her cowboy got her into while making wedding plans. Next thing I know you'll be asking for food as well."

"Um. I was thinking about coffee." He was hoping she couldn't read past his façade.

"Men." He held her, and with fears they never shared, they

kissed one long, last time, until whenever—and wherever—they would meet again.

Chapter Fourteen

Rourke gazed across the rugged land en route to Rawhide, wondering for the hundredth time how a land of such rugged grace could hold so many foul people out for their own gain. It was like watching the debris of the East slowly wash out to the West, like in the Army when a pool of foul gravy would soak into that one clean piece of bread. He wondered if there was a place to ride far enough to be away from it. Perhaps the future would simply hold more and more people and less and less room for cowboys and riders. Well, the future would be what it was. First, he had to live to see it.

As the town materialized from the flat land around it, Rourke tried to plan for what he might find. The beard had grown in. Hair was a good disguise. His best guess was that in the noise and crowds of everyday chaos, no one would notice him. He was right.

Bear Wallace was the same. He warned Rourke the Nestors were at the Last Chance. He also told Rourke a man who Rourke knew was Evans had been around looking for him.

Rourke talked to Star. "Good horse," he told the animal, wondering why he never told his best friend how much Star really meant. One last pat. When a man goes out to find trouble, he never knows if he's coming back. Rourke wasn't looking to die, but he could either find the Nestors or wait until they found him. He could hear his boots crunch the dirt; feel his pulse start to race; feel his muscles relax as once again he walked through life for a meeting with death.

The Last Chance was half-filled. Hazy sunshine streamed in through filthy windows. The daytime piano player may have been even worse than the nighttime one. Rourke looked along the bar. The Nestors were not in sight. The black, curly-haired woman Rourke hoped had left town was there. She sashayed up to him boldly, her eyes cold but her phony smile as wide as the wings of an eagle.

"Well, cowboy, what brings you back to town so soon?" Louise Callahan said loudly, swaying her hips. She hushed her voice. "Smile back at me now, there, cowpoke, so your friends who are waiting for you over in the corner behind the door there in the shadow don't think much about it. You probably don't want to turn your back on them." Her voice resumed its usual tone. "Walk this way, cowboy. Let me help you cut the dust of the trail."

He could trust her or think she was leading him into a trap. Trust won. He kept his hand in the small of her back as though he was pushing her. She turned her head and laughed at him. "Not so fast, cowpoke. Girl needs a little drink, first." Then she turned all the way around as they reached the end of the long bar. "Been there all day and yesterday. One, two, or all of them. I wanted to warn you. I owe you. Now let's finish this little play. Wait here."

She started up the stairs. After about four steps, she turned. "You comin' tenderfoot, or do I have to show you how to do everything?"

All eyes in the Last Chance were on her, including those of the three Nestor brothers until Rourke appeared in their view, holding the Remington revolver with a steady, relaxed hand. Their eyes went from the muzzle to Rourke, and back. Rourke closed in slowly.

"Guns up on the table, boys." No one moved. Rourke cocked

the gun. "You really think I can't kill all three of you?"

One of the men nodded. Three Colts appeared on the table. Whatever else was under the table was anyone's guess. At least one knife, Rourke thought. Maybe one of those little guns in a boot top.

"Now both hands, boys, all of you."

They complied. Rourke holstered the Remington, and leaned on the edge of the table. All it would take is one of them to push it over and the ball could open then and there. Rourke was almost hoping they would try it.

The silence in the Last Chance was complete. Gunfighter against gunfighter happened rarely. One scrape of a boot on the floor and the lead would be flying. No one wanted to make that noise.

"Rourke." Henry, the black-bearded oldest brother with a gravelly voice, did the talking for the Nestors. Rourke knew the story. Orphaned in Kansas, Henry had raised the two younger ones himself by teaching them to be tougher and faster than the next man. Henry Nestor looked Rourke up and down, noting the blood stains that looked fresh. Men who followed the trade of gunfighting knew each other. They mostly held one another in respect, all knowing the day might come when their paths would cross with fatal consequences. His inspection for weaknesses completed, Henry Nestor spoke. "Been lookin' for you. Seems you been interfering in a man's business and the man don't like it none."

"Found me." Rourke felt the thrill of the challenge sliding down his spine. This was his world, now. He waited. Patience was survival. The ones with icy nerves lived; the ones who gave into fear died. He stood with his back to the door, inviting the world to shoot him. Henry Nestor waited, too. They had all learned the same trade in the same hard school.

"Man says you stole his horses," Henry Nestor rumbled at

last from around his beard.

"Man lied. Not stealin' when you take from a thief, Henry. Then again, you boys'd know all about that, wouldn't you?"

"There a meaning in those words of yours, Rourke?" piped up Stanley, the squeaky-voiced smallest brother whose temper was even shorter than his stature. When the fight came, Stanley would likely draw first. It was something to remember.

"Funny place, this Wyoming range," Rourke spoke again. "Seems like folks come out here with big plans to become big men no matter who they got to step on. Not my business. I want me and mine left alone."

"You and yours? You a family man now, bounty hunter?" sneered Carl Nestor, the deadliest brother. He killed because he enjoyed it. Henry and Stanley were common riders who took to killing because it paid better than riding the range; Carl was a killer plain and simple.

"Woman. Her pa, the blacksmith. They been ridin' with me."

"Heard about them. Got no bone with them," Henry Nestor said, making a gesture at his younger brother that warned him to shut his mouth. "Drunk and a girl don't mean nothin'. They got nothin' to fear from us. But we got business with you. Got hired for a job. Got a job to do until it's done. Way it is, Texas. Don't know if I would change it if I could, but since we took the man's money it's too late anyhow."

Carl Nestor had a funny look on his face, as though he heard the fine speech but it had no connection with anything he was thinking. He drummed his fingers on the table. Stanley's right hand was twitching.

Rourke looked about the room, casually, as if inspecting the wood and lamps and tables hushed with cowboys who realized they were seeing the opening act in a drama that did not have much longer to play out. He could kill the Nestors easily now. He was sure of it. But they would not be the only ones to die.

The saloon woman was watching him as if she was reading his mind. He could see her scouting places to duck for cover. Then he shook his head.

"Fella runs this place, figger he works real hard to make it pay. Figger if we got business to tend to, maybe we ought to tend to it outside, Henry. Hate to shoot up the man's place, get you boys' blood all over the floor."

Henry Nestor felt the pressure of the words. "You push too hard, Rourke."

"You can always, leave, Henry. You can ride out now while you can ride and take your brothers with you."

"Took the man's money to do the man's business, Rourke," Henry rumbled. "Don't like you much besides when you come right down to it. Way it is. Figger Carl and Stanley ain't gonna want to ride away anyhow."

Carl was grinning—an animal at feeding time. Ready to spring. Rourke nodded. "Likewise, Henry, likewise. World of difference in my book between killing a killer and killing anyone for the money, but I know a man has to eat. Don't plan not to accommodate you boys, so don't worry about that. But see here. Streets in this fool place can get busy with women and children, Henry. Men in here come by for a drink and most of 'em don't deserve to get killed for it."

He raised his voice for the challenge. "There's a place by the gallows tree past the stables. Not far from there to the graveyard, so the fellas carrying your bodies won't have far to travel. Give you a choice. Be a man and meet me there in an hour, or I'm coming back in here and kill you all."

Rourke turned and sauntered out, slowly. As if three killers with no morals were not watching him from their table.

"Hey, cowboy!"

He turned. The curly-haired woman was still on the stairs. She blew him a kiss. He tipped his hat, flipped her one of his

$20 gold pieces in hopes that would get her partway to Denver, gave the Nestors one final look, and left. He could hear the echoes of his boots on the warped wood floor as he walked, then the swish of the batwing doors as they closed behind him. One hour. Then, it would be over.

Cal had seen dust clouds dancing on the horizon from the first light of day. The cloud moved along the trail that led to their hiding place. On the flat lands, there were only so many places to look. She told the men. O'Toole grinned. He made a comment about having dinner served early. Her pa took her aside. He spoke in a soft, gentle way unlike their usual banter. "Daughter, you know you can ride out."

"You know I won't do that."

Zeke nodded. Cal didn't like the way he was acting; as if he'd already seen the future and it was grim. "Didn't think you would. Let's get ready."

The captured rifles and the ammunition had been arranged. There was nothing left to do but wait. Cal wondered what Rourke was doing. She had seen gunfights. She knew that in the end, it was over in a second. She swallowed past a lump in her throat. Pa had never taught her much in the way of prayers. She said the best one she could think of as she gazed across the flatlands.

Riders came into view. She forgot Rourke. Arms silhouetted against the sky pointed toward their refuge. A group of 40 or 50 horsemen began moving slowly on the floor of the valley beneath them. She reached for a rifle.

"Not yet, lass," said a grinning O'Toole, brogue firmly in place for the coming fight. "When they are close enough so that even a Yankee couldn't miss, we open fire. They think we are easy pickings, sweet lass. We do not want them to learn differently until we teach them a sound lesson."

She still grabbed the gun. Her nerves were jumpy. Holding onto the rifle seemed like a good idea.

"Daughter." It was Pa. O'Toole moved away. "Like I told you. Like I taught you. Like that fool Rourke taught you. Hear?"

How many hundred times had he told her to do something that way? She felt a rush of emotion. She blinked and fought it back. "I hear, Pa."

"Good girl." Zeke put his hands on her shoulders. A man not given to softness, he kissed her hair. "Good girl."

His eyes were wet. He looked as though he had something to say. Then a shout came from the riders below. They had seen the old mine entrance and the cave. They were fanning out, taking this seriously. The lead riders were about 100 yards away.

"Steady, lass, steady," chimed O'Toole. "I'll take the center and your pa can take the right. You take the left. Aim and make those first three count. Then, we give them everything we've got."

The posse moved closer. Some of them dismounted and approached on foot. They were armed and scanning the sides of the cliff. They had minutes at the most.

"Lass," whispered O'Toole, "Start the dancin'."

Cal sighted on one posse member, a thief she remembered from Rawhide. She took a deep breath, just as Pa and Rourke had taught her. Then she slowly squeezed the trigger. She didn't see the man die. She moved to the next target, hearing the eruption of noise around her as Pa and O'Toole joined in. A thunderclap of gunfire responded from the valley below. The fight of her life had begun.

CHAPTER FIFTEEN

The dark coolness of the stable was welcome for Rourke as he waited to meet the Nestors. He cleaned Star's stall and fed his friend. He told the horse how they would spend the winter. He heard his name whispered. Rourke drew his gun even though he knew the voice.

"Evans?"

The preacher moved closer, hands in the air to be sure Rourke knew he was friendly. "I've got good news, Rourke. Your friend is on his way back. He says he can clear all of this up. Apparently Harwood had some big secret deal with the Army. Anyhow, he said to wait for him."

"Andy?"

"Yes. Apparently he doesn't know anything that's gone on."

"But Andy's someplace else. How could you get in touch with him?"

Evans made a mock show of annoyance. "Rawhide got connected to the telegraph last month. I got word to the fort; they found him in that boomtown they call Cheyenne. He'll be here in a couple of days. He'll bring the Army with him and then it will all be taken care of. There's no need to meet those men. The town knows what you're planning. Do you have someone to help you kill them if they show up? I mean, it is suicidal to do anything else. You would have three against one. I'm not much of a shot but I can be there with you."

Rourke was touched by the man's courage, but shook his

head. "Never liked crowds." He was silent a moment. "Andy says to let it go?"

"Yes," said Evans. "The telegraph message said to wait for him."

Rourke swallowed. It felt wrong. He could think on it later. "Got to go, Preacher."

"Why?"

"There's a world you don't know, Preacher. Them Nestor boys, they're not gonna care about anythin' except trackin' me down. They got paid to kill me. They're gonna do it or die tryin', same's as I would if I got paid to kill them. No law can end that, Preacher. Maybe Andy can get here in time to help Cal, so you ought to head out that way to warn them. Cal ain't used to killin. It's a trade that wears on a soul."

"I can back you up, Rourke. I can find others."

The gunman smiled thinly. "My play, Preacher. I called the tune, I'll dance to it. If it don't come out right, maybe you can say a couple of words to square it with God. I never set out to do nothin' bad to nobody that didn't deserve it. So put in a word?"

"Rourke, I don't think . . ."

"Just do it, Preacher, will you? Better tell Cal that if things don't come out right, she ought to light out with Zeke. Don't want her riskin' her fool neck for nothin'. Mebbe Thomas will help them."

Evans looked at Rourke, knowing the man was set on a course that could no more be changed than the order of the seasons. "Well then, Rourke. I'll ride out there. When I come back, I will let you know that they are fine. Perhaps the posse never found them. We will all survive this, Rourke."

"You do that, Preacher." Rourke grinned loosely. "Help Cal."

Evans had seen grins like that in the war. They were found on soldiers who had already left the world behind and were at peace with that, even as they were ready to charge. Life and death no longer mattered as much as dying like a man. He wondered if Rourke didn't care or had accepted that he would lose. Both were discomforting thoughts as he rode away.

Rourke watched the preacher leave. It was time. This was as good a day as any. He was glad Cal wasn't around. There were things he didn't want her to see.

All Cal was seeing was dust. After the first fusillades, the posse had found such cover as its members could find among rocks and stunted trees. They sporadically traded shots with Cal, Zeke, and O'Toole. A respite of quiet followed. They could hear voices. Then it seemed every gun opened on the rocks at the mouth of the cave.

"Devious it is they are, lass," called O'Toole. "They want us away from the edge, or ducking, so that they can rush us."

He had barely said the words when they could see shapes moving. The posse was rushing them. Zeke moved to the edge of the cave, stood up, and fired almost straight down the side of the cliff. He let out a noise. Holding his chest, he staggered against the rocks. O'Toole kept firing. Cal, screaming, ran to her father.

"Proud of you, daughter." He was gasping. She could see at least three wounds. One was by his heart. Bright red stains dripped onto her hands. "Like your mom. Girl! Girl!"

"I'm here, Pa." She held his hands tightly.

"I love you, girl," he whispered. He strained to move, then limply slumped, eyes fixed and empty. The guns roared. Cal didn't hear. Everything she could see was shrouded by a mist of her loss. Cal knew Pa had feared dying old and alone and sick— had feared it worse than anything else. But she didn't want him to die. She held his hand, as if that could bring him back.

"Pa!" she screamed. "Pa!"

"Lass," called O'Toole, urgently. "I need you, lass."

Men with rifles had reached the bottom of the path to the cave. They were climbing up the first part of the zigzag path. Others behind trees and rocks kept up a covering fire. Cal felt the first wave of defeat as she left her father and went to O'Toole.

"Lie down flat, lass," O'Toole said. "When I stand over you and shoot, they will stop a minute to duck and take cover. Then they will all aim for me. When I duck back, you shoot. Your Rourke and I played this game in the war. Shoot fast. Shoot straight."

She moved, obedient even in heartache. She watched O'Toole, who looked unconcerned and almost happy. He, too, had a battle frenzy about him. "Now, lass," he called, standing over her and firing as fast as the rifle would work. She picked targets and fired. She hit at least two men before O'Toole jumped back.

"Other side, now," he called. "Faster. They'll be waiting."

They did it again. Two more men dropped. After a surge of gunshots, silence descended. O'Toole peeked out. No one was moving. It was late in the afternoon. O'Toole knew what came next. They would wait until night and then every man would rush the cave. He looked at Cal. He wondered if the girl would run or stay. He was of a mind to stay, but he'd wait a bit to talk with her. They still had a few hours.

Cal, sitting in silence by her father's body, had come to the same conclusion that darkness would bring an attack. If she was going to die, she wanted to die next to Pa.

"O'Toole," she called softly as the dimming of the day started to deepen the gloom of the cave.

"Yes, lass."

"We're not running."

"Yon Rourke will be angry with you. He wanted you safe."

"I'm not leaving Pa." O'Toole knew the tone. It sounded like

Rourke. Well, he'd wait and see. Enough darkness to cause mischief was still a couple of hours away. Anything could happen.

CHAPTER SIXTEEN

Rourke leaned against the gallows tree. The Nestor boys approached. He wondered about the men who had been where he was, with their last sight on earth a jeering crowd come to watch a man die. For a moment, he wondered if a tree felt all the misery around it, like the Indians said, or if it was only a tree. He chuckled, then sobered; he'd have to ask Star. Cal would surely think he had gone crazy then.

Evening was drawing near. Townsfolk had gathered. Everybody wanted to see. Nobody wanted to see too well in case a gunfighter didn't shoot straight. Shame, he thought, that this couldn't have happened in the middle of the day so everyone could have a good view.

A north wind picked up. Rourke took off his battered hat and left it on a branch. He liked the wind in his hair. He gave Cal one more thought, then put her out of his mind. Not now. Later. Doubts and fears and mortality were gone. The wind breezed around him. He was ready.

The Nestor boys walked slowly. Rourke moved away from the tree, a plain challenge and target even in the fading light. He stood with his hand by his gun, waiting. The Nestor boys walked on. Their fingers danced the way gunmen did so they could move as fast as possible in the split second that separated death from life.

There were no challenges. They had all walked out here before, to the place where men dared other men to kill them.

They felt little, if they felt anything at all. Not even hate. Just men in a time and place where the price being paid was kill or be killed.

Henry Nestor walked in the middle, eyes on Rourke. The others kept pace to the steady brother who held it together. Stanley had a sawed-off shotgun slung over his left shoulder on a strap. Carl wore two pistols. Two were for show. Shoot one right, you have everything you need. Three on one. He wondered what it would be like to have the odds on your side. He'd never known. He never would.

The Nestors spread apart as they walked closer. They knew how to do the job, he gave them that. Man didn't live long in the territory in the trade of a gunfighter without knowing how to kill. The wind gusted. He felt the cold edge of a norther once again. A smile welled up unbidden. Lorraine loved those hard cold winds. Maybe the wind meant that she was with him. Maybe it was time to finish this.

Rourke ambled forward with the deliberate pace of a man who was ready to be done with a chore. One is not supposed to brace three. One of them rules that don't matter, he reminded himself.

Rourke's movement checked the Nestors, who had expected him to stand and wait, perhaps using the huge trunk of the gallows tree as cover. He caught the glances among brothers as the unexpected planted in his opponents a seed of doubt, a ghost of fear of the unexpected, a possibility of an unknown trap. Then Henry nodded again and they continued walking toward each other. They were fifty yards apart. Rourke liked to be closer. The boys walked closer; Rourke walked as well. Blow that horn, Gabriel, he told himself. It's time for someone to die.

Death was in Cal's mind as she looked at her father's body and then at the posse men below. They were waiting for the inevitable darkness. She might live if she ran. She would die if she stayed. O'Toole might die as well. She could not be responsible for that.

"You think we should run," she said to O'Toole. It was a statement, not a question.

"Lass, I think we should stay here and kill every wee one of them for the pure enjoyment of it, but I don't know if my shooting hand is up to the job. It gets a wee bit tired without a drop, you know."

He made her smile. He and Rourke. What a pair. Well, she thought, at least she had good company at the end. "Pa hid a bottle in his bedroll. Even though he was supposed to give it up, I know it's there. Help yourself."

O'Toole made appreciative noises, scrambled to the back of the cave, then coughed and spat. "Somebody laced it with water, lassie," he fulminated. "Unspeakable."

They were quiet awhile. "O'Toole?"

"Yes, lass?"

Her voice quivered. "If you're still alive, don't let them take me alive. I know what happens to women when they fight back and they lose. You understand?"

"Now, lass. None of that talk. You should be planning the wedding. There should be something to drink, at the least, for the occasion. Leaving things like that to said Rourke, leads to important details being omitted. The man could never rescue whiskey in the war in the proper fashion, which led to no end of suffering among those of us who did the work and had the thirst, as it were."

She knew he heard her. She waited. She wanted to sit next to Pa and cry. There was no time. There was never time. She wondered where Rourke was; why he hadn't come. She had accepted she was going to die. She would take them with her. If Rourke didn't come, then he was either already with Pa or was going to be there soon. Everybody she loved was dead. She might as well join them.

Four sets of boots crunched Rawhide dirt. The Nestor boys were now twenty feet away. Rourke stopped. They did as well. Rourke felt the sudden urge to smile. He knew it was his body preparing for what came next and his soul rising to the bait of dancing with death. In this moment, he was free beyond all constraints.

He looked Henry in the eyes. One of them had seconds left to live. They both knew it. Henry kept an unblinking glare locked on Rourke. Rourke stared back and saw it in the eldest Nestor's eyes. The hard stare was part of the ritual. Then it happened.

Stanley Nestor moved first. He shifted the shotgun to spray Rourke with deadly lead. The Remington fired first; Stanley's head snapped back from the bullet that left a hole in his forehead. The shotgun went off as he fell. Pellets flew toward Carl Nestor, who was drawing his guns when the ground at his feet turned to rippled dust from the blast of the shotgun. Both guns fired wildly. Rourke's second and third shots slammed him backwards with the force of a mustang's kick.

Two down. But one remained. Henry Nestor fired four times in quick succession. The bullets sailed toward Rourke's head where he would have been standing if he had stood his ground. Rourke threw himself to the ground and rolled in the dirt. He came up firing his last three shots. A bullet sailed high over his head. He pulled the throwing knife from his boot and took aim.

Henry Nestor slowly wobbled forward. The man's face blended surprise with pain. His gun was in his right hand. Its aim was wandering. The weight of the iron was more than Henry's hand could bear. It pointed at the ground and fell there. Henry toppled to his knees, then face down in the dust.

Rourke rolled him over. Two hits in the chest. Rourke didn't know he had been holding his breath until he exhaled loudly. It sounded like a tornado. The gunplay had barely lasted a minute. It was quiet now.

Henry Nestor was trying to talk. Blood bubbled from his dust-caked mouth. His breath rattled; his eyes darted, and his face was white. The blood began to seep onto the ground. His eyes looked up at Rourke.

"We'll bury you boys together Henry," Rourke spoke, not unkindly, as he squatted down next to the dying gunfighter. He had to kill them, but now that it was over, it seemed a waste. He lifted the man up. Henry licked his lips. The dying were always thirsty. "Let it go, Henry. Whoever's waitin' for you across the river is gonna see you soon. Think about that, not what you leave behind."

Henry's eyes saw something other than the Wyoming sky. He mumbled a woman's name. Rourke waited. Henry's eyes bored into Rourke's face. There was something more Nestor was struggling to say.

"Judas." The word from Henry's dying mouth was clear. Then Henry Nestor's arm jerked toward Rourke. He grabbed him tightly. Whatever hadn't been said mattered to the man. Rourke bent to catch the whispered final words.

Rourke closed Henry Nestor's dead eyes and laid his head on the ground. Rourke folded the man's hands and went into Henry's pockets, where he pulled the gold pieces that had been their pay. Rourke spared him one last look, walked past the other two bodies, and walked toward the stable.

"Make sure they get buried decent, Bear," he said as he mounted Star, throwing some of Henry Nestor's gold pieces into the man's massive hands. "Get it done right. I'll be back. This ain't finished yet." He rode off in a gallop. Three bad men died because worse ones were on the loose. It was high time to set things to right. He urged Star to gallop. There was more business that had to be done. But first, there was Cal.

Darkness had fallen. Neither Cal nor O'Toole had spoken in an hour. Instead, they had loaded every gun. Her handgun, the new one Rourke gave her, was in her belt and ready. She still had lots of shells for the gun, and was planning on using every one of them. She could hear noises below.

She kicked her boot on the rocks. O'Toole didn't come. "O'Toole," she whispered fiercely.

"Easy lass. Move away now. 'Tis time for a surprise."

O'Toole, pushing a good-size boulder, moved closer to the edge. He went back and rolled a second one to the lip of the cave. "We can hide behind these for cover, lass, if we want, or roll them down on the poor lads when they're getting close," he said, a smile breaking white in the darkness. "That Alamo Rourke talked about will be nothing to this!"

Cal could feel his irrepressible spirit rouse her to battle. This must have been how he and Rourke fought their way through the war—defying the odds and making light of death. "Let's light up the night, Thomas," she said.

They took positions behind the boulders. "Lass?"

"O'Toole?"

"If there is not time later for such things, after the dancin' is over, 'twas a pleasure doing business with you, lass."

"All mine. Shoot straight."

He saluted. She thought of Rourke. Her eye started to mist. Not now, she told herself. Make them do the crying.

A posse member fired. Another. Then several more. It was time! Cal and O'Toole fired back. O'Toole hummed an Irish ditty as he fired methodically into the darkness.

"A lovely way to pass the time, lass," O'Toole said once when changing a rifle for one with ammunition.

"You and Rourke enjoy the same amusements." Cal smiled back. Bullets from below knocked rock chips off of the roof of the cave. Firing from below escalated. This was their last stand!

It was not. Eventually, the flare of firing flickered away. Whatever plans the posse had been developing, they had been foiled. Cal could hear arguing. She guessed the posse would wait them out—or starve them out. Maybe they could escape after all if the horses were where they had been left. Maybe not. Morning would tell. It would be enough, she thought, just to see the light after this darkness.

CHAPTER SEVENTEEN

Time crawled. The night refused to end. Cal crept to the edge of the cave. If she could ignore the men there to kill her, the night could have been beautiful. Every star God had ever made was on display. O'Toole was checking the cave for any ammunition they might have overlooked, because their last scrape had used up a lot of bullets. They had enough left for one last charge—if that. Cal's initial elation at survival had faded into a grimmer assessment of their chances. They were weary, worn, and wounded from dozens of small cuts inflicted by rocks and ricochets.

"O'Toole."

"Lass."

"Thank you."

"For what, lass?"

"Staying."

"Lass, it's a hard time in a hard world. The rules out here don't mean as much as the wind. Rourke is a friend, lass. He saved me life. The poor man is sadly afflicted with the need to do right in a world that always does wrong, but you can't reform him. Lord knows I tried in the war. Now rest."

Cal could hear every sound from the valley floor. Nothing much. Then one sound caused her to focus on the dim distance. One horse, riding hard. A messenger?

Should she tell O'Toole that someone was riding fast toward the posse? Another attack would be coming. He had slouched

217

against the wall of the cave, apparently asleep. She shook her head at his ability to nap.

"Only resting, lass," he said, stretching. "A trick we all learned in the war—sleeping while we were awake. Are you here to tell me breakfast is cooking?"

She told him about the rider she had heard. But there was nothing now. Maybe it was nothing. She started to relax. Then she heard it again. A lone horse. Galloping. A shrill scream. Gunshots! She grabbed a rifle. The gunfire was not aimed at the cave. It was aimed at the posse!

Yellow dots of flame from the barrels of the guns looked like the winking bolts of an avenging angel. Whatever was going on down there, somebody was attacking the posse. In the desperate hours before dawn there was new hope in her heart.

Rourke guided Star with his legs as he fired every round he had from the Remington and the spare Colt. There was no time to reload. He put both pistols back in their holsters and pulled out the Winchester, firing at anything that moved.

Rifle fire from the cave joined in. It intimidated the posse, who were probably already dispirited from lack of success, lack of sleep, and too much liquor. The greatest enemy of all—fear— had conquered the posse. The results were swift.

"Don't shoot," came the first voice. Others took up the chorus. The sweepings of the Rawhide streets had signed up for some easy money to round up an old man and a young girl, not put their lives on the line. They all surrendered.

"Throw down the guns and raise your hands high," Rourke roared, putting the rifle in its scabbard and reloading his pistols while there was a lull. "Now, or every mother's son of you dies."

Rourke fired over their heads, in case someone was thinking of a sneak shot under the cover of darkness. "I saw that," he said, hoping no one called his bluff. "Anyone else tries anything, you're all dead."

He called up to the cave. "Thomas, if your siesta is over, can you come down and round up the prisoners? Cal? Zeke? Cal!?"

"Aye, sir, your Generalship, sir," responded O'Toole's lively banter. "The lass and I will be there as soon as we dress to prepare for company. A little tired we are from all of the dancin' and fiddlin' but perhaps if there's a wee drop to be had I might bestir meself."

"Hey, cowboy!" called Cal, putting up the front Rourke would expect. "O'Toole and I were planning a final attack for the morning and you ruined it!"

"Want me to leave so you two can have all the fun to yourselves?"

"Don't trouble yourself!" she called down. "You'd only get lost and we'd have to rescue you." The façade grew tiresome soon. "Oh, Rourke!" she exclaimed softly, too softly for him to hear as she walked down the path. "Why weren't you here sooner?"

In time, twenty sullen men were grouped together under O'Toole's watchful eye. Cal had started a bonfire for light. A handful of posse members had been wounded beyond caring. Unmoving shapes dotted the valley floor. Cal counted twenty bodies.

As the peak of crisis flattened, Cal took Rourke aside to tell him the bad news privately. "They got Pa," she said, trying not to cry again. "It was quick. He's up there. I . . . I figgered I was gonna join him during the night, Rourke. I pretty much thought you already had."

"Not today, Cal. Not today." He put his arms around her, then pushed her aside as a horse galloped across the Plains. "Get down; get behind cover." Rourke held the Remington sighted on the rider racing like a fool in the dark.

"Hello! Hello! Rourke?" It was Evans. Rourke, relieved, answered.

The preacher rode into the glow of the firelight and looked around him, slack-jawed. "How did you get here before I did?" the preacher asked. "I . . . oh, I could never find my way."

"Preacher, could you help Thomas keep an eye on those folks? Take a gun. Don't matter if you can shoot or not, the fight's out of them."

Evans helped guard the posse members. Rourke and Cal walked up to the cave to see Zeke. In the light of the match Rourke struck, Zeke looked peaceful, at last. He had lived life on his own terms, and had never bowed to the world around him. He had taken its blows without complaint. Now he was past all of it.

Rourke put an arm around Cal's shoulders. He was too tired for fine words. They sat on the cave floor a few feet away from Zeke. The sky in the east was promising a dawn Cal had thought she might never see. The light would be coming soon. She could close her eyes and rest.

A gun fired below them. Two answering shots rang out.

Rourke and Cal clambered down from the cave. Evans was running and yelling, panic-stricken. O'Toole? Where was Thomas? He was standing against the rocky face of the path that led up to the cave, on the other side of the group of posse members from where Evans had been stationed. He was holding his ribs. There was a gun smoking in his hand. A few feet away, one of the posse members was lying flat.

"Thomas!"

"Hello, lass," O'Toole gasped. Red drops landed on his shirt. "A wee bump, laddie. What's a wedding without dancing?" O'Toole wore a smile Rourke had seen on too many faces during the war—faces already seeing what waited beyond. "I'm dry, Rourke. Me old grand would be aghast. There should be a wee drop for the groom's man."

"Thomas, sit down. Let me see what's wrong."

O'Toole slid down the rocks. The gun slipped from limp fingers.

"Move a step and I will kill you," Cal snarled at someone behind Rourke.

Rourke pulled up O'Toole's shirt. He'd been shot in the chest. Blood was flowing steadily over Rourke's hands.

O'Toole's voice was just above a whisper. "Your Captain-Generalship Lordship and Excellency . . ."

"Thomas, don't talk. Let me stop the bleeding."

"Them damn horses. Thievin' will be the death of ye is what me old grand would tell me. Don't you worry, sir. I've got a drink waiting on the other side, sir. Saint Peter himself will have a bottle for a thirsty man."

"O'Toole!"

Rourke was using his jacket trying to stop the blood, but it was useless.

"Laddie," O'Toole winced and breathed in raspy gasps. "We've seen too many wounds to be tellin' tales. I never wanted to die old. Your lass . . ." O'Toole swallowed. "I never betrayed ye, laddie. Never. Not me. Kill them all, laddie. Kiss the lass for me . . . at the weddin'." His head dipped.

"Thomas?"

For a second, Rourke thought O'Toole saw him. A smile passed across the bloody stubble of O'Toole's face and froze there as the light faded behind O'Toole's eyes. The war was finally over for Thomas O'Toole—the war he had waged against every rule he ever met, a war that was leading him places Rourke had feared would cost him a friend.

There was a noise behind him. Boots scuffling. Rourke drew even as he knelt over O'Toole's body.

Evans threw up his hands. "I thought we took all their guns, Rourke. I . . . I'm sorry."

"Don't fret on it, Preacher," Rourke replied sadly. "Thomas

always said that if the rules caught up with him one day, he would escape. He did."

Cal, after dumping on the ground a few extra pistols that had not earlier been surrendered, stood next to Rourke. "I want to bury Pa. We can bury Thomas with him. Then we finish it, Rourke. Me and you. We got a score to settle. First we got to bury our dead decently."

He nodded. Rourke had seen men die in the war, and he never believed where they were buried determined what happened to their souls, but he would have done anything Cal wanted.

To her, one piece of dirt was as good as the next. Pa was gone. No ceremony would bring him back. He was with God and her mother now and she was glad he had made it home. She was glad he was free. But she would always miss him. Children buried their parents; it was the natural order of life. Knowing that didn't make it easier.

Rourke thought of O'Toole—the laughter in the face of death at Murfreesboro; the piles of food "liberated" at Chattanooga. The irrepressible friend who always had his back. And at the end, Rourke had feared betrayal. What was the world becoming, he asked, when you bury a friend you almost lost because you couldn't trust anyone?

The blue in the east was starting to lighten. A tiny scimitar of moon poked over the hills in the west, barely visible. "Injuns tell a story, Cal. They say that a moon like that rises when the Spirit they worship comes to collect the souls of the dead and take them to where there's no cold and no war and no pain. Kind of like the Ferryman of the Dead. Zeke's time, girl. Thomas' time, too. Maybe they are lookin' down on us."

Cal waved to the stars, then sobbed. "Maybe he wasn't much of a father the way some people look at things, but there was never a moment of my life that I didn't know that he cared for me. I'm never going to know that again." Rourke had no words for that. He held Cal when she cried. Whoever was responsible for this was going to pay.

Riders! He grabbed his guns; Cal was scrambling for hers.

"Rourke! Caledonia!" A woman's voice?

"Here, Abby!" Cal called.

About twenty riders appeared. "Gil said there was only one place that would be easily defended. Crazy Fritz's old mine!" she said. "We agreed that if Green Hills was not going to come to us, we ought to take it to them!"

Riders from both ranches, including Treadwell's sons, were there. Cal blinked back tears. People who had lost everything came to help her. Eastern people would never understand—this was what living in the West was all about.

"Rourke, who are these people?" asked Harrison, waving at the remnants of the posse.

Rourke explained that they were Rawhide's loafers and drifters; the only ones who took up Owens' offer. Rourke set the ranchers and their riders to watching the posse members. If only they had been there a couple of hours earlier. Perhaps Thomas would be alive. No. Do not go back. Thomas should have died a hundred times in the war. So should he. What was, was.

Evans was overseeing the digging of a grave at the foot of the cliff using tools found in the old mine. The posse members were good for something. Rourke and O'Toole laid Zeke and Thomas in the grave together. Evans stood over the grave as Cal, dry-eyed, looked on. Evans looked at her, at the land that saw all human frailty and looked on in impassive, rugged beauty, and felt again the smallness of life in the vastness of creation. What could words add to this?

"There is no greater love than to lay down one's life for ones that we love," Evans said. "We commend our brothers Thomas and Ezekiel to you, O Lord. We will see them again when we cross the river to rest with them in the shade of the trees with You. They were good men who loved the life you gave them, and enriched the lives of others. We thank you for sharing their lives with us."

Rourke took the shovel and covered Thomas and Zeke, taking care that the dirt not make the sounds he remembered too well from the war when frozen soil met the hurriedly buried dead.

The posse members, a pitiful lot in defeat, told the story. Owens had recruited them and paid them. They didn't mean any harm; they thought they were chasing rustlers, if they thought at all beyond the free whiskey and reward money. The ranchers and their riders guarded them as they set off for Rawhide. Rourke and Cal had other plans.

"We got plenty of help," Harrison offered.

"It's personal," Cal replied.

Cal and Rourke were riding across the flatlands along a familiar trail when Cal pulled up sharply. "Cal?" Rourke called out, riding back. Then he realized her face was a mass of wetness. He lifted her out of her saddle and onto Star. They rode at a walk; he held her like a child. He could feel the dampness spreading into his shirt as she buried her head into his shoulder. Rourke stopped riding, dismounted, and carried her to the shade of an oak. He stroked her hair and held her.

"Rourke, what are we going to do?"

"Make them pay."

Cal felt a chill. This was not the man who teased her and kissed her; it was the man she heard snippets about—the remorseless killer who never rested until he tracked down his quarry. She wasn't sure what that meant for them, for tomorrow. But for now, this man was the man she needed. "Rourke? I don't want them to talk their way out of this."

He nodded. That was the plan, anyhow. He hadn't quite been sure about the women. The war left scars. Screaming women fighting off raiding troopers was one of them. But these women were not victims. They schemed; their plotting led to Zeke's death. He hoped he could remember that when it counted.

CHAPTER EIGHTEEN

Green Hills was unchanged and appeared deserted. Rourke hoped the Treadwell woman and her boys were safe with the riders guarding the posse. Then he thought of Thomas and Zeke. He could not even protect his own! Then he looked at Cal. Revenge would never bring Zeke back, but it was all he had to give. And Thomas? Cal had told him the way the Irishman had kept her spirits alive during the shootout. He could have run any time. Rourke felt shame that he hadn't trusted his friend more.

"Rourke? You got something like a plan or do we ride in and kill anything that moves?"

Rourke outlined the plan. He would ride up to the house and take them from the front. Cal would find a spot above and behind the house on the hill. Whatever happened, she was not to show herself until the end. If they surrendered, that was one thing. If not, Cal would come at them from one side, Rourke from the other. Rourke expected none of them would fight. Cal was hoping they would.

Rourke watched the girl move through the tall grass and trees. He didn't worry that she would not be ready. He was worried she might be a hair too ready. He hadn't told her everything. There was something he needed to know for sure. He'd been wrong about Thomas O'Toole. He did not want to make another mistake.

Rourke readied the Winchester in his hands and nudged Star

forward. He was about forty yards from the house when two horses bore down on him—one from each side of the house where they had been hiding. Rourke had thought it looked too easy. He downed the rider on the right with his first shot. The second was intimidated by his partner's death and put up his hands.

"Throw down the guns," Rourke ordered.

A rifle opened from the house. Somebody inside was yelling. The shots went wide. Had to be Easterners shooting, Rourke thought. Time to show them what shooting really was.

Rourke methodically turned the rifle on the house. Glass windows carted from St. Louis at phenomenal cost were shattered in seconds. He swiveled back to cover the Green Hills rider. "Want to die, boy, or you want to live?"

The rider threw his rifle into the brush. Rourke ordered him to lie face down, arms out. The young man's horse ambled away. Rourke turned back to the house. No one inside had answered his fire.

"Get out here now, all of you," he called. "I know you're in there." Nothing. He shouted louder. "Get out here!" No answer. They had to be hiding, trying to line up a shot without being spotted. Well, he had asked nicely. Enough words. He reloaded the rifle. Time for his brand of talk.

Rourke kicked Star into a gallop. After three trips back and forth across the house's once-immaculate and now pockmarked front, not a shard of glass remained. Dust from the bullet-riddled walls was starting to blossom where the windows had been. Shots had been fired, but they were not close. Out of range, he reloaded for another pass.

"Last chance before I come in there and kill you," he called. He could hear voices inside. No one emerged.

Before he could open fire again, Harwood opened the door, followed by two women, dust-covered and coughing. They stood on the porch with empty hands in the air. They were covered in plaster dust and cowering in defeat. Rourke was not close enough to see what was in their eyes.

Rourke dismounted. "You, join them," he said to the rider. The young man, who had not moved, scuttled over to join the hapless group, his hands shoulder high in the air.

Keeping his rifle trained upon them, Rourke barked the most important question. "Where's Owens?"

"Gone," replied Harwood, still choking on plaster dust. "Left us behind. Heading for San Francisco."

Cal moved closer as the Harwoods talked and whined to Rourke. She was sure they lied. She wanted a clear shot at the back door. Owens had been Rourke's friend. Betrayal hurt him deeper than he let on. Rourke wasn't telling her everything. Maybe Rourke didn't want to kill Owens because of O'Toole. But she was more than ready to do it for him.

The back door's knob turned. The door opened soundlessly. Owens. The coward closed the door quietly. He moved onto the porch, a rifle in his hand. That was the game—pretend to surrender so Owens could pick off Rourke. Owens had taken off his shoes. He didn't get two steps. Cal pulled the trigger slowly. The rifle's boom seemed overly loud. Owens was slammed to the porch. His rifle clattered across the wooden slats.

Rourke ran around the house, leaving the Harwoods behind. "Cal?" he called out.

"He had a rifle, Rourke," she called. Grim-faced, she moved down to meet him. "He was going to shoot you down from hiding; that's what a real good friend he turned out to be."

Rourke rolled him over. Blood had seeped from Owens' mouth and caked on the plaster dust that clung to his face. The wound was mortal. Cal didn't miss. "Why, Owens, why?"

"Money to be made, Rourke. Had to borrow to bury the judge. The inheritance . . . was worthless." He was gasping.

"You never understood . . . money out there waiting. There's money. Big money. Big money. We were going to be . . . money . . . rich and powerful, Rourke. Rich . . . powerful . . ."

As the life faded from the young man, Rourke looked sick. The judge and the judge's son were like family. Cal was transfixed watching Rourke. Out of the corner of her eye, she saw motion. Something moved behind Rourke!

Two guns fired together. Rourke spun around and drew his Remington. Elizabeth Harwood was on her knees, swaying and moaning. A tiny wisp of smoke rose from the small pistol in her right hand. She was staring past Rourke. Cal fired again. The woman soundlessly collapsed like a rag doll. The gun skittered along the porch.

"This new toy here really does shoot a mite to the left, Rourke," Cal said with no more emotion than discussing last year's weather. "Just a mite. Maybe I can do better on the next one. Should only need one shot." She looked him in the eyes with the anger still hot on her face. Cal had settled a score he didn't know had existed. "Told you once before that them Eastern women can't do nothing right," she said, holstering her pistol. She walked over and prodded the body with her boot. "Leave her for the buzzards."

"Law gets funny about dead folks, Cal," Rourke replied. "Throw her on a horse. The law in Rawhide can decide what they want to do with her."

"Not digging her any grave, Rourke," Cal said.

"Not askin' you to, Cal."

"Ain't gonna pick her up if she falls off the horse."

"I understand, woman!" he snapped. He took a deep breath. "Cal, we have to bring in her body. Law gets in a fuss over rich folks. Way it is. Keep them covered while I see what's in the house."

"Not liable for what happens if they move, Rourke."

Rourke looked at the Harwoods and the rider. "Then you all better sit still." He went inside.

Chapter Nineteen

Rourke let the lone Green Hills rider leave after he buried his comrade. The rider, not much more than a boy, had no idea what his outfit was all about, Rourke decided. Even if he did, there had been enough killing.

The Harwoods talked plenty on the ride to Rawhide. The plan had been hatched back in New York City. Harwood would push other ranchers out of business or into warfare with each other, then use the power of the territorial government to own the range. Harwood insisted he had no role other than to be the front. His wife was actually his wife, more or less. They had been in cahoots together for years back East. Their supposed daughter worked for the group's anonymous leader. She had recruited Owens back in New York City, and had enlisted the Harwoods as fronts.

Rourke was astounded when Harwood told him the real goal had nothing to do with horses. "By spring, there will be trains running from Wyoming to the East that can ship our beef to all the big cities. All that grazing land these fools have never used right can be range for cattle. Even if we have to drive them a day's ride to the trailhead, they will be a lot fatter than longhorns driven up from Texas. The money to be made will be beyond anyone's wildest dreams. I had hoped that it could all be done without any violence, Rourke. I am not a violent man. But this Wyoming Territory of yours is a violent place."

Red Jim had been working for them, but he became too wild.

Rourke had thrown a scare into them, because no one knew what Red Jim had told him. They were afraid he would spot the scheme so he was to be set up as a patsy who could take the blame. They confessed everything they knew or suspected. They begged repeatedly for their lives, having seen Cal in action and heard her ask Rourke more than once for permission to kill them both. They knew Rourke by reputation. They kept eying the younger woman's body as it jostled across the back of a horse. Rourke figured they were telling the truth. Nothing like staring at a dead body to encourage people to speak the truth.

When they reached Rawhide, Rourke told Cal to deliver the Harwoods to jail.

"Cowboy?" She was solemn as she looked at him.

"Got to see a man about a horse," he said. "Don't kill them yet."

"I'll think about that," she replied, motioning the Harwoods along down the main street.

Rourke rode Star to the stable, took off his saddle, and tossed it aside. There was a sense of finality in him, as if everything that had been was passing away. Get on with it, he told himself. Get the job done. Then move on and move out. He checked the gun. Full. It was time for a reckoning.

Dickinson's home was deserted. Rourke pounded on the door. The frightened clerks at the territorial offices assured him they had not seen Dickinson in days. Rourke went to find Wheeler.

A crowd had gathered by the town jail, across the street from the Last Chance. The defeated posse had arrived a short time ago, attracting a crowd. Its members were sitting on the duck-boards by the jail, waiting. A squad of soldiers had arrived. But on whose side? Andy Dickinson was talking fast and gesturing to someone standing at the far side of the press of people.

Rourke saw the Eastern suit, the derby hat, and the waxed

mustache. He tried to look past them to find a man he used to know. Wheeler was standing by the jail looking at the Harwoods with undisguised contempt. Cal was pointing at the Harwoods and talking to Wheeler. An Army officer was there too, looking angry. Rourke could read the look the soldier was giving Dickinson. The Harwoods looked frightened as the red-faced officer yelled. Well, they were getting what they deserved. No, he thought again, they were alive. Zeke, Treadwell, and Thomas were not.

Andy Dickinson moved smoothly around the crowd surrounding Wheeler. Rourke watched him study the Harwoods intently. Rourke had no intention of accosting the man. The law was the law. When it was handy, it ought to be respected. The Army could dispense justice. Papers from the Green Hills house hung facts on the story the Harwoods had told. Rourke looked for the shoulders with the largest amount of gold braid. He headed for them. He wanted to speak to the officer Thomas said was not corrupt.

Dickinson was moving to intercept Rourke. He was extremely animated as he spoke to passersby and his eyes flickered between Rourke and the Harwoods. When Andy was next to him, Rourke smelled liquor on Dickinson's breath and saw sweat on his forehead.

"Rourke, I got here as fast as I could. I had no idea Owens was in cahoots with these people. The Army is grateful, Rourke, for all you have done. I was completely fooled! We need to discuss a new owner for Green Hills, and with what I already told the Army and my influence as assistant territorial administrator, I think it could be you! Think of the possibilities for your future, man!"

"It's over, Andy," he said in a flat, dead tone.

"What do you mean?" Dickinson looked genuinely puzzled.

"Judge's son wasn't smart enough to have thought of this

himself. Don't know why you set me onto him, but if I had to guess, you wanted him to take the fall if things went bad. You told me once you had connections in New York City where this evil got brewed. You put this together, Andy. Cal's pa is dead. My old friend is dead. Pete Treadwell is dead. You got to answer for that."

"Rourke, you have had some hard days. You don't know what you're saying. A man in my position has connections in many places. Whatever these people are saying, you have to consider who they are—sweepings of the East!"

"I do know. You set me up to do your dirty work, like you set up Owens and Red Jim, but it got out of hand. It's over. Them Harwood folks talked like birds singing. But that ain't all, Andy. Before he died, Henry Nestor told me who hired him. Even men who do somebody else's dirty work got more principles than you."

Dickinson's smile fell away. "Rourke, you can't make allegations like that without proof."

Rourke sighed. Until that minute, he had hoped that Andy would convince him that he was wrong. Now, he knew. The man he thought was his friend had changed into someone he didn't want to know. "Judge was the only one I worried about needing proof. There ain't no court in the world ever gonna hear about this, Andy."

"Are you threatening me?"

"Promising."

"Rourke . . ."

"You and all those Eastern dreams about money. You got the world out here for nothin' Andy. There's enough land, enough sky, enough wind out here for everyone to share. You got greedy."

Dickinson laughed. "Rourke, you are a fool. I am the assistant territorial administrator. Do you really think that a tale about rustlers and conspiracy will hold water? It will be my

word against the word of criminals you yourself have turned over to the Army. You cannot get the words of a dead gunfighter admitted to a court. Will anyone believe stories told by corrupt Army officers or a scout who stole for them? Rourke, you have nothing."

Dickinson threw an arm over Rourke's stiff shoulders and led him across the street. "Rourke, heed the advice of a friend. No one is going to care. Men are getting rich, taking control of the future, and dreaming big dreams. This territory will be a state soon. Some people I know very well will have power beyond what you can imagine. You don't understand what opportunity there is here. You do not have the ability to fathom how much a man like me can change this Territory for the better. A few horses and a few lives are nothing in the big picture, Rourke. You stole horses in the war. No one called you a rustler then! You killed men in the war. You are not a murderer! Sometimes plans go astray, Rourke. Do not lose out on the future by look-ing back. The people I know in high places can make life so much better for you, or so much worse. You must consider your future, if you are going to be responsible for that young lady."

Dickinson's voice had grown in volume and confidence as he talked. He had persuaded men to do his will before. He could do it again. The lure of power and wealth was universal.

Rourke looked at Dickinson for a long time without speak-ing. A sigh like the last breath of a dying man escaped Rourke's lips. A false smile bloomed on Dickinson's face. It widened as Rourke nodded.

"A night's rest will make a world of difference, Rourke. In the morning, you will thank me."

"I guess a man has to know when it's over, Andy. Everything ends."

Dickinson frowned at those words. He nodded to someone behind Rourke. Lloyd Jeffries emerged from the crowd, hands folded on the buckle of his gun belt. Rourke turned his back on Dickinson. As he moved to face Jeffries, he caught sight of Cal. She watched him as she talked with Wheeler. Panic transformed her face. She grabbed for her gun. Above and behind him a woman screamed. Gunfire exploded on the street. Rourke acted on instinct.

Dickinson was open-jawed and staggering. He gripped a derringer in his right hand. He was looking away from Rourke. Lloyd Jeffries returned the look. Jeffries' unfired gun was pointed at Dickinson, as though the reeling man was a threat. Red dripped from Dickinson's mouth and from the hole in his chest where Rourke's bullet landed. Cal was yelling. To Rourke, the sound was like a muffled, distant thunderstorm. Was she hurt? He lurched in her direction, then recoiled. Ten feet from her, the Harwoods lay in the street. They had been shot and wounded. Had Cal shot them?

Wheeler tipped his hat to a woman with long black curls who was leaning out of a window above the Last Chance. She was pointing at something. Rourke looked. In the middle of the Rawhide street lay Caroline Dickinson. A shotgun was next to her. Rourke had not seen her. He looked up at the woman above the Last Chance. He tipped his hat to Louise Callahan as well. She was too busy blowing Wheeler a kiss to notice him.

Lloyd Jeffries moved closer. "Runnin' a game on the Army sounded like fun, Rourke. Don't get that much fun often. Guess the fun had to end." He paused. "Man hired me. Man wanted too much for what he paid. I ain't a back-shooter, Rourke."

"Owe you again."

Jeffries shook his head. "My cousin, Earl, saw him with the Nestors. They killed some of our kin in Nebraska. I'd call it even. Heard about your friend, the Irishman. Liked him. Sorry."

They watched Dickinson die. He stared at Rourke, face contorted. His mouth making inarticulate sounds. His right arm tried to raise the derringer. Dickinson took one final step, half-fell trying to take another one, and fell face down. The gun slipped from his hand. The assistant territorial administrator lay in the dirt of Rawhide's street.

Rourke stood over the dying man without touching, without speaking. He watched silently as the red stain spread into the dirt, then stopped. He watched a tremor slide through the body, disconnected from it as though it was somebody else standing over a friend—a friend who had betrayed him.

Rourke holstered his gun. Something hazy and wet was making it hard for him to see just then. Bystanders who had backed away at the sound of the gun were now surging forward.

Jeffries melted away.

"Lloyd!" The man turned. "Pete Treadwell's widow needs good riders, Lloyd. Steady work and good work."

"Maybe," replied Jeffries. "Maybe, Rourke. Maybe Wyoming's getting too small. One of the cowboys said down in New Mexico, place called Lincoln County, they need cowboys who can shoot. Maybe we can start fresh. The range here has a long memory. Don't want no more Wyoming winters anyhow, Rourke." He pulled the brim of his hat as a salute and was gone. Lloyd and his cousins rode away to another place, another job.

He was being pushed and shoved as townsfolks ran to see what they could see. Someone grabbed his arm, hard. He pulled away.

"Do that again, cowboy, and I kick you where it hurts!"

Rourke blinked. Wet eyes saw Cal, inches away.

"You hit?" He shook his head. "Darnedest thing. That fancy lady gave the Harwoods both barrels. Got 'em pretty good. I thought she was coming for us. Wheeler's woman warned us, but he was too slow. I downed her. Why'd she do that, Rourke?"

Rourke understood. With him dead, with the Harwoods dead,

the case against Dickinson would melt away. Then the Dickinsons could hold onto their power. Then Cal understood. Caroline had seen everything she had ever wanted falling apart. She was not going to sit by and watch it all be taken away. Cal knew that feeling. She just shot straighter.

Rourke stared at the corpses. Cal put her arms around Rourke. He was unresponsive. She heard him curse, then looked behind her.

Wheeler was striding forward with an Army officer in tow. "Colonel Kilpatrick, this is Rourke."

"Sheriff, can't this wait?" asked an exasperated Cal.

"Let's get it done, Cal," Rourke said, gently. Rourke ran down the scheme. "The Army was the ultimate buyer for all the horses, Colonel, with the new forts you are planning. When the range was clear of horses, Harwood and Andy and Owens were going to grab the land and make a killing raising beef. We got papers from Green Hills. Andy's house will have some. Don't matter now. Guess no jury's gonna hear a word of it, even if the Harwoods live."

Kilpatrick promised to see to the matter. He mentioned something about the land and a reward. It didn't matter. Nothing mattered. He'd killed a friend who was already dead to him, only Rourke didn't understand that yet. Thomas dead. Zeke dead. Andy gone. Judge's son gone. Gone and dead.

Vacantly, Rourke watched Wheeler and Kilpatrick fade into the crowd. Until a few minutes ago, this had been important; this had been his whole life. Now it was over. He didn't want to ever think about it again. He wanted to find Star and put so many miles behind him that his thoughts could never ride the trail back. Rourke pushed through people, making his way to the stable.

"Rourke!" Cal ran after him. "Forget something?"

He didn't stop. "Like what?"

"Me." She stepped in front of him.

Rourke took off his battered hat, running his fingers through his hair again. "It ain't I don't care, Cal. I never thought I would feel for a woman again like I do for you. I just shot a man I thought was a friend. I don't know what comes next. The Army will be cleaning up this mess for weeks. I don't want to be around. They will say somebody won. Nobody won, Cal. I don't know about the future, girl. I thought I did. I thought I knew a lot I never did. When you lie out there with the stars, you think everything is possible. When you wake up, none of it is real. None of it." He put his hands on her shoulders and gently moved her aside.

"I'm real, Rourke," she told him. "All that is real." She waved her arms toward the mountains. She dug her hand into his arm. Hard. He winced. Her nails hurt. There, she had his attention. She needed to help him, to reach him. He hurt so badly it was painful to see.

She blocked his path again and glared right into his eyes. "You know, Rourke, they tell me there's a place up north where nobody bothers a soul for months on end except an Indian looking to see if there's anything worth stealing." She was staring right into his soul. "Think maybe we should find it, Rourke, you and me and Star? See if the winter way up there past the settlements is really what they say?"

He seemed to really listen. "You know what you're saying, girl?"

"Figger somebody's got to take care of you since you'd have gotten shot today without somebody to warn you." There was a challenge in her eyes. There was more. "Listen, cowboy. I don't know if I want to travel with nothin' the rest of my life like I did with Pa, or try to find land and raise horses or children or potatoes, or rob banks, but I know that me and you have to stay together, Rourke. I lost everyone else. I'm not losing you, too."

There was a catch in her voice.

He looked away. Wheeler was walking toward them. The colonel wanted something. There was something he had to sign. He could see in that instant that there was a whole world of things closing in. The law. The rules. The papers. The men in Eastern suits and the men in Army uniforms. He had no choices. He grabbed Cal's arm roughly and led her away.

"In a hurry to get up north right this blessed minute, cowpoke?" she asked as they entered the stable. Wheeler was hard on their heels. Rourke was dragging her forward even as she stumbled. "Some girls may not want to be dragged into a horse stall, Rourke! 'Specially a girl with a pistol she knows how to use!"

Rourke laughed. It was a sound Cal had not heard since before Pa was shot. Wheeler, wheezing, caught up with them. He started to speak.

"Sheriff!" Cal heard that voice of command Rourke didn't use often. "This is what you do. You search this town. You find that preacher—Evans. He's got to get me 'n' Cal married legal. I don't care where he is or if he objects. Drag him if you have to. Try not to shoot him. Right now! And tomorrow—tomorrow, Sheriff, you understand—tomorrow and not one moment before that, you search every square inch of this town to find that man the colonel wants to see. Got that? Tomorrow!"

Wheeler grinned. "That durn preacher finally showed up? 'Bout time! Guess somethin' good comes out of somethin' bad," he said. "I'll start looking right now, Rourke. I will that. I sure will." He lumbered away.

Cal and Rourke walked out through the stable's open rear doors. Not a person was in sight. They looked across the flatlands to the hills far from the debris washed into Wyoming by the greedy who didn't know riches when they saw them. One far-distant mountain had already been crowned by the first snow. The future was out there, beyond that mountain in some place they had never been.

"Cal?" murmured Rourke, as they stood with his arm across her shoulders.

"What is it, Rourke?"

"I want the preacher to say the words because people are funny about things like that. A proper girl ought to get a proper wedding even if it isn't big and grand. And if it ain't the way you pictured it, girl, nothin' ever is. I can't make life be what it isn't gonna be."

"Cowboy, I've had enough of anything that Eastern people call proper." She was trying bravely to smile.

Rourke never talked about his emotions. It was hard to do it now. "For all the things the preacher fella reads from the book, Cal, there ain't only one thing that really matters."

"What's that, Rourke? Coffee?" She enjoyed seeing him tongue-tied. She flashed him a real smile this time, the kind that had come to mean so much to him.

He realized as he smiled back that the old life was gone. The man who rode the Territory with a gun and nothing to lose was as gone as if Red Jim had killed him. A man had to change. Poor Zeke knew that. The past was gone. Maybe it would look better some other day. Now, it was a weight to be rid of like an elk shedding antlers. He wondered what he would become; what they would become. Land? Potatoes? Horses? Young'uns? Thoughts for another day.

"Well, it's nice of you to offer to brew up a pot, but that wasn't what I was thinking, Miss Caledonia MacReynolds."

"Then what's the one thing that matters, Rourke?"

He took her hand. They walked farther away from the scar of the town and the waste and ruin of people bent on having something that would not last. Sunset's fading remnants shone above their heads in red and purple streaks that would soon fade to inky swirls across the blue-black sky.

He lifted his arms as though he could hold the sunset as well as her. "This. All this. This is what matters, Cal. It ain't the money, the owning, or the taking. It's the living, Cal. It's all this free range that don't fit into words I can say. Last few days, I wondered if everything I ever knew in this world had changed on me. I wondered if every sunset we saw together would be the last one. It don't make no difference if it is, as long as you stand with me."

"You, me, and all that out there, cowboy," Cal whispered, feeling the mystery of the land and its wildness grow in her and fill her. "That's the deal. Forever."

"Forever," he replied.

They stood for a few more moments. There was work to do and life to live, but the wildness of the Western sky, the power of the prairie wind, and the vastness of open range were calling to both their souls. Stained with violence and hope, the land would hold their lives in the hollow of its mysteries, for as long as vermillion sunsets would fill the Wyoming sky with more than a man could hold.

"Come on, cowboy," said Cal at last, pulling him as she turned toward the stable.

"Aren't we supposed to be waitin' on the preacher, Cal?"

"Life isn't for waitin', Rourke," she said, with a smile as wide as the span of an eagle's wings. "He can catch up. Anyhow, way I hear things, once the sheriff finds the preacher, me and you got to wait in line! I don't want to wait, Rourke. I don't want to see another minute of Rawhide. For me 'n' you, paper and words and such ain't gonna matter. Let's ride, cowboy. We waited long enough. Let's get out of here!"

He let her lead him into a future as uncertain as tomorrow. But for this moment it was enough to feel the wind in his face, bathe in the fading of the light as though it were a new baptism of hope, and—beneath the glory of the Western sky—ride into their dreams.

ABOUT THE AUTHOR

Rusty Davis is a freelance writer who joined the Cowboy Nation riding the range at age six when Westerns were only on TV at 7 a.m. on Saturdays. You can contact him on Facebook or via email at Cowboyrusty99@gmail.com.